The Lost Survivor

Other Doherty Mysteries

The Mill Town

Sam Kafrissen

The LOST SURVIVOR

A Doherty Mystery

By **Sam Kafrissen**

International Digital Book Publishing Industries

Florida, USA

ISBN: 1575500566
ISBN 13: 9781575500560
Library of Congress Control Number: 2015907257
International Digital Book Publishing, Incorporated, Clearwater, Florida

Cover Photo: Ahavath Shalom Synagogue
West Warwick, Rhode Island

For Those Who Survived

1959

Chapter One

Doherty shifted his body, trying to find a more comfortable position. In doing so he banged his bad knee against the steering wheel and let out a curse. It was difficult for a five-foot, ten-inch man to get any sleep splayed out across the front seat of a 1955 Chevy. Giving up on that notion he lifted his head above the dash just high enough to see that the sun was about to make its daily appearance over the water. His watch said it was twenty-five minutes after six. He'd been curled up in the car for five hours, of which he'd slept for maybe one.

He hadn't planned on spending the night in his car, but when the couple he was tailing drove down to the beach to shack up for the night at a no-tell motel he wasn't left with much choice. He didn't know if he'd have enough time to go back to West Warwick and beat it back down here before the couple left. So now his back ached, though not nearly as much as his bladder. He unfurled himself and stepped outside. It was early and the morning air put a chill on the back of his neck. He opened the passenger door to block the view of any cars passing by and relieved himself on the asphalt. It wasn't a pretty sight though he felt much better afterwards. Looking over the top of the car he still saw no action in room six where the man and woman had disappeared the night before.

Doherty had a sour taste in his mouth and could have used a stick of gum. Instead he opted for a cigarette. The tobacco made him feel lightheaded. While smoking he looked at his reflection in the car window. The hair on the back of his head was sticking up at an awkward angle. He wet his hand and tried to tame the sleeper's cowlick. Even in the smudged glass he could see that he needed a shave and that his shirt was wrinkled. He straightened his tie and got back into the car. Checking himself in the rearview he saw the gray hairs that were beginning to take up space around his ears. His barber, Bill Fiore, had remarked about them the last time he was in Harry's for a trim. Doherty couldn't really see them from the chair that sat a good ten feet from the mirror that spanned the length of barbershop's wall. From this close, however, there was no mistaking their presence. What did he expect given that he was pushing thirty-nine?

He turned his attention back to the motel but there was still no action. He finished the cigarette and leaned his head back hoping to catch a few more winks. Just as he was drifting off he saw some movement through the blinds that covered the room's window. Someone split them just enough to let in a little daylight. Doherty hoped he hadn't been spotted since his car was the only one in the beach lot. He sat up and tried to crank himself fully awake. Some vague images were moving around inside the room.

About ten minutes later a man opened the door and stepped outside. Doherty hadn't gotten a good look at him when they arrived last night in the dark. Now he could see that the guy was of medium height and weight with black hair neatly combed straight back from his forehead. He was wearing a white dress shirt without a tie or jacket. He lit a smoke and turned back to the room to say something to the woman inside. Then he climbed into the late model Oldsmobile 88 parked by the door and drove off.

Doherty gave him a few minutes and then ambled over to room six. He knocked on the door in that old shave-and-a-haircut cadence of four quick knocks, a hesitation and then two more. He was hoping the man and the woman had a special signal, and even if they didn't, she'd still think from the rhythm of the knocking that it was Grimaldi returning for some reason. The door opened and a tired looking woman wearing only a sheer slip stood inside the room. She froze for a second when she realized the man who'd knocked wasn't Grimaldi. Doherty quickly tried to introduce himself; she closed the door before he could finish. Still, he'd had time to take in the sight of her wearing only a slip with nothing underneath, her breasts all but spilling out of the top.

He waited patiently. A minute later the door opened again, though only a crack. It was enough for him to see that the woman had put a man's trench coat on over the slip.

""What do you want?" she asked nervously.

"My name's Doherty. I'm a private investigator. Your husband hired me to find you." Nothing more was said. Nothing more needed to be said.

After some thought the woman swung the door open and invited Doherty in. The bed sheets were all twisted up and pieces of clothing, both men's and women's, were strewn about the room. The place smelled of cold cream and sex. The woman sat on the bed and pointed at a chair for Doherty to sit. He chose to remain standing. His legs needed stretching after a night in the car.

"Your husband would like you to come home," he said matter-of-factly.

"Why?"

Doherty shrugged. "I don't know. That's between you and him. I was just hired to find you. And now I have."

Her husband was an oafish, heavyset construction worker who'd come into Doherty and Associates two days earlier wanting to hire him to find his missing wife. He mentioned that he'd heard Doherty's specialty was finding people who are *lost*, which it is. The poor slob said his wife had run off with some "nogoodnik," named Richie Grimaldi. Doherty quoted Leo Carney his fifty-dollar rate plus expenses and the client forked over twenty-five as a deposit.

Finding Marilyn Carney hadn't been much of a problem once Doherty was put onto Richie Grimaldi. Grimaldi was the kind of guy who preyed on unhappy housewives looking for a good time. From what Doherty could tell the guy was mostly in it for the sex, though occasionally he took the poor broads for some money as well. You might say he was a gigolo but that would've given gigolos a bad name. His usual MO was to promise these women a good time; usually a trip up to New Hampshire to look at the leaves or down to Atlantic City to look at the ocean, depending on the time of year. What they often ended up with was a night in a cheap motel like this one, or if they were really unlucky, a dose of the clap.

Doherty noticed an open bottle of Cutty Sark Scotch on the dresser and poured himself a couple of fingers without it being offered. Anything to kill the rancid taste in his mouth. He couldn't exactly ask Mrs. Carney if she'd let him use her toothbrush.

"Where's Grimaldi gone off to?"

Marilyn Carney got up from the bed and stood in front of the mirror above the dresser. She brushed at her limp brown hair, though without much enthusiasm. She wasn't a bad looking woman except for the fact that life was wearing her down faster than it should. In any case, she was on the other side of thirty and apparently saw no way back except through an occasional tumble with a guy like Grimaldi. She put the brush down and picked up a pack of Salems and lit one. Salem cigarettes were the new menthol sisters to Winstons. Doherty sparked a Camel and soon the room smelled of burning tobacco rather than cold cream.

"He went into town to get breakfast. Said his night with me left him with a 'he-man's appetite.' I think that was suppose to be a compliment." Doherty sensed that instead it left her feeling used.

"Do you think he'll be back soon?"

"He'll be back when he feels like it." She then turned away from the mirror above the dresser and looked directly at Doherty. "He won't be in any hurry now that he's had his way with me."

"Did he promise to take you on a nice trip somewhere?" Mrs. Carney didn't answer. "I think you ought to know this isn't the first time Richie Grimaldi's done this kind of thing."

"Don't worry, I'm smart enough to know I'm not the only woman he's promised things to. I've been married a long time, but that doesn't make me stupid. It's just … it's just that he made me feel like somebody for a change – somebody besides a cook and house cleaner."

"Do you want to go home? If you do, I'd be happy to take you."

"You don't have to do that. I know when Richie comes back he'll have some story about how something's come up and we can't go on that car trip after all. Then he'll suggest that maybe I really should go home to my husband."

"Truthfully, it usually is that way with Grimaldi. What would you like me to tell your husband?"

Marilyn turned back to the mirror and began to touch up her face. The raincoat slipped open a notch and Doherty got a good look in the mirror at what was underneath. She caught his eye in the reflection and made no attempt to button up. "I'll take care of Leo," she said sadly. And with that Doherty left the motel.

Grimaldi's big finned car was not hard to spot. It was parked a few spaces down from the diner on the strip across from the sea wall. It was still early spring so there wasn't much morning action in the shore community. Doherty pushed his way into the diner. Most of the other patrons were locals: fishermen, handymen and short haulers. They gave Doherty a quick once over and then went back to their lives. There were six spiral seats with red plastic cushions and chrome trim in front of the Formica counter. He took a seat next to Grimaldi. The place smelled of grease and eggs.

Grimaldi was reading the sports pages and shoveling some over-easy fried eggs into his mouth. He wore his black hair greased back and had a thin little mustache. He was a good-looking guy in a seedy sort of way. Doherty ordered coffee and a blueberry muffin.

"What do you think, any hope for the Sox this year?" Doherty asked as an icebreaker.

Grimaldi looked his way, sized him up pretty fast and said, "Don't matter. It'll be the Yankees in the end anyways. It always is."

"I don't know," Doherty said. "With Jensen and Runnels and this new kid Malzone at third, the Sox don't look so bad."

"Could be, but I don't know how much Williams's got left. Two stretches in the service can take a lot outta ya." Grimaldi was apparently comfortable with sports talk.

"You from around here?"

Grimaldi scanned the diner, his eyes resting momentarily on the locals. He let out a short laugh and said, "Do I look like I'm from around here?" Doherty didn't respond right away. "No, I'm from up in East G. How about yourself?"

"West Warwick."

Grimaldi snickered. "The old mill town, huh. Now there's place that's seen better days. So whaddya do over there? You don't look like a mill worker."

"I'm an investigator."

"An investigator, huh," Grimaldi said through a mouthful of toast, acting like he was impressed. "What exactly do you investigate?"

"I mostly find people that are lost. Right now I'm looking for a woman who's run off with some slimeball that's not her husband."

Grimaldi stopped in mid-bite. "Is that so," he said. His jaw muscles had gone rigid. "So did you find this lost housewife?"

"Matter of fact I did. Found her shacked up in some cheap motel over by the beach. She didn't seem too happy to be there."

Grimaldi folded up his paper and swiveled in Doherty's direction. "What is this, some kinda shakedown?"

Doherty slowly sipped his coffee and didn't bother to turn to look at Grimaldi. "No, not at all. I just thought if you're done with the woman you might want to return her to her husband."

"Suppose she don't wanna go?" Grimaldi said, trying to sound tough. Doherty wasn't sure if it was a question or a challenge so he let it go.

Grimaldi smiled and shook his head. He then threw two bucks on the counter and beat a hasty exit. Doherty took his time finishing his coffee, giving the man a good head start.

Fifteen minutes later he was parked in the same spot where he'd spent the night. In a short time Richie Grimaldi and Marilyn Carney came out of room six. Grimaldi was very animated, gesticulating with his hands in the way Italians often do when they're excited. Doherty watched them drive away and then took himself back to West Warwick.

Chapter Two

He didn't roll out of bed until after noon. Once he'd bathed and shaved, he shoveled down some leftover chop suey from the Hong Kong before heading into town. As he expected, his secretary Agnes was at her post when he arrived at the office.

Her eyes gave him a good going over before asking, "Tough night last night?"

"You might say that – if spending it curled up in the front seat of a Chevy qualifies as a tough night."

"Jeez, what happened? Was it because of that Carney woman?"

"Yeah, she and her boyfriend decided to spend the night in some no-tell motel down by the beach. Once I tracked them there I didn't have much choice but to keep an eye on things till something broke."

"And did it?"

"Eventually. Early this morning the sleazebag she'd been shacking up with went out by himself for breakfast. That gave me an opportunity to spend some time talking with the wife. To tell you the truth she doesn't seem be living on the sunny side of life."

When Doherty first hired Agnes Benvenuti as his secretary he'd done so to give his operation some class. For a long time the only thing he let her in on about his cases was what he put into the official reports he wrote that she then typed up. But in time he came to trust her judgment more and more, especially where women were concerned. Lately he'd begun to regularly bounce ideas off her about his approach to the cases he was working.

Agnes nodded as if she knew what Doherty meant by this last remark. "Do you think she'll go home to her husband?"

He considered her question carefully. "Hard to say. It's clear Leo no longer floats her boat but what else is she going to do?"

"Did you talk to the guy at all?"

"I followed him to a diner and braced him there. I think I pushed him hard enough to rescue the missus, though by that point it probably didn't matter. This Grimaldi character was already done with her. By now he could be working on some other unhappily married woman. In any case, if Mrs. Carney doesn't go home we may be hard pressed to collect the rest of what her husband owes us."

"Well at least you won't have to pay me for the next few weeks."

Agnes would be taking three weeks off because her husband Louie was coming home from the Merchant Marines. Louie was on shore for three weeks out of every four months and since he didn't know his wife had a job, she kept up the charade of being the happy homemaker while he was on leave. It wasn't like Agnes worked for the money since Doherty only paid her sporadically. By her own admission she took the job to get out of the house. After a while she told him the cases really began to interest her. Doherty knew he'd miss Agnes but wouldn't say so because he didn't want her to feel bad about taking the time off. Besides, it wouldn't be long before Louie got her pregnant and she'd have to leave the agency for good.

Doherty asked Agnes if she'd type up the Carney report before she left for her *vacation*.

"You know, boss, if you need me at any time over the next three weeks all you gotta do is call my sister Lucille and she'll get the message to me. Louie usually gets bored sittin' around the house watchin' TV. Sooner or later he'll go into Providence to hang out with some of his merch buddies at the hall. They'll hit some bars and Louie'll stagger home drunk like he always does. So it's not like I'll be on lockdown the whole time he's home."

"I appreciate that, Agnes. And I will let you know if I need you for anything, I promise. In the meantime enjoy having your husband home and don't go worrying about Doherty and Associates. We'll be here when you get back."

Doherty retreated to his office where he spent the next hour scratching out his notes on the Carney case. He'd have Agnes type them up for the files and also put an invoice in the mail to Leo Carney for the balance of what he owed. When he was done he dropped the pages on Agnes' desk. She took them with a smile.

Around four he could hear her tidying up in the outer office. He knew she wasn't sure about Doherty's housekeeping skills and didn't want to leave the place unkempt in case any clients came in while she was away. When he walked out to her space she handed him the typed copy of the Carney file and told him she'd drop the bill in the mail on her way home. Doherty noticed that she had put the plastic casing over the old Remington on her desk.

She saw him looking at the typewriter and said, "You oughta learn to type, boss. That way you could do your own filin' while I'm away."

Doherty smiled. "But then I'd have no reason to have a secretary, would I? You're the main reason I don't learn any of those clerical skills." He then reached into his wallet and extracted twenty of the twenty-five Leo Carney had given him and handed it to Agnes.

"Here, this should tide you over till you get back."

"You don't have to do that, boss."

"Oh, go on, Agnes. Take it. Go buy yourself a dress in case Louie decides to take you out for a night on the town."

Agnes then did something she'd never done before. She gave Doherty a quick hug. Afterwards she was noticeably embarrassed and left quickly.

Doherty retreated to his back office and took up an article he'd been reading in Sport Magazine. It was about last year's World Series hero Bob Turley, the Yankee pitcher. The story was the usual puff piece meant for fans who worshipped baseball players as if they were clean living demigods. It was accompanied by a picture of Turley and his beautiful family and another of him in the fancy Corvette he won for being the series MVP. The next story was about some racecar driver named Sterling Moss. Doherty wasn't much interested in car races, nor was he interested in reading a story about somebody named Sterling.

He was ready to pack it in for the day when there was a light knock on the outer door. Then he heard a man's voice say, "Hello. Is there anyone in?"

Doherty came out of his office. Standing just inside the door was Mr. Mendelson, the owner of Francine's, a women's clothing store near the corner of Main and Washington. He'd made Mendelson's acquaintance last fall when he briefly dated Millie St. Jean, a girl who worked in his shop. It was another one of Doherty's relationships that ended badly.

"Mr. Mendelson," Doherty said as he stuck out his hand. "You're a sight for sore eyes."

"Nice to see you again, Mr. Doherty," Mendelson replied with a smile. The owner of Francine's was a small man with a head almost devoid of hair. There was a curtain of gray around the edges but that was about it. His handshake was firm though his paw was so small that it was engulfed by Doherty's mitt. Mendelson was wearing a beige raincoat and was nervously fidgeting with a hat that he held in his other hand.

"Are you here on business?"

Now nervously twirling the hat by its brim, he said, "As a matter of fact, I am."

"Well, why don't we step into my office?" Doherty thought to ask Mendelson about Millie, then discarded the idea. He didn't want to queer any business that might transpire between them, especially since Leo Carney'd been his only client in the past month.

Not wishing to be distracted by Mendelson's hat twirling any longer Doherty took his lid and hung on his antler rack alongside his own.

"So what can I do you for, Mr. Mendelson?" Doherty was hoping beyond hope that this visit didn't have anything to do with Millie.

"I'm here about one of the men in our minyan."

"Your what?" Doherty asked, knowing only that a minion was some kind of follower or dependent.

"Our minyan.* You see, whenever Jews hold a religious service of any kind we need ten adult men to be present. That constitutes a minyan. Anyway, at our shul, I mean our synagogue, we have a group - usually thirteen or so men at any given time that we can call on whenever we need a minyan. Occasionally someone drops out or moves away and then another man steps forward to take his place. Though lately it's been getting harder to gather one as the Jewish

---

* A glossary of Yiddish and Hebrew words appear in the appendix

population in town keeps shrinking. I believe you know one of our former members, Bernard Pressman."

Pressman was an elderly man, a retired lawyer, who disappeared last fall. Shortly afterwards, Pressman's wife hired Doherty to find her husband. It turned out he was suffering from dementia and had simply wandered from his home and couldn't find his way back. It wasn't a difficult job locating the man, as the lost soul had never left West Warwick.

"Yes, I remember. How is the old gent doing?"

Mendelson shook his head. "Sorry to say Eunice had to put Bernie in a nursing home up in Edgewood a couple of months ago. Some of the other men and I go to visit him now and then, but he hardly knows who we are anymore."

"And the wife?"

"She's doing about as well as can be expected. Her daughter and son-in-law moved in with her, so at least she's not alone. That way she gets to stay in her own house." Doherty knew all about being alone, given that he hadn't had any companionship besides Agnes since he and Millie broke up.

Abruptly changing the subject Doherty said, "Why don't we get back to your missing minyan?"

Mendelson smiled and let out a small laugh. "It's not the minyan that's missing; it's one of our members. His name is Meir Poznanski."

"When did he go missing?"

"According to his wife, it's been almost two weeks now."

"Did she report it to the police?"

"Yes, she did, after a few days. She filled out a missing person's report at the new police station and they said they'd put out an APB, whatever that is."

"It's an *All Points Bulletin*. To be honest with you, I wouldn't put too much faith in the West Warwick Police Department. They only seem to be on their toes when there's a bar fight or when the DeCenza machine wants something done."

"Oh, I wouldn't be so hard on the police. I'm sure they're doing all they can."

"Trust me, Mr. Mendelson. I know whereof I speak. I was on the force for three years. I'll confess I could use your business. But that aside, I can promise you you'll get better results hiring me than depending on the local cops. I do have to ask one question first though: How come it took the wife a few days before she reported her husband missing?"

Mendelson was uncomfortable with this query and it took him some time to frame an answer. "The Poznanskis don't get on too well," was all he came up with.

"Marital problems?"

"I suppose. Meir and Edith are very different kinds of people. Edith is very outgoing, very sociable - involved in a wide variety of community and religious activities. And Meir, well, Meir tends to keep to himself."

"Do you think he could've run off with another woman?"

Mendelson shook his head. "I would find the idea of Meir having an affair very hard to accept."

"Don't be so quick to dismiss it. I see a lot of that in my business."

"I'm sure you do, but Meir is what I would call a *tortured soul*. You see he was in one of those concentration camps during the war. Apparently before the war he had a whole other family over in Poland: a wife and two children. Every one of them killed. Meir is the only one who survived. I don't think he's ever recovered from that. I don't think he ever will," Mendelson added sadly.

Like a lot of GIs who served at the tail end of the war, Doherty was required to watch the films of the concentration camps after they were liberated. What they showed was something beyond his comprehension. The brass thought that by showing the GIs these films it would make them feel better about all the Germans they killed. The films, like the war itself, just left Doherty with a sense of despair about the human race.

"So, do you want to hire me to find this Meir whatever his name is?"

"Well, here's the thing. We, the members of the minyan, would like to hire you as a group. We'll pay you from our treasury whatever it costs. But we don't want Edith to know that we've done this. Would that be satisfactory with you?"

Doherty shrugged. "It's a little unusual since most of the time some family member hires me to find a missing relative. But if that's the way you and your minyan want it, then it's fine by me."

"Good. Now we would like you to meet with us as a group. We hold a little service every Sunday morning at the synagogue followed by a breakfast. Do you know where the Ahavath Shalom Synagogue is?"

"Sure, I know where it is. Down Main just after the fork at the Richfield station."

"Can you meet us there on Sunday morning around ten? That won't interfere with your going to church, will it?"

This last question brought a smile to Doherty's face. "That won't be a problem, Mr. Mendelson. I haven't been to Mass on a Sunday in quite some time."

Mendelson then rose and gave Doherty a weak smile. They shook hands and that should have been the extent of it, except before leaving Mendelson turned at the door and said, "You haven't asked about Millie."

Doherty was dumbfounded and just stood there, awkwardly staring at the little man. Finally he asked, "Is she still at Francine's?"

"Oh yes, she's still with us." There was an uncomfortable silence, which Mendelson broke. "I think I should tell you, she's getting married."

"What?"

"I said she's getting married - sometime this summer."

"But... but, she's already married," Doherty sputtered. Millie's husband Gerard was a brain-damaged vet from the Korean War. Last Doherty knew he was still alive though in a vegetative state up at the Howard Institution in Cranston.

"Apparently she was able to get her marriage annulled. Not being Catholic, I don't know how those things work. She told me Judge DeCenza was instrumental with the church in helping her get the annulment. Millie thinks the Judge even spoke to the cardinal himself on her behalf."

Doherty shook his head. "My God, is there no limit to that man's reach?"

He'd had some unpleasant dealings in the past with Judge Martin DeCenza, whose Democratic political machine ran just about everything in West Warwick. However, Doherty'd been able to gain some leverage with the Judge that allowed him to keep his distance from him and his political operation, or so he thought. He now wondered if DeCenza's involvement in helping Millie St. Jean obtain an annulment was another subtle blow the Judge wished to strike against him.

"Who's the lucky man?"

"A fellow named Gene from her church. She tells me he's an insurance man. But ..."

"Yes?"

"She stills talks about you fairly often. In fact, it was Millie who first suggested that we hire you to find Meir. I can't help but feel that she still has a warm place in her heart for you."

"Why don't we leave Millie out of this and stick with me finding your friend, okay," Doherty said, trying to banish the girl from his mind.

"Then I will see you on Sunday morning at the synagogue. And Mr. Doherty, bring your appetite. We serve a mean breakfast."

Chapter Three

It was a relatively warm day so, as was his custom when the weather permitted, Doherty chose to walk through Arctic to the Jewish place of worship. By walking nearly everywhere around town he was able to make the acquaintance of a lot of local merchants and men and women who worked for them. It was one of the small pleasures that came with living in the mill town. It was also good for his practice. Although the churches in West Warwick did a robust business on Sunday morning, Doherty knew the Jews did most of their praying on Friday night and Saturday morning.

As usual the town was locked up tighter than a drum on this Sunday. Only a few spas were open so that the townspeople would have somewhere to buy their Sunday papers and cigarettes. West Warwick was a pretty solid workingman's town, but on Sunday everyone did their best to dress up for church. The men wore suits or at least jackets and ties while the women dressed as best they could in their finest dresses. Even the young boys donned jackets and snap on ties like the parochial school kids wore every day. The girls wore frilly little dresses along with their Mary Jane shoes.

There was a crowd spilling out from the eight o'clock Mass at St. James' as he passed by on his way into town. Doherty had attended school at St. James' in the building adjacent to the church until he was forced to leave after eighth grade when his old man could no longer make the parochial school payments. Along with St. John's, St. James' was one of the largest Catholic churches in

Arctic. Other villages in West Warwick had their own Catholic sanctuaries, but none was as big as these two, either in size or number of congregants.

St. James' had once been the sole domain of the Irish until the town began to attract a growing Italian population. For a long time St. Anthony's down in Natick had been the preferred place of worship for the Italians who clustered in that part of town. But once more people of that nationality began to move into Arctic they elected to share a piece of St. James' with the Irish. When Doherty was young his family and other old line Irishmen complained constantly about this encroachment of the Italians, though never to their faces. Since Italians still represented a small slice of the town's population they tended to keep to themselves and still held most of their christenings, marriages and funeral Masses down at St. Anthony's. St. John's church, and to a lesser degree St. John's school, which sat behind it, were still the province of the French-Canadians, who made up the bulk of West Warwick's diminishing mill workers. As a kid Doherty had been friends with a boy whose mother was French-Canadian and father Italian. Every Sunday his buddy Johnny went to Mass at St. John's with his mother while his brother Ray went to St. James' with his father. Such was the clannishness of the town's ethnic groups.

Doherty had not been to St. James' since his mother's funeral. There were a lot of reasons why he'd fallen out with the good fathers and sisters. Some of it had to do with the brutal nature of their schooling methods. The day his father lost his job at the Royal Mill and could no longer afford to send him and his sister Margaret to Catholic school was one of the happiest days of Doherty's life. He thrived in public school in a way he never had under the nuns at St. James'. Margaret, on the other hand, was devastated and didn't recover from the transfer until high school. She even flirted for a while with becoming a nun, a choice their pious mother strangely did what she could to dissuade her from. She was still harboring such notions when she started dating a boy named Larry during her junior year at Deering High. He was nothing to write home about and they broke up after going steady for five months, but it was enough to turn her away from the convent. His sister is now married with two kids and lives out in Minnesota. Doherty exchanges cards with her at Christmas time and she always sends him a box of candy as well. For years he has promised to go out there to visit with her and her family but has never gotten around to it.

The other reason Doherty deserted his Catholic upbringing was the war. Having seen the devastation in Europe and the films of those terrible camps, he lost all faith in God. He had been schooled in the church of a merciful God. Merciful, that is, if you were Catholic. Then he witnessed and did things that were so horrific that he could no longer believe that man was created in God's image. Or worse, if he *was* created in God's image, then God himself must be anything but merciful. He remembered many a Sunday over there when a chaplain would show up to lead the men in a religious service or a Mass. Then a few hours later they would be blowing enemy soldiers to smithereens. He could never understand how a merciful God would let something like that happen, let alone countenance it.

He was relieved to be away from the crowd at St. James' and these thoughts. He turned down Main Street and headed toward the place where the town's small Jewish population worshipped. He passed by the neo-classical Centreville Bank. If he squinted when he looked at it head on he could imagine it was a Greek or Roman temple. Likewise with the Post Office a block further on, built during the Depression with federal money used to put men idled from the mills back to work. Across the street from the bank was the Donut Kettle, then Benny's Auto Parts store and a few doors down St. Onge's, Arctic's premier men's and boy's clothing store. Along the same block was Grant's, one of Arctic's three Five and Ten Cent stores along with Newbury's and Woolworth.

Further down was the First National market, where Doherty's mother always did her weekly grocery shopping. He remembered well the times she took him with her to haul the grocery bags out to the trunk of their beat up old Hudson. He vividly recalled the wooden slat floor in the First National and the fruits and vegetables that had fallen out of their bins onto that floor. Most of all he remembered the vast variety of food the store had to offer, much of which his family couldn't afford. Back then Doherty's mother had to economize on food, never knowing how much of his paycheck Peter Doherty would pass across the bar at Paddy's or one of Arctic's other watering holes before coming home. Too often the stews she cooked up for her family were a thin gruel made up mostly of potatoes. Once the war started his mother had to scrimp even more to stretch her ration coupons as far as she could. She was relieved when Doherty was drafted, knowing that for the next few years at least, Uncle Sam would be feeding her strapping son instead of her.

At the fork where Main and Providence split sat the Richfield station, once owned by Arnie Rosenberg, the father of Doherty's only Jewish boyhood friend, Joey Rosenberg. Joey's father had once been a professional wrestler and there were pictures in his office of him in his trunks striking menacing poses. To a young Doherty, Arnie Rosenberg looked like a giant, especially in comparison to his own emaciated father. Joey said that his father once wrestled Gorgeous George and lost in a close match.

The Jewish synagogue was only a short block on the right further down Main. He'd never been in such a place before so he didn't know what to expect. As was his usual pattern he arrived early for his appointment. He often did this to give himself an advantage by catching his clients or his prey off-guard. The synagogue was a small building compared to the large Catholic churches in the town. It was even smaller than the few Protestant houses of worship that still remained in the predominantly Catholic enclave. West Warwick still had a church for every ethnic group and one in each of its small villages.

Ahavath Shalom Synagogue sat right on Main Street just outside the commercial center of Arctic. It was a square building sided by brick on the outside. It had stained glass windows on its front facing Main but without any biblical scenes on them. Legend had it that the building was once the site of a barroom, still the town's most popular place for worship. The big, wooden front doors were closed so Doherty didn't know whether he should knock or just walk in. Not wanting to cause a stir he chose the latter, careful to edge the large, heavy door open just enough for him to slip inside.

Facing him was a long corridor that led to two sets of stairs, one going up to a second floor and another going down to a basement. To the left was another large door standing partially open onto the main sanctuary. Doherty heard some low murmuring from inside and peeked in to see if the minyan was in there. He had to admit what he witnessed startled him. A group of about a dozen men and a young boy were standing in a semi-circle praying in a language that Doherty figured was probably Hebrew. It certainly wasn't English or the Latin that was used in the Catholic Mass. Most of the men were wearing skullcaps and shawls. A few wore their own fedoras. In addition, each wore two small boxes, one tied to his forehead and another to the inside of his upper left arm. At first Doherty was embarrassed to witness this scene though he couldn't take his eyes off of the men either. The boxes connected to their left arms were fastened by a thin leather strap that wrapped around their arms from the wrist to the bicep. To do this the men had folded up the sleeves of their shirts about as high as they could go.

As they prayed the group continually bowed ever so slightly at the waist. In front of them was a raised platform surrounded on all sides by balusters. Beyond the platform was a closet in the wall with a heavy curtains partially opened on each side. Emblazoned on the curtains were embroideries of two lions on either side of tablets, which Doherty took to be the Ten Commandments in Hebrew letters. To the right of this closet was a large upright candelabrum with the six-pointed Jewish star at the top. To the left of it was a white flag with blue stripes and the same large six-pointed star in the middle. This he knew was the flag of the Jewish country of Israel.

From the rhythm of the prayers the men all seemed to be chanting something different. Occasionally someone would announce an "amen". Even as he continued his bowing one of the men noticed Doherty. The box attached to his forehead bobbed as he prayed. Feeling slightly embarrassed, Doherty backed away from the open door, yet stayed close enough to watch and listen to the disorderly chanting. Finally the group gathered together to say a prayer in unison that had a lot of words beginning with what sounded like "Yis." In this one they all bowed deeper than before and wore solemn looks. Doherty began to feel like he was witnessing some secret ritual he wasn't meant to see.

There was a bench in the hallway so he took a seat and waited for the service to come to an end. The door to the sanctuary swung open and he could see the members of the minyan unwrapping the boxes from their heads and arms and placing them in small cloth bags. Doherty had to admit that he was fascinated by the hocus-pocus of the service. Having never been in a synagogue before he wondered if the Jews engaged in this kind of ritual at all their gatherings. He reminded himself that a Catholic Mass with its altar boys dressed in their cassocks and rochets and priests swinging the thurible incense burner on its long chain and then doling out communion wafers and wine would likewise seem strange to outsiders. Still, what he'd just witnessed at Ahavath Shalom outdid anything he'd ever seen at St. James'.

The men soon filed out and headed toward the stairs that led down to the basement. A few of them looked suspiciously at Doherty as they passed though most were too engrossed in conversations of their own to give him more than a passing glance.

Finally Mendelson emerged and when he saw Doherty greeted him warmly. "Ah, Mr. Doherty, so glad you could make it," the little man said as he shook his hand while patting Doherty on the shoulder with his other.

He then escorted him downstairs behind the other members of the minyan. Doherty was surprised at how the men who'd been engaged in such solemn prayers just a few minutes before were now so boisterous and convivial with one another. They all took seats around a large breakfast table. Mendelson pointed at a chair for Doherty to sit in beside him. Given that the men were all wearing dress shirts and ties he was glad he'd chosen to wear his suit to the synagogue. To his right was an older man who looked at Doherty with disinterest and loudly slurped his coffee without offering a greeting.

Mendelson stood and tapped his spoon against his coffee cup to get the group's attention. What had been a cacophony of chatter only seconds before slowly dissipated.

"I have invited the investigator we spoke about, Mr. Doherty here, to join us at our breakfast," he announced. "I have suggested to you that we hire him to find our Meir and …"

A stout older man at the other end of the table interrupted, "Not all of us have agreed to this, Morrie. Personally I still don't see why we have to bring in a goy to help us find one of our own."

Doherty was about to speak up for himself but Mendelson held him back, placing a hand on his shoulder. "Mr. Doherty has come here in good faith. I suggest we eat first and afterwards we can air any grievances we might have. Then, if we agree, hopefully we can provide Mr. Doherty with the information he needs to successfully complete this job for us."

The stout man was not satisfied and grumbled as he went back to his meal. This gave Doherty a chance to survey the food laid out on the table. There was a large basket full of round rolls that looked like donuts. Beside it were two tubs of cream cheese. In the middle of the table arrayed on large platters were fishes of various kinds. Some were whole fish with a crisp golden skin, others were just squares of some kind of white fish, while still others were slabs of light reddish salmon laid out in thin slices. Surrounding the fishes were freshly sliced tomatoes and red onions. Another plate at the far end of the table held an assortment of Danish pastries. Except for the tomatoes and onions, Doherty was not familiar with any of the food on the main platter.

The men filled their coffee cups from a large urn that sat on a side table. The young boy sat with a full glass of orange juice in front of him. The kid seemed nervous and distinctly out of place among the grizzled adults, many of whom were sorely in need of a shave. Mendelson brought over a cup of black coffee for Doherty and one with cream for himself.

The little man reached for one of the rolls, cut it in half with a large serrated knife and handed it to Doherty. Although it looked like a donut, the dough was hard and shiny on the outside and only slightly softer inside.

Noticing Doherty's confusion Mendelson smiled and said, "It's a bagel. You eat it with a schmear of cream cheese and some fish if you like." Doherty watched carefully as the other men slathered up their bagel halves with generous amounts of cream cheese from the two tubs. One of the cheeses was plain white; the other had some kind of green herb mixed into it. Doherty opted for the plain. Mendelson forked some of the lean, raw looking salmon onto his plate and asked Doherty if he'd like some.

"What is it?"

"It's lox."

"Locks?"

"Lox. L-O-X. It's salted smoked salmon. Comes mostly from Nova Scotia. Try it, you'll like it."

Doherty cut off a small slice and gently placed it on top of his cream cheese covered bagel. He noticed that some of the men had also heaped slices of tomato and red onion on top of their open-faced bagel sandwiches. Others had used two bagel halves to make a closed sandwich of the fish. Conversation grew louder and it was clear everyone was having a good time. They talked baseball, complained about their wives, groused about business and even about the synagogue's rabbi. That was something Catholics never did outside of their own family - complain about the parish priest, no matter how much they disliked him.

The cheerful atmosphere in the room made Doherty feel more comfortable, though he was still thinking about the strange service he'd witnessed upstairs in the sanctuary.

Mendelson asked Doherty if he liked the food and Doherty said that he did, though it was a far cry from his family's traditional meat and potatoes Sunday meal.

"Where do you get food like this? Certainly not here in Arctic."

Mendelson laughed, "No, you can't get food like this here in town. One of the men has to go into Providence to get it. In fact, Meir used to pick it up at a deli on the East Side every Saturday. He's not orthodox so he could drive on Saturdays. Most orthodox Jews don't drive on the Sabbath. A lot of the men here are not orthodox either though the synagogue itself still is. When he didn't show up last Sunday with the bagels and lox, that was how we learned he was missing."

Doherty then leaned toward Mendelson and asked in a quiet voice, "That service you had this morning – is that a ..." He was searching for the right word. "Is that a typical Jewish service?"

"Oh, so you saw us up there did you? The service was a traditional morning service, though not a Sabbath service. Those we only hold on Saturday mornings. On Sundays it's become a tradition in our minyan to don the tefillin as a kind of ritual. Those are the little boxes we tie to our head and arms. It's not required, but since we seldom have a morning service during the week, we've chosen to wear the tefillin on Sunday. We like to do it especially if we have a bar mitzvah boy among us."

"I'm afraid you're losing me here."

Mendelson laughed, realizing Doherty knew virtually nothing about Judaism. "The little boxes we wear on our heads and on our arms near to our heart are called tefillin. The ceremony of wearing them goes back to the Bible. We wear the tallits, the prayer shawls, at all services, as well as hats. Most men wear yamulkes, the skullcaps you see, though some of the older men prefer to wear their own hats during services. I believe in your services men are required to remove their hats, are they not?"

"Yes, always. They remove all headwear in church as a sign of respect. So, what exactly is a bar mitzvah boy?"

Mendelson took a bite of his bagel and fish and waited until it was fully chewed. "When a Jewish boy reaches the age of thirteen he is considered ready for manhood, though he's not really, not these days anyway. But in biblical times he was considered a man by then. So we have a ceremony to commemorate this passage called a bar mitzvah. It's his symbolic passage to manhood. Probably serves the same purpose that a Confirmation plays in the Catholic faith. But in Judaism the boy has to prepare for the ceremony with study. He must learn to read and speak Hebrew and he must participate in certain rituals, like this morning's putting on of Tefillin. On the big day he is called to the Torah and he must read in Hebrew. So, his bar mitzvah training is a pretty lengthy and arduous process."

"And it's only for boys? Girls don't do this bar whatever?"

"Not here at Avahath Shalom because we are an orthodox congregation. In some of the reformed and even conservative synagogues they now let girls pass through a similar ceremony marking their adulthood. Here the girls and women are kept separate, even at our services. I personally believe it's one of the reasons our synagogue is losing members. Some modern Jewish women don't want to abide by the old rules. I hear such complaints from my own wife and daughter."

The breakfast soon wound down and the men began to light up cigars and cigarettes. Doherty took the liberty to spark up one of his Camels. Plates were cleared and more coffee was poured.

Then Mendelson called the group to order. He tapped his coffee cup again and rose to speak. "As you all know our good friend Meir Poznanski has recently disappeared. And like all of us, his wife Edith is very concerned. I have taken the liberty to ask Mr. Doherty to join us this morning and to listen to what we can tell him about Meir. And then if we agree, we will officially hire him to find our lost friend. Mr. Doherty comes to me very highly recommended."

"Recommended? Recommended by who?" barked the heavyset man who earlier had challenged Doherty's presence.

Mendelson stammered for a few seconds. Doherty was about to say something when Mendelson blurted out, "He was recommended to me by Judge DeCenza." That set off a loud murmur among the men and took Doherty by surprise.

Judge Martin DeCenza, the boss of the Democratic Party in town, controlled just about everything in West Warwick from patronage jobs to who got licenses to run saloons to the police themselves. One of the reasons Doherty left the police force was that he no longer wanted to be an errand boy for the

DeCenza machine. The Judge had put Doherty on the ropes last year until he uncovered a dirty secret about DeCenza and a crooked real estate deal that led to someone getting murdered. Doherty had used this knowledge as a means to end any dealings he'd have with DeCenza, or so he thought. That was until the other day when Mendelson brought the Judge back into Doherty's life by telling him how DeCenza helped to arrange Millie St. Jean's marriage annulment. And now he was telling the men in the minyan that it was the Judge who recommended Doherty for the job of finding their missing member. He was not comfortable with this surprising turn of events.

Mendelson broke the spell by singling out a man named Milton, who was Meir Poznanski's brother-in-law and employer. He asked Milton to speak first on behalf of Meir. The brother-in-law quickly rose from his chair. He was squat man with a large belly that drooped over the waistband of his trousers. His hair was dark and wavy and he wore an exceptionally colorful tie. Once on his feet he flashed a broad smile that indicated he was comfortable speaking in front of this group.

"As everyone here knows, I own The Bargain Store down on Washington Street. St. Onge's it's not, but we do a good business – mostly in our children's clothes. The Bargain Store's motto is 'service with a smile'," he said flashing his broad grin again as he did. There were a few snickers among the men. Milton raised his hand and said, "I know, I know. Service with a smile is not what you think of when you think of my brother-in-law who works for me."

"Meir couldn't sell a glass of water to a man in the desert," shouted a small man with glasses and a bow tie. That drew some loud guffaws from group, and even a smile from the bar mitzvah boy.

"If you ask me that man is meshugana," said a deep voice from the far end of the table.

"Please, please boys, let Milton continue," Mendelson interjected.

"I took him into the business because he married my sister, God bless him. In Poland, he was a university scholar and a teacher. But here I tell him Jews can only make a living by selling. In America, he could not be a teacher because when he first came here he spoke only Polish and Yiddish. And as for retail, well, he's not so good in that either. I try to teach him about the shmatte trade, but for business he knows from nothing. Most of the time he acts like he's too good for the kind of people who come into our store. So I send him to Providence as often as I can to meet with the wholesalers and to pick up our new merchandise."

"That doesn't explain where he might've gone," Mendelson said.

Milton shrugged, "With him it could be anywhere. When he goes up to the city he often doesn't come home till late at night. But I don't ask any questions. Frankly, I'm glad when he's out of the store for the day. When he's in the store he scares the children. Always yelling at them for running around and through the racks. I tell him 'Meir they're just being children', but he won't listen to me. I say, 'Meir, don't yell at the kids, they're our best customers'." The men all laughed and the brother-in-law sat down clearly pleased with himself.

"Does anyone else have anything they'd like to add to what Milton has just said?" Mendelson asked. Doherty slid a small pad out of his pocket and made a note to speak at length with this brother-in-law. He kept the pad under the table where no one could see it.

The conversation spun around the room, with each man weighing in with his view of Meir Poznanski. The overall impression Doherty got was that none of the men was particularly fond of the missing man or friendly with him. Mostly they were upset that he hadn't picked up the breakfast food the previous weekend. The consensus was that Poznanski was an unsociable person, who tended to look down on the other men in the minyan. He was not interested in the things that they were, which was mostly the synagogue, sports, family, and above all, business.

Finally someone came to Poznanski's defense. A tall, almost cadaverous looking gent with thinning hair stood and spoke. "Boys, we must not forget what Meir went through during the war. None of us can know what that would do to a man."

"Hey I was in the signal corps. I fought for over a year against the Japs," the small man with the bow tie objected.

"Please, Moishe. Being in the signal corps in the Pacific was not like being in Auschwitz," another man objected. The signal corps guy grumbled but let it go.

The conversation was beginning to run down until one of the men turned to the bar mitzvah boy and said, "So boychik, what do you think of all this?"

The boy's cheeks turned bright red and he looked around the table obviously embarrassed. Doherty wondered if the kid thought this was part of his bar mitzvah training. Finally he mumbled, "I dunno." That ended that.

Mendelson now stood hoping to bring the session to a close, but was immediately interrupted by the gruff voice of the stout man. "Let's hear what the goyim has to say. What about it mister investigator?"

Doherty took a sip of his coffee and slowly rose. He looked directly at the large man who'd hurled the insult his way. "If you men want to hire me I will find this Meir Poznanski for you. I can guarantee you that I'll do a better job of looking for him than the police will."

"And why's that, Irishman?" his adversary asked. The silence in the room was deafening.

"Because finding lost people is what I do best. I'll find your man, but I can't make him come back here unless he wants to. That's how it works. And if he's broken the law I won't protect him."

"Meir break a law? Now that would be a first," his brother-in-law said. His comment broke the tension in the room and they all laughed.

Some of the men soon began to rise and Doherty figured it was probably a good time for him to leave. Mendelson walked him up the stairs and out to the sidewalk in front of the synagogue.

"You'll have to excuse Irving," Margolis said referring to the man who'd challenged Doherty. "He's just a tough shelled old turtle. He likes to think of himself as the leader of the minyan and today I'm afraid I stole some of his thunder."

Doherty lit a cigarette and shook hands with Mendelson. "I understand," he said though he wasn't sure he did. "If your minyan still wants to hire me you can come by the office to sign an agreement form. If not, well, I still enjoyed the breakfast. You sure can't get food like that in Arctic." He knew if Mendelson did come by he'd have to find out how Judge DeCenza got involved in this business.

Chapter Four

Mendelson showed up late Monday morning. In addition to his hat he was also clutching a thick envelope in his hands.

"There's a hundred and thirty dollars in here," he said without prompting as he handed the envelope to Doherty. "Everyone contributed something except Irving Leibowitz, which was not unexpected. For some reason he resents dealing with Gentiles unless, of course, it's to sell them curtains and drapes in his store. For that I apologize."

Doherty took the envelope and tossed it on his desk. "No reason to apologize. I'm sure there are still people in this town who won't go into any of the stores owned by Jews. Old prejudices die hard. I guess it's the way of the world."

"Can I ask how you're going to proceed from here?"

"You can ask but I'm not going to tell you. You see in this business it's better that I keep my cards close to the vest. It's how I prefer to operate. I will tell you that looking for your friend will be my number one priority as of right now. But I need something in return from you, Mr. Mendelson."

"Please call me Morris, or Morrie if you wish. I'd like to think we're on friendly terms now."

"Fine. But I need to know how Judge DeCenza became involved in this case."

Mendelson did not hesitate. "The truth is we went to see him first, or at least I did."

"Why was that?"

"Well, the Judge has always been very friendly toward our community. I'm sure it's mostly because he wants our votes, and maybe even some of our money come election time. Everyone knows he runs things here in this town so I guess we thought if anyone could get the police off their duffs to help us it would be him."

Doherty considered whether what Mendelson was telling him made sense. "And what did he want in return?"

Mendelson looked confused. "Nothing really. Just our votes in the next election. And maybe, if we could find it in our hearts, some contributions to the Democratic Party."

"Then how did my name enter into the conversation?"

The client was nervous and didn't answer right away. "He said that he could only help us if Meir Poznanski was lost somewhere in Kent County. His reach did not go beyond that. Otherwise, he said, he would be stepping on someone else's toes. That was how he put it. He was the one who suggested we hire a private investigator."

"And that's how my name came up?"

"Oh yes," Mendelson said smiling now. "He said you were the best man around for the job. Said you'd scour the entire state if necessary to find our Meir." Mendelson was fidgeting again.

"Is that why you asked Millie about me?"

He nodded. "I knew if I asked Millie right away I might be opening up some old wounds. She's a good girl and I didn't want to bring any more hurt into her life than I needed to. But when I did mention your name she had nothing but good things to say. I got the distinct impression she rather enjoyed talking about you after all these months."

"I'll tell you what," Doherty said as he lit a cigarette and leaned back against his desk. "I'll take the job and do my best to find your man. But you've got to promise me something in return."

"What's that?"

"We leave Millie out of this. I don't want us talking about her any more, okay."

"Sure. Whatever you say."

"And you say nothing more to the Judge about this case either, not a word. I do not want him meddling in my affairs. If I even get a hint that he's nosing around, I will return your money and have nothing else to do with you and your minyan - ever. Do I make myself clear?"

Mendelson was taken aback by the vehemence of Doherty's ultimatum. Nevertheless he stammered, "I think I understand, but..."

"There are no buts about it. If you hire me the Judge stays the hell out of this or I walk away, and you find somebody else to search for Poznanski. Got it?"

"I got it," Mendelson said not entirely sure that he did. Doherty then pulled one of his standard contracts out of his wooden filing cabinet. Meldelson read it carefully and signed it on behalf of the men in the minyan. For all practical purposes, Morris Mendelson was now the client of record.

Once the little man was gone Doherty slipped a five spot out of the envelope and walked up to the Arctic News for lunch. Afterwards he made a pit stop at The Bargain Store for a face-to-face with Meir Poznanski's brother-in-law. Although the store was only a few short blocks from Doherty's office he'd never been in it before. He'd passed by it on numerous occasions given that it was on the same block as the Palace Theatre, where Doherty frequently went to the movies.

Milton Orlovsky wasn't kidding when he said his store was not St. Onge's. Upon first glance the space itself had a warehouse feel to it. The floors were not carpeted, but rather bare wood with thin planks that trapped dirt between them; dirt that would remain no matter how much sweeping or washing was done. Almost all of the merchandise hung on cheap metal racks that ran the length of the open space. There were racks for men's topcoats, suits, sport jackets, slacks and shirts running along the right side from front to back. On the opposite side were mostly children's clothes on comparable racks but at a lower height. Beyond the children's apparel were racks of women's coats and dresses. Doherty suspected that Orlovsky kept his stock of women's clothing to a minimum so as not to cut into Mendelson's business at Francine's. Maybe the Jewish merchants in Arctic really did function as a community. The whole place was lit by florescent lights that gave the store an unappealing glare.

Orlovsky was busy with a mother and her two small children so Doherty grazed along the racks of men's slacks and sport coats. The merchandise was decent enough and neatly presented. When he looked at the labels none was from a manufacturer he'd ever heard of. Most of the wool garments felt thin and insubstantial to the touch. Doherty was no fashion plate but this stuff was even below his usual purchase line. Still, it would suit the small town mill workers and clerks who needed dress-up outfits for special occasions like weddings, funerals, christenings and First Communions.

The proprietor looked pleased with himself as he turned in Doherty's direction. The woman was departing the store with two large bags in her hands, though not before having to reprimand one of her children for running back and forth through the center of the men's suit rack. Orlovsky was in shirtsleeves and suspenders and was wearing another colorful tie as he had at the synagogue.

"A good sale?" Doherty asked.

"A very good sale. Service with a smile," Orlovsky said as he flashed his enamels. "What can I do you for, Mr. Detective?"

"I'd like to talk in private. If this isn't a good time…"

Orlovsky waved his hand in front of him. "Not a problem. This is the slow time of the day anyway before the kids get home from school. Though I am a little short on help now that brother-in-law is no longer around. Wait here for a minute."

Orlovsky walked toward the back of the store and called out to someone named Arnold. A tall, pimple faced kid with a very pronounced Adam's apple appeared virtually on the run.

"Arnold, can you take care of things out here for a while? I have to conduct some private business in my office." The kid's head was bobbing up and down the whole time his boss was addressing him. Arnold wore gray slacks, hiked up so far that his pants and shoes were inches apart. The tie he wore was badly knotted and rested a good two inches below his neck, and his shirt could have used some pressing.

After a few words with the kid, Milton Orlovsky led Doherty through the back of the store and into a small office. The room was dusty and had the acrid smell of cigar smoke. Orlovsky plopped down in a chair behind a cheap wooden desk that was scarred in several places. He offered Doherty a seat on the visitor's side. The stub of a well-chewed cigar sat in a glass ashtray on the desk. Orlovsky picked it up and stuck it in his mouth and lit a match, almost burning his nose as he tried to get the cigar going. Doherty struck up a Camel and it wasn't long before the small room was heavy with smoke.

"Do you like jokes, Doherty?" Orlovsky began.

"Sometimes. As long as they don't involve drunken Irishmen, cheap Jews or oversexed Italians."

Orlovsky tipped his chair back and let out a roaring laugh. "You know, jokes can be very useful in this business. A man comes in thinking he might buy a suit but isn't sure. I chat him up a little, tell him a joke or two, and the next thing you know he's had a good laugh and I've made a sale."

Doherty wasn't about to deny The Bargain Store's owner the chance to tell a joke, especially if it would help get some information out of him.

"A priest, a rabbi and a minister walk into a bar..."

"I don't like those kind of jokes either," Doherty said.

Orlovsky took the cigar out of the corner of his mouth and pointed it at his visitor. "What're you, one of them sensitive types?"

"I just don't find jokes about clergymen very funny, that's all."

"Okay. Here's one you'll like. A guy walks into a saloon with a dog. He puts the dog up on the bar and says to the bartender, 'This here is a talking dog. If you give me a drink, I'll get him to say something.' The bartender is skeptical but pours the guy a shot anyway. The guy downs the shot and says to the dog, 'What's on top of a house? The dog barks 'roof, roof.' Now the bartender is really skeptical, but the guy convinces him to pour another shot. Then he says to the dog, 'What does sandpaper feel like? And the dog barks 'ruff, ruff.' The bartender is starting to get angry, but indulges the guy one more time. This time the guy asks the dog, 'Who's the greatest baseball player of all times, and the dog barks 'Ruth, Ruth.' By now the bartender's had enough. He grabs the guy and the dog and tosses them both out onto the street. They're sitting on the curb and the guy turns to the dog and says, 'What the hell was that all about? The dog looks at him and says, 'I guess I shoulda said DiMaggio.'"

Orlovsky laughed uproariously at his own joke, even though Doherty was sure he'd already told it a dozen times. Nevertheless, he laughed along with the jokester, despite the fact he'd also heard the joke before.

"So Mr. Mike Hammer, what can I do for you?" Orlovsky asked, his cigar now burnt down so far it looked like an extra knuckle in his hand.

"I wanted to ask you about a couple of things that came up the other day at the synagogue breakfast."

"Sure. Go ahead, shoot."

"When you talked about Meir marrying your sister, you punctuated it by saying 'thank God'. Why the 'thank God'?"

Orlovsky leaned across the desk and said, "When you look at my face, what do you see?"

"Excuse me?"

"My mug, what do you see? First you can tell that Clark Gable I'm not, right? I'm not even Humphrey Bogart for that matter. Am I right?"

"I still don't follow."

Orlovsky laughed then produced his 'service with a smile' grin. "I'm an average looking guy with a good personality and a winning smile. I'm not bragging. It's what people've told me my whole life. It's why I'm so good at selling those off-the-rack shmattes out there. The point is, Mr. Doherty, I got the looks in the family and that ain't saying much. My sister Edith - you know what they say about her? That she's got a good personality, she's got a lot of spirit, she's a good sport, things like that. When it came to giving out looks, God passed over Edith and went right on to the next girl in line."

"Why did Meir marry her then?"

"My first thought is to say that's a mystery right there. I know the men told you all about Meir and his life back in Poland so I won't go into all that. Edith met him at a singles dance at the South Side Jewish Center right after the war. She liked him right away because he was European and kinda formal. Not like the other men, always on the hustle. If you ask me she liked him because he was the only man there who asked her to dance. In those days his English was not so good, but she didn't care. They dated for a while and the next thing you know they got married."

"How did you and your family feel about that?"

Orlovsky shrugged. "Oy. I think my mother was just happy there was a man out there willing to marry Edith. My father, he was another story. He worried that Meir wouldn't be able to provide for her and a family. That's why he asked me to take him into the business. I didn't want to but hey, he was family. I couldn't say no."

"And how has it worked out?"

"The marriage or the business part?"

"Either, or both."

"Meir has given Edith two wonderful children. She kvells about them all the time. To be honest with you, sometimes I wish my own kids were so terrific. You saw my son Arnold out there. A good boy but a bit of a schlemiel. His mother and I wanted him to go to college but his grades weren't good enough. So him I have to put to work here as well. If you want to know the truth, Mr. Private Eye, I don't think there's any love these days between my sister and her husband. I happen to know for a fact that they sleep in separate bedrooms. She says it's because he snores too loud. I snore too but my Dora says it's 'music to her ears'. You give a woman what she needs, she puts up with a little snoring," he added with a toothy grin.

"Do you think Meir may be seeing another woman?"

"Our Meir? Another woman?" Once again Orlovsky let out one of his belly laughs. "Who would want him? Except for Edith, and even she has no use for him anymore. If you ask me, I think Meir lost all his human feelings in the war. Now he acts like a prisoner serving out his sentence here on earth. I'd have more sympathy if he wasn't such a know-it-all."

"What about with the business? Have there been troubles here between the two of you?"

"Troubles? Meir has been nothing but trouble since the day he walked into this store. If it wasn't for my sister I would've thrown him out on his tochis a long time ago. I shouldn't say this 'cause you'll probably take it the wrong way, but I'm glad he's missing. And if he never comes back I won't be so sad for that either. Does that make me a schmuck? If it does I don't really care. I'm tired of having to clean up his messes all the time. I got a business to run here, not a home for mental cases." Orlovsky had worked himself up into a lather and Doherty wasn't sure he wanted to take this part of the conversation much further.

"You said at the synagogue that he went into Providence once a week. What did he do there?"

"Twice a week," Orlovsky corrected. "He went every Thursday on business for The Bargain Store and every Saturday to get the bagels and fish for the Sunday breakfast at the shul."

"Where exactly did he go on these Thursday trips?"

"He went to pick up our goods at the wholesale warehouse in Davol Square. I'll give you the number where you can find these people. Or better still, why don't you drive up there with me on Thursday? I haven't been to Davol in a while and I could use the company. I'll introduce you to our wholesaler."

Doherty nodded in agreement, though he wasn't sure Orlovsky's presence would help or hinder this part of his investigation.

"Before Meir'd go up there I'd place all the orders and bargain on the prices over the phone. All Meir had to do was make sure he picked up the correct merchandise and that everything we ordered was there. You know, sometimes these gonifs will try to short-change you if you're not careful," Orlovsky explained. "I gotta tell you every week I'd say a prayer that nothing would go wrong before the goods got back here to Arctic. I'd keep my fingers crossed that Meir wouldn't screw something up or get into an argument with the wholesaler."

"And you said he'd usually come back late at night on those days?"

"That's what my sister told me. Personally I didn't care what he did as long as he had the right goods and nothing was damaged." Orlovsky shuffled through his desk and pulled out two invoices from the wholesaler The Bargain Store bought clothing from. He handed them to Doherty who took down the name on his pad before giving them back. They didn't really tell him anything.

"What about on Saturday. Where does he go for the Jewish food?"

Orlovsky looked at Doherty and smiled as if he was still savoring the minyan breakfast. "Katz's Deli on Rochambeau. It's up on the East Side. We been dealing with them for years. We send Meir 'cause he knows his way around Providence. He lived there before he married Edith. Most of the other men don't like to drive into the city or won't on Saturday because it's the Sabbath."

Doherty stood to leave, figuring Orlovsky had already left his inept son too long running the store on his own. "Is there anyone else you can think of I should talk to?"

Orlovsky likewise rose and stubbed out the cigar that had already died quite a while ago. "You should talk to my sister."

"But Mr. Mendelson said that our business should only be between me and the men in the minyan."

"Doherty, how long've you lived in West Warwick?"

"My whole life."

"Then I don't have to tell you what a small town this is. Well, my friend, the Jewish community is even smaller. Mendelson was a fool to think my sister wouldn't find out about us hiring you. In fact, I'd be willing to guess that she knew all about you even before Mendelson gave you our money. So go talk to Edith. But I gotta warn you before you do, she won't give you service with a smile, like me." Orlovsky then flashed his classic grin and led Doherty out to the front.

Chapter Five

Doherty arranged by phone to meet with Edith Poznanski the next afternoon. The family lived on Greene Street up a steep hill directly across Main from the synagogue. It was part of a fairly new development of houses clustered over a hillside that was open fields and woods when he was a kid. The whole area had been cut into small housing lots since the end of the war.

The Poznanski's house was set down on a plateau. Although the address was listed as Greene Street, the front door actually opened onto Youngs Avenue. The yard was a little overgrown, though it was still early spring and the gardening season was not yet in full swing. He assumed that in time the hedges would be cut back and the lawn would be mowed, though perhaps not if Meir Poznanski didn't return.

Doherty pushed the doorbell but didn't hear a ring, so he resorted to knocking. After a short wait a large woman opened it. He flashed his business license just to let Edith Poznanski know he was on the up and up. She invited him in and led him into the kitchen. As he followed he noticed a number of large cartons containing clothing strewn about the living room. His first thought was that Edith Poznanski was a hoarder.

"You'll have to excuse the boxes," she said in a loud voice. "I'm putting together some old clothes for the Hadassah rummage sale. Do you have any old clothes you'd like to donate?"

Doherty thought about the paltry threads that barely made a statement in his closet. "Probably not, but I'll check when I get home," he said as a courtesy.

Edith Poznanski must have stood five-nine if she was an inch. She was a big woman, but not fat by any means. She was what people usually described as 'big boned'. She had a nest of reddish brown hair that was so thick no hairdresser in Arctic would've been able to tame it. And it didn't look like she ever tried herself. As her brother had advertised, she was an unattractive woman with a horsey face marked by a ruddy complexion. She had one of those bumps on her jaw line that would no doubt sprout hair as she grew older. He could see why she hadn't attracted any boys at Deering High, though most of them weren't any bargains to begin with. She was wearing a brown crew neck top with matching pants and a pair of white Keds on her large feet. It was evident she had not dressed up for Doherty's sake.

"Please, please sit," she said moving a carton off one of the Naugahyde covered chairs that surrounded a breakfast nook. Doherty took a seat. Edith asked if he'd like a cup of coffee and he accepted.

"How about some rugelach to go with the coffee?"

"I'm not sure what that is."

The woman offered a crooked grin that revealed large front teeth that went perfectly with her horsey mug. "It's a Jewish pastry. Nothing more than some rolled dough with jam, dates or raisins inside. They say I make the best rugelach in West Warwick." She put out a full plate of the small rolled treats. Doherty was hooked after the first bite.

"These are delicious," he said.

"I told you. You can't get them this good, not even from a bakery in Providence."

After finishing the pastry Doherty asked, "Can we talk about your husband now?"

"It's why you're here, isn't it?" She pushed the plate of pastries closer to him, tempting Doherty to have another. "Go ahead, eat." It sounded more like a command than an offer. Still, it didn't stop Doherty from munching on a second roll up. Edith poured herself another cup of coffee and pushed her fingers through the bush that grew atop her head.

"Do you have any idea where your husband might've gone?"

Edith Poznanski shrugged. "I don't know. The only place I could imagine Meir running off to is Poland. Even though he knows that the glorious Poland he's always talking about isn't there anymore. Otherwise, where else would he go? He's got no real money of his own and as far as I can tell he hasn't taken any money out of our savings account."

"I hate to ask this but could your husband be seeing another woman?"

Edith sipped some coffee. "Not such a farfetched question. You see Meir and I don't really live in the married way anymore if you know what I mean. Once the kids were born, I guess we just lost interest in each other. I know I'm not anybody's ideal of a woman, and well, Meir has been like a eunuch to me for a long time now. Don't get me wrong, I'm not complaining. He gave me two wonderful children, which is more than I ever could have hoped for."

"What's his relationship like with your kids?"

"My son Frankie is a star in the Little League. He's the biggest boy on his team and a pitcher. Every game he strikes out so many of the other boys. He's that good. His teammates call him 'Poz' and Frankie loves that. At first I dragged Meir to the games – to see his son play baseball. I tell him it's the American game and he should learn about it. So what does that husband of mine do? He sits in the stands among all the other parents and reads *The Jewish Exponent*. It's a Jewish newspaper written in English," she explained. "I say to him, 'You're embarrassing our son', but he won't listen. Finally Frankie asked me not to bring his father to the games anymore. He says he doesn't want the other boys and their parents to know we're Jewish. I say there's no hiding it, we *are* Jewish. After that I leave his father at home because we don't want to be seen as that kind of Jewish."

Doherty didn't know what she meant by this last remark but he let it slide.

"What about your daughter?"

"Rhonda. My Rhonda is a very clever student. And thank God, she's has her father's looks, not mine. When she gets older she'll have plenty of dates; it won't be for her like it was for me. Though some of the local boys will be put off because she'll be so much smarter than them. Thankfully Rhonda is average size. Frankie is big like me, but that's not so bad for a boy. By the time my son gets to high school he'll be one of the best athletes in town, mark my words. "

"How do they get along with your husband?"

Edith Pozananski picked up a rugelach and began to gnaw on it. "In a word, they don't. Not now anyway. It was better when they were young. Most days my husband comes home from the store and we eat dinner. He's mostly silent except when he asks Rhonda about her studies. He never says anything to Frankie about his sports. After dinner he goes into the den to read the paper. Then he either falls asleep with the paper or in front of the television. A lot of nights he hasn't moved from that spot when I go to bed. We sleep in separate rooms now. I tell the children it's because their father snores too loud. I don't know if they believe me, but at their age I don't think they really care one way or another. Sometimes when I get up in the middle of the night I find Meir still sitting in front of the TV with the test patterns on the screen."

"Is he sleeping?"

"Mostly. Though there are times when I find him sitting there wide awake just staring at the television, or looking out out the window. I tell him to turn off the television and go to bed. He says he has to stay up in case *they* come."

"They. Who are they?"

"That's the thing, he never says who *they* are. Just that they might come."

"Do you think this could be some kind of flashback to his time in the concentration camps?"

"Perhaps. But that doesn't make any sense. All those years since we first met nothing like this ever happened, and then all of a sudden he thinks some people are going to come get him. I just don't understand him anymore - and to be honest with you, I'm not sure I really care to."

"Is there anything else about his behavior recently that might be a clue as to why he's gone missing?"

"There's one other thing, but you've got to promise not to say anything about this to my brother. He already thinks Meir is meshug in the head."

"I promise."

"Meir's been hoarding food under his bed. I was cleaning his room last week and I found bits of bread and some rotten apples under there. I told him he's got to stop doing this, otherwise he is going to attract mice."

"What did he say when you confronted him?"

"He looked at me with a blank face and said he didn't know what I was talking about."

Doherty asked Edith Poznanski if he could smoke and she agreed. He offered her a Camel but she declined. "What can you tell me about his trips to Providence on Thursdays and Saturdays?"

"What's there to tell? All I know is what Milton tells me. That Meir goes to the city to pick up the dry goods from the wholesaler on Thursdays. He often comes back late at night on those days."

"Did you ever ask him where he's been all day?"

"I did at first and he gave me some vague answers about visiting old familiar places in Providence. After a while I no longer bothered to ask. On most of those days it was more peaceful not having him around. If he's seeing some other woman I don't really care. I just don't want the children to find out about it."

"And on Saturdays?"

"On Saturdays he goes to Katz's on the East Side to pick up food for the minyan breakfast. Those days he doesn't stay late because he's has to put the fish and the cream cheese in the fridge before it goes bad. It was a week ago Saturday when he told me he was going up to Katz's and never came back. I called the Providence police. They took down my information but didn't seem much interested. They told me to call back after a week if he still hasn't come home. I told Milton that Meir was sick when he didn't show up for work on Monday. I thought he would come home in a day or two. When he didn't I had to admit that he was missing and asked my brother and Morris Mendelson to help find him."

"Why did you wait a three days before you told them your husband was gone?"

Edith blushed, though it was hard to tell given her ruddy complexion. "To be honest with you, Mr. Doherty. I was relieved not to have him around for those few days. I told Frankie and Rhonda that he was staying in Providence on business and that satisfied them. Now they know he's missing. I didn't tell Milton because I didn't want my brother to fire him."

"Have you and your husband ever discussed divorce?"

"Never. I think we just got used to the way things were and left it at that. But when he started acting strange lately that's when I became concerned about his health. I started to think that maybe he wasn't right in the head. I mean I didn't really know him all that well when we got married. And lately, he's been even more of a stranger to me. Do you think he might be having a nervous breakdown?"

"That was my next question. This doesn't sound like any case I've ever worked. Most of the people I search for go missing because they're running away from something or someone. You know, a jealous spouse, a crazy lover, bill collectors - people like that."

"Can you find Meir?"

"I'll certainly try. That's what the men in the minyan hired me to do. Do you want me to find him?"

A look of uncertainty passed over Edith Poznanski's face. "I don't know. I suppose so, at least for his own sake. I guess I'd like to know that he's okay and not sick somewhere or lying dead in an alley."

"If I do find him would you like him to come home?"

She did not respond right away. Then she said reluctantly, "No, I don't think so. I think I've had enough already of Meir."

Chapter Six

On Thursday Doherty accompanied Milton Orlovsky to Providence to meet with his main wholesaler. He had offered to drive, but Orlovsky said they should take his car because it had a bigger trunk, which he needed to carry his goods back to West Warwick. Half way to the city Doherty wished he'd insisted on driving. Milton talked the whole time, constantly sprinkling bad jokes into their conversation. He also kept lighting and relighting his smelly cigar, all the while paying little attention to the road. On two occasions they almost got into accidents when he swerved into the oncoming traffic while cursing his cigar.

When they got to the city Doherty tried to direct Orlovsky toward where he thought Davol Square was, but the driver insisted that he knew the way. As a result they got lost three times. Doherty understood why the owner of The Bargain Store was so willing to let his brother-in-law make the weekly runs to Providence. He obviously had little experience driving into the city. They finally found their way to Davol and after some searching located the warehouse of the wholesaler. With some halting maneuvering Orlovsky eventually was able to back his car up to the loading platform. Doherty was relieved to exit the vehicle after a harrowing hour in captivity.

The main wholesaler was a short, fat Italian guy named Fraterelli. He was probably in his mid-forties and had a thatch of black curly hair atop his wide head. He was wearing dusty blue work clothes. Fraterelli was a little put out when Doherty flashed his license and asked if he could have ten minutes of his time in private.

"I got a business to run here," he objected.

"This won't take long," Doherty said, accompanied by a look that indicated it would be in Fraterelli's best interests to talk to him. He was ushered into the wholesaler's office while Orlovsky had his weekly order loaded into the car. Once inside the cubicle both men lit up cigarettes and stared at each other for a few uncomfortable seconds.

"I'll be brief," Doherty began. "What can you tell me about Meir Poznanski, the fellow who usually comes to pick up The Bargain Store's order?"

Despite the cool weather the fat man was noticeably sweating. "I ain't got nothin' good to say about that guy. All I can tell you is he shows up regular to pick up the stuff and he don't know nothin' about this business. That's why all my dealin's are on the phone with the brother-in-law out there. Why, what's happened to the other guy? Did he get fired?"

"If only. It appears that the regular pick-up man is missing. You wouldn't know anything about that, would you?"

"Me? Why would I know anythin' 'bout him bein' missin'? The guy hardly talks when he's here. He picks up the goods, signs the invoices, that's about it. Sometimes he makes a snooty comment about the quality of the clothes. Kind of a stuck up bastard if you ask me."

"According to his wife he doesn't come home on those days till late at night. Do you have any idea where he goes after he leaves here?"

The fat Italian sat back and raised his hands. "How the hell would I know what he does once he leaves here? Alls I know is what I just told you. Hey, I'd like to help you out but I don't know nothin' else."

Although Doherty was pretty sure Fraterelli was telling the truth he went on. "He doesn't say anything about having friends here in Providence or asks about where certain places are? You know, like restaurants or men's stores, stuff like that."

Fraterelli shook his head. There was obviously nothing more to say. Just then a young guy stuck his head in the office door. "Hey boss, we got a problem out here."

Fraterelli sat up straight. "What kinda problem, Carmine?"

"Shaky and his boy are here and that Jew from West Warwick won't move his car. And you know how Shaky can get."

"Shit," Fraterelli said as he stood up. "Sorry, mister, I gotta take care of this."

Doherty followed Fraterelli out to the loading dock where Milton Orlovsky was engaged in an argument with two toughs. Things didn't look like they were going in a good direction. Fraterelli placed his sizable body between Milton and the one the kid called Shaky. The guy was tall and skinny and somewhere in his thirties. He wore a blue fedora at a rakish tilt and had a crazed look in his eyes. Doherty grabbed Orlovsky by the arm and began to edge him away from the fracas. Orlovsky was uttering some Yiddish expletives under his breath as Doherty pushed him.

"I was here first. Half my load's in the car already," Milton protested. "Who do those guys think they are?" Doherty had a pretty good idea of who they were, which was why he kept moving his Jewish companion further away from them.

"One of them called me a kike, the dirty bastard," Orlovsky said a little too loud for his own good. Hearing that, Shaky's boy began to head in their direction. Fratterelli would have intercepted him, but he was too busy trying to calm down the one called Shaky.

Doherty pushed Orlovsky back and stepped in front of the kid walking toward them. As he did he sized the guy up and saw that although he was much younger than him, Doherty had a good twenty pounds on the kid.

"What did that sheeny say about us?" the young guy said trying to push past Doherty.

"Leave him alone. He doesn't know what he's saying; he's just upset."

"How about if you step aside, friend. Or are you one of them Jews too?"

"Actually I'm one hundred percent Irish even though that's neither here nor there." Doherty gave him his best graveyard stare. "I'll get my buddy to move his car so you and your friend can load up your van and be out of here."

The kid took another step forward and Doherty placed his hand on his chest and looked him straight in the eye. "We don't want any trouble. If I was you I wouldn't come any closer."

The two men dead eyed each other for nearly half a minute. Then the one called Shaky shouted, "Hey, Marco. Get over here and help me load up the van. Leave them Jews alone."

Marco gave Doherty one last hard stare then turned and headed back to the white panel truck. They had pulled it up so close that Orlovsky couldn't have gotten into his Olds to move it even if he wanted to. Doherty and Orlovsky watched as the two men loaded suits into the van. When they were done Fraterelli peeled some bills off a wad he was holding and gave them to Shaky. The guy smiled at Fraterelli and gave him a soft slap on the cheek.

After they pulled away Doherty and Orlovsky made their way back to the loading dock. Fratterelli was really sweating now. "Sonsabitches," he muttered under his breath.

"What was that all about?" Milton asked.

"Just load up the rest of your stuff and get the fuck outta here," Fraterelli said, not even trying to mask his anger.

Still incensed from his face-off with Marco, Doherty put a strong grip on Fraterelli's fleshy arm and said, "That's no way to talk to a paying customer."

Fraterelli gave him an angry look but didn't pull his arm away. "Payin' customer, my ass. Your payin' customer just cost me two C notes and three extra suits."

"Who are those guys?" Milton asked again, truly perplexed by what just occurred.

"Who the fuck do you think they are, shlomo?" The three men looked at each other, though no one said anything. Then the fat Italian pulled his arm out of Doherty's grip and said, "They're the price I pay to do wholesale business here in Providence. They come by once, maybe twice a month and take a half dozen of my best suits. Sell 'em right outta that fuckin' van for less than I pay for 'em."

"I don't understand," said Orlovsky.

"Well maybe your tough guy pal here will explain it to you on your way back home. Now do me a favor, finish loadin' your car and get the fuck outta here before they decide to come back. And another thing my Jewish friend, find the lost guy and send him next time. At least he knows enough to keep his mouth shut."

Chapter Seven

Doherty planned to get up to Katz's Deli by mid-day on Saturday, but that idea was short-circuited when Leo Carney unexpectedly showed up at the office. Aside from wanting to pay off the balance of what he owed it was clear from the get-go that Carney needed to talk. Doherty ushered the client into his office. He took his seat behind the desk while Leo fished through his pockets for some cash. It was only then that Doherty noticed that Carney was wearing something other than his work clothes.

"You look good today, Leo. What's the occasion?"

His visitor looked down at his feet as he handed over thirty-two dollars and some change. "I'm tryin' to be a little more dressed up when I'm not workin' on account of the wife," he said almost as an apology.

"Does that mean Mrs. Carney is back home?"

Leo squirmed a little in the guest chair. Doherty offered him a cigarette and he took it. "After she came home we had a long talk. You know, I think we both been pretty unhappy for a while now, mostly 'cause we aren't able to have kids. I guess I been kinda takin' our marriage for granted these last coupla years. I shoulda seen how miserable she was."

"Look Leo, I'm not one to talk being that I've never been married myself. Your wife seems like a good woman and if it's going to be just the two of you, then maybe you should try a little harder to make things…" Doherty was searching here for the right word. "More exciting. Not the usual humdrum"

Leo Carney looked confused. Doherty continued, "You know, like take her out every now and then. Buy her a nice dinner, go to a movie or a club. Show her a good time. Women like that. Maybe even buy her flowers or candy once in a while."

"You mean like even when it's not her birthday or our anniversary?"

"Yeah. Like sometimes you should surprise her in little ways. And another thing, Leo, don't spend all your time off the job wearing your work clothes."

Carney nodded his head at this last remark. "I been tryin' to do that. You know, dress up nice, 'specially on weekends like now."

"It's a start, Leo. Your wife struck me as a pretty nice girl. And when I found her she sounded like she really wanted to go home," Doherty lied, all the while recalling the image of Marilyn Carney in the motel room wearing only a sheer slip after a night of sex. "Try to make her feel special even when you don't have to."

"What about that guy she run off with?"

"Forget him. He was only using her. He's the kind of guy who takes advantage of unhappy married women. I took care of him. Trust me, neither you nor your wife will ever see him again."

Leo Carney seemed satisfied with this last remark and stood to leave. "I can't thank you enough, Mr. Doherty," he said as they shook hands.

"And don't forget what I said. Treat her right and your wife'll never leave home again. But if you take her for granted, well, you never know what'll happen."

It was nearly four by the time Doherty located Katz's Deli. It was up on the East Side of Providence north of the College Hill area where the schools are located. He'd never been to this part of the city before and was surprised at how many stores here catered to the Jewish trade. Some of them even had Hebrew letters on their signs along with the English. He'd only recently become acquainted with the Jewish community in West Warwick and they tended to maintain a pretty low profile. In this part of Providence the Jews seemed to be in the majority.

Once inside the deli Doherty noticed that Katz's was smaller than he thought it would be. The place smelled of pickles, fresh baked bread and smoked meat. There were two large glass display cases with a counter in between. One case had a variety of fishes and cream cheeses in it, including the various fishes Doherty had seen at the minyan breakfast. The other case contained mostly pink cold cuts, many of which Doherty had never seen before. The top shelf of that case had some cooked items, primarily meats of unrecognizable origins. Lining the wall to the right of the glass cases were several metal bins containing bagels, rolls and different kinds of breads, all unsliced.

The deli was crowded and noisy. Each customer took a number out of a machine and gabbed loudly as they waited their turn. Many of the conversations were a mix of English and Yiddish, a language Mr. Mendelson had explained to him was a combination of German and Hebrew with some unique words of its own thrown in. To Doherty it sounded a lot like the German he'd heard the Kraut POWs speaking during the war. As he stood patiently in the back surveying the scene Doherty observed that most of the customers were heavyset women in a range of ages from their twenties to their seventies. There was much jostling among them, though generally of a good-natured sort as each waited for one of the two women working the counter to call her number.

The serving women wore white aprons that hung around their necks and tied at the waist and had food stains on them. One looked like she was somewhere in her late forties. She had her dark hair pulled back into a tight bun and wore a severe expression on her face. Doherty watched her deal with the customers in a terse manner, rejecting any attempts at small talk and never smiling as she went about her business. The other was younger and shorter. She couldn't have been more than in her mid-twenties, had dark skin and tightly curled black hair that was cut short and close to her scalp. Unlike the older woman, she bantered easily with the customers, occasionally dropping a Yiddish word or expression into the conversation. She had dark eyes that sparkled when she smiled and she laughed easily with each customer. As she did the older woman made disapproving remarks about her behavior that the younger one ignored.

Realizing that he might be standing in the crowd forever, Doherty finally took one of the numbers and rehearsed what he would say as he moved closer to the counter. When his turn came the young girl looked up at him and let out a friendly laugh. She was quite short so even a guy of Doherty's rather average height towered over her. As a man in Katz's among all the women he was already conspicuously out of place.

"So what'll it be, big fella?" the girl said with a grin on her face.

"I need to talk with you," he said hesitantly. "But now doesn't seem like a good time."

"What are you, some kind of salesman?" she asked.

"No, I'm a private investigator," Doherty said flashing his card. He could sense that the women waiting behind him were growing restive.

The young girl looked at the older one who was now giving Doherty the hairy eyeball and said, "Come back at six. That's when we close. She'll be gone by then so I'll be able to talk freely," she added in reference to the older woman.

Doherty left the clamor of Katz's and drove south down to the College Hill area. He parked on Thayer Street and walked up and down the three blocks of stores and eateries, admiring the coeds as he did. He passed the Avon Cinema, which was showing two French language films. One was called *Four Hundred Blows* and the other was advertised only in French as *Les Enfants du Paradis*. From his time in Paris Doherty knew that the title translated into Children of Paradise. He'd never seen a foreign language movie before and wasn't sure how people who only spoke English would know what was going on in them. He assumed you'd have to be pretty fluent in French to understand either of these movies.

It started to drizzle lightly so he stopped in at one of the many bookstores that lined Thayer. After perusing the shelves for a while he bought a copy of another book by the Hemingway guy who wrote the one he was currently reading. That book was about a solitary fisherman in Cuba who catches a big fish while out on his own, only to have great trouble bringing it back into port. All the while the man keeps thinking about Joe DiMaggio. Doherty liked the fact that the Cuban man was a baseball fan. The new book was called *A Farewell to Arms*. He figured he'd give the author another go round. The book jacket said that this Hemingway fellow had won a Nobel Prize for literature in 1954.

He returned to Katz's before six and sat in his car across the street smoking while the last stragglers left the deli. He saw the older woman put on her coat. She had a few words with the younger one and then marched out of the store, her back ramrod straight. A few minutes later the young girl, still in her apron, came to the door and looked out. Then she flipped the sign that said *Open* over to *Closed*. Doherty climbed out of his car and crossed the street. The door wasn't locked; he knocked anyway and when the girl saw who it was she opened it right away. She greeted him with the same infectious grin she had earlier.

There were three small tables inside that he hadn't noticed earlier, mostly because of the crowd of customers who'd jammed the place. The girl pointed for him to sit at one.

"Would you like something to eat?" she asked.

Doherty held back, wanting to say 'no' though the smells inside the deli made that almost impossible. He hadn't eaten since breakfast yet didn't want to put the girl out after a hard day at the counter.

She smiled again and said, "Okay, how about a sandwich? What'll it be: pastrami, corned beef, roast beef? You don't look like the beef tongue type."

"I don't know."

"You're not Jewish are you?"

"Afraid not. Irish on both sides."

The girl let out a pleasant chuckle. "Then maybe we should stick with the corned beef. The Irish eat corned beef, don't they?"

"Every St. Paddy's Day – boiled to death, with cabbage."

"Well this won't be like that, but you'll like it anyway. Rye bread and mustard all right?" Doherty nodded and the girl went back behind the counter to make him a sandwich. She reappeared a few minutes later carrying a tray that had a thick corned beef sandwich on it along with some coleslaw and a large pickle to the side. She also handed him a cup of black coffee. She'd brought herself a coffee and a cherry Danish. She wiped her hands on her splattered apron and sat down with him.

"So bubbie, what can I do for you?"

"You work here all the time?"

"Only on Saturdays. It's all I can take working alongside the bitch," she said, obviously referring to the older woman.

"She a relative of yours?"

The girl laughed. "You might say that. She's my mother. We don't get along. Never have. She's always treated me like shit, though over time I've gotten used to it. It's the way she treats my father that I can't stand. This is his deli; he's Katz. When they're here working together she acts like she's the boss and he's the hired help." The words were coming out in rapid fire. "He won't work on Saturdays because it's the Sabbath, so it's just her and me. By the way, my name's Rachel, Rachel Katz. And you are?"

"I'm Doherty. My first name is Hugh, but everybody just calls me Doherty."

"Okay, Doherty. Now eat your sandwich. It's the last one I'll be making till next Saturday, so enjoy it." The girl then pulled a pack of cigarettes out from under her apron and lit one. Doherty began to wolf down his corned beef sandwich.

"You're a hungry man, eh Doherty."

"I haven't eaten since breakfast."

"That's another reason I can tell you're not Jewish. Jews never miss a meal. They might miss an anniversary or temple on the high holidays, but they never miss a meal."

"So, Rachel, what do you do when you're not slinging corned beef?"

"Would you believe I'm a teacher? I teach English over at Hope High."

"Aren't you a little small to be teaching in a high school?"

Rachel Katz laughed at that. "That's what everybody asks me. So every year I get some big basketball or football player to be my protector. Soon as the other kids find out who he is they stop giving me a hard time. To be honest with you, I think my students kind of like me. They think I'm cute and they like my sense of humor. That's one of the ways we Jews have always protected ourselves – with our humor." Doherty thought their humor hadn't worked so well for them during the war.

"Are you married?"

"What kind of question is that? Are you flirting with me, Doherty? Boy, the bitch would love that. Me going out with an Irishman."

"I'm sorry. I was just trying to make conversation. You seem so easy and breezy, it makes me feel a little awkward."

"Really? It must be the five cups of coffee I've had today." She took a sip from her cup and eyed him over the edge. "So are you?" she asked.

"What? Easy and breezy?"

"No, silly. Are you married?"

"No, I'm not. Never have been either," he said sounding more defensive than he meant to.

"The bachelor type, eh. I was almost married once. I was engaged for almost a year to a nice Jewish boy. Even my mother liked him."

"What happened?"

Rachel took some time to consider her answer. "I don't know. I guess you could say I didn't like the way he smelled. I know that sounds kind of superficial, but when you start thinking about how you could be living with a guy for the rest of your life and you already don't like the way he smells, you know it's only going to get worse. So I broke it off. My dad understood; my mother was furious. I think more than anything she just wanted to get me out of the house."

"You still live with your parents?"

"Yup. It's kind of embarrassing. I'll be twenty-seven in July. Most of my friends are married and have kids and I'm still living with mom and pop. Pretty sad, huh?"

Doherty didn't know how to respond so he didn't.

"Have you always been a private eye?"

"Not always. I was a kid for the first part of my life."

"Okay, smart guy. Sorry I asked." They both went back to their coffees, though Rachel eyed him pretty closely as she did.

"I'm only teasing. After I got out of high school I worked at Quonset Point till I got drafted. Then I was in the army for a little over two years during the war. I went back to Quonset after I was discharged. I left there to become a policeman in West Warwick and stayed on the force for a few years before going into business for myself. That's about it. My life in a nutshell."

"Sounds more interesting than mine. I went right from Classical to RIC and then into teaching – and working as a part-time deli waitress, of course. I'll probably stay at Hope till I get pregnant. They don't let girls continue to teach once they start showing. I suspect it's because they don't want the kids to think about what she did to get that way. First I'll have to get married, though - unless some guy knocks me up," she added with a smirk.

"You got a pretty smart mouth for a schoolteacher."

"I got a pretty smart brain too, Mr. Private Eye. I graduated third in my class at Classical. Highest girl in my grade."

"Then why did you become a teacher?"

"I don't know. I guess it beats working. You grow up slinging sandwiches in a deli you get a pretty good idea what it's like to work hard for a living. I've seen what it's done to my father. Compared to this, being a teacher is a breeze."

It might sound strange but I really like teaching. It's fun, for now anyway. What about you? Do you enjoy your work?"

Doherty thought about the question as he worked through the last of his sandwich. "Yeah, sometimes. I mean I always liked solving puzzles and my job is sort of like that. Sometimes it's sad though. Most of my clients hire me to find a lost spouse or missing loved one. It usually turns out that one of them is cheating on the other. Either that or they're trying to run away from a dead end life."

"No murder cases like in the movies?" she teased.

"I had one – just last fall as a matter of fact. It was in all the papers. A prominent real estate guy from Warwick and a big deal in the Republican Party got killed right before the election. You might've read about it."

"I think I remember that story. So did you find out who killed him? Did you crack the case, McGraw?"

"Not directly. The guy who killed him was a small time hood connected to the mob. It was all because of a business deal that had gone bad. The whole thing was pretty complicated, too complicated for me to explain right now. Plus, I still have to protect some clients who were involved in the mess."

Rachel took one last hit off her smoke and stuffed it out in the now empty coleslaw bowl. "Whatever you say, Doherty. How was the sandwich?"

"Very good. First time I've ever had corned beef that wasn't boiled with cabbage."

"Would you like some more coffee?"

"Sure."

While Rachel Katz went to fetch up another cup for each of them Doherty extracted the photo of Meir Poznanski from his wallet that his wife had given him.

When she sat back down Doherty placed the picture in front of her on the table. "Ever see this guy in here?"

She looked at the photo and immediately smiled. "Who, Meir? Of course I have. He comes in every Saturday for bagels and fish and pastries for his minyan breakfast. A very nice man."

Doherty looked at her strangely. "Did I say something wrong?" Rachel asked.

"No, it's just that you're the first person I've spoken to who said Meir Poznanski was a nice man."

"Poznanski? Is that his last name?"

"Yeah, and he's gone missing. He's the person I've been hired to find."

"I was wondering why that other fellow came in the last two weeks. He was here this morning; a little guy with hardly any hair. He seemed pleasant enough, but when I asked him about Meir he turned away and had my mother wait on him. My mother never asks anybody about anything. The deli is all business and no pleasure to her."

"Did you ever talk to Meir when he came in? Did he ever say anything that would indicate he was in some kind of trouble? Anything that could be a clue as to why he's gone missing?"

Rachel shook her head. "Not really. We would just talk about the weather or the quality of the fish; things like that. He was always very formal. I could tell from his accent that he was European. We get a lot of Europeans in here – mostly older people. You know, people who were refugees from the war. They're always very formal, even when they're being arrogant. She was very nice too."

"She?"

"His wife. She came with him, every Saturday."

Doherty was suddenly very confused. "What did she look like, this wife?"

"I don't know. Dark hair, probably dyed, dark eyes. Nice looking. I'd say she's in her forties, like him. Always dressed well as if she'd just come from temple or out shopping. She's European too. Her accent is thicker than his though her diction is very precise. As an English teacher I pick up on things like that. Is she the one who hired you to find him?"

"I can't tell you that. But I will tell you that the woman who came in here with Meir Poznanski is not his wife. I met with the wife the other day and she doesn't fit the description you just gave me."

"Wow. They sure had me fooled. She wore a wedding ring and often had her arm wrapped in his. Do you think she's his mistress? I understand that's pretty common among Europeans."

Doherty wiped his mouth and stood. He pulled some money out of his wallet but Rachel stayed his hand. She said the sandwich was on the house. It was the most she could do to help him find the missing man. He then handed her one of his cards and said, "If either of them comes in again, could you give me a call. My home number's on the back in case you can't reach me at my office. My secretary is currently on vacation so…"

"Will I see you again?" Rachel asked perhaps meaning more than Doherty understood.

"Sure. I guess so. Next time I come in I'll try the pastrami."

"Have it hot. It's better that way." They shook hands before Doherty left. He caught himself holding her digits longer than was necessary.

Chapter Eight

He felt like he'd hit a wall. All potential leads so far led nowhere. Unless Doherty could find the woman who'd accompanied Poznanski to Katz's he wasn't sure where to turn next. The wife had been of little assistance, and the fact that she seemed not at all upset that her husband was missing didn't help. Fraterelli, the wholesaler at Davol Square that Poznanski dealt with on Thursdays, appeared to be nothing more than a person he did business with. And judging from what had occurred at the loading dock, someone with plenty of troubles of his own. Unless Poznanski'd had a violent run-in with the booster named Shaky that path apparently led nowhere as well. The key was the woman that accompanied Meir to the deli each week. Somehow Doherty had to track her down.

Rachel Katz had said something about how Poznanski's lady friend was always dressed as if she'd just come from temple. That might've helped until he discovered that there were six different Jewish synagogues in Providence, three located on the East Side alone. Plus Mendelson had told him that most Jews didn't regularly attend synagogue either on Friday night or Saturday morning as Christians did church on Sunday. As a result he couldn't exactly park himself outside a synagogue and scan the crowd for someone who fit the woman's description as he might've done outside St. John's or St. James' on a Sunday morning. On top of that he had only a vague idea what this mystery woman looked like. It was a description that probably fit dozens of Jewish women her age in Providence.

On Monday Doherty sat in his car outside of Francine's at a quarter to six, hoping to catch Mendelson as he closed up shop for the night. In this business he preferred to confront people when they least expected it because it gave them little opportunity to fabricate a story on the run. What he didn't want to do under any circumstances was run into Millie St. Jean. When Millie exited the store at five to six Doherty's heart sank, as did his head below the window line of the Chevy. The last thing he wanted was for her to see him. He hadn't spoken to Millie in five months, though he never stopped thinking about her that whole time. For a second he thought about stepping out of the car to walk with her as she headed down Main to catch her bus. He caught himself, knowing that whatever happened afterwards wouldn't go as he wished.

Ten minutes later Mendelson emerged from Francine's. He was bending down to lock the door when Doherty slipped up behind him.

"Evening Mr. Mendelson," he said.

"My goodness!" the little man squealed as he jumped out of his crouch. "You scared the living daylights out of me." Doherty said he was sorry though he didn't really mean it.

"I was up at Katz's Deli the other day and the young girl who works the counter there told me you've been picking up the breakfast goods for the minyan the last two weeks."

Mendelson straightened up and ran his hands down the front of his trench coat. He was trying to regain his composure. His voice did sound calmer and almost indignant when he said, "Well, someone has to do it now that Meir has flown the coop."

"What do you mean 'flown the coop'?"

The little man hemmed and hawed for a moment. "Well, you know, since he's ah… disappeared. That's what I meant," he added in a tone that indicated he was not so sure it was.

"When I spoke at length with the young girl at Katz's, she told me she asked you about Meir and you immediately turned away and got her mother to take your order. Why did you do that, Mr. Mendelson? Is there something you know about Meir that you're not telling me?"

Mendelson wanted to be on his way, though he couldn't leave before answering Doherty's questions. He fidgeted as he tried to think of a good answer.

"Did you know about the other woman? Is that why Meir often stayed in Providence until late on Thursdays when he went to pick up The Bargain Store's goods? Did you know she accompanied him to Katz's every Saturday?"

Mendelson's look was now downcast. He stared at the sidewalk. Finally he looked up at Doherty and said, "Yes, I knew. Meir told me about her."

"Is that why it was the minyan and not Poznanski's wife that hired me? Did she know he was seeing someone else and didn't care anymore whether he came home or not?"

"I can't answer that. I will tell you the men were shocked when Edith didn't tell anyone that Meir was gone. Even Milton was dumbfounded. Usually when a man leaves his wife she tells someone: a friend, a family member, someone. Edith told no one. We don't even know what she said to her children."

"How long have you known about this other woman?"

Mendelson looked embarrassed and wouldn't make eye contact with Doherty. He tried to edge away but the larger man blocked his path.

Reluctantly he admitted, "I've known for several months. He told me about her just after the New Year."

"And you didn't think to pass this information on to me when I was hired to find him?"

"I thought you'd find out about her in your own way. I mean, you're supposed to be the ace detective. I was hoping you'd uncover his relationship with her without involving me. I couldn't let Edith and the other men know what Meir had revealed to me in great confidence. I didn't think it was my place to betray his trust."

"Not even after he disappeared?" Mendelson didn't answer. He just stood there looking foolish. "Who is she?" Doherty asked.

"That I don't know. Honestly, I don't."

"Is he involved with her romantically?"

"No," Mendelson said softly. "According to Meir their relationship isn't like that."

"Then what is it like?" Doherty asked, louder now.

"She is someone he knew over there during the war – from before he came to the States. That's all he would tell me. He kept saying she was someone who understood him. She was not 'like the rest of us' were his exact words"

"Is there anyone else who knows about this? Anybody from the minyan?"

Mendelson carefully considered the question. "Gordon might know. Gordon Titleman, the one who spoke on Meir's behalf at the minyan breakfast. The tall, thin fellow. He's probably the closest thing Meir has to a friend here in West Warwick. Gordon lives down in Centreville. You can find him in the phonebook," he added in a nervous voice.

Doherty was growing angry with Mendelson. Angry with him for not being honest in the first place and angry for not being any help in identifying this other woman. However, there was no more to be said tonight, so he stepped aside and let the little man continue on home to his little family.

Doherty phoned Gordon Titleman and they agreed to meet for breakfast the next morning at the Veteran's Square Diner at the lower end of Main near the Centreville Bridge. The diner was a greasy spoon built out of an old trolley car. It seated only ten people at a time. By 9:30, when the two men met, the morning crowd had pretty much cleared out. Doherty arrived first and ordered two eggs over easy with bacon, toast and coffee. Titleman was late and told Doherty as soon as he arrived that he couldn't stay long, he had to get to work. Titleman ordered coffee and buttered toast to go with it.

Titleman was wearing a beige wool sport coat with a white open collar shirt under it. His hair was thin enough that his pink scalp shone through it. Nevertheless, he was a pretty handsome guy. Tall and stately looking. They exchanged pleasantries though Doherty was determined to get down to business knowing that Titleman's time was limited.

"Did you know Meir Poznanski was seeing another woman up in Providence?"

Titleman sipped his coffee, apparently in no particular hurry to answer Doherty's question. He began slowly. "As you know, Meir was in the concentration camps during the war. He lost the whole of his family in Poland to the Nazis. Most people never recover from something like that. I thought it was a mitzvah when he married Edith Orlovsky and made a new life for himself here in West Warwick. I knew he was a damaged person; we all did. The other men, the ones in the minyan, they've been very hard on Meir. Most of them are practical businessmen. Shopkeepers to a great degree. They see Meir as a self-satisfied intellectual while most of them never even finished high school.

Me, I'm an engineer," Titleman added as a way to indicate that he thought he was a cut above the other members of the minyan. "I understood Meir. He's a scholar. And as I'm sure you know, there's little place for scholars here in West Warwick, Jewish or otherwise."

Doherty finished his eggs and ordered more coffee. "That's all well and good," he said, "but you're getting off the track. What about this other woman?"

"In all the time I've known Meir he's been searching for *others*. For people who shared his dreadful experiences. I believe he needed that to help him make sense of what happened over there."

"And that's what this other woman is? Someone who can help him make sense of the past, of the concentration camps?"

"She's a survivor like him. That's all I know about her. I don't even know her name. I only know that she too was a victim. He never told me how he found her or what they do together, but apparently she gives him something that no one else in the world can, including his wife. He never told me anything else about her. I got the feeling that he didn't want to share her with any of us. Does that any make sense to you, Mr. Doherty?"

"I don't know what would make sense to people who survived those camps. Life itself might not even make sense after something like that."

Titleman finished his coffee and picked up the check. "This is on me, Mr. Doherty. It was nice to see you again," he added as they shook hands. The breakfast hadn't advanced the case any, though it did give Doherty a better understanding of Meir Poznanski. Still he wasn't sure it would help him find the lost man.

Back at the office Doherty sat at his desk staring at the pack of Camels lying near his elbow. It showed a very noble looking animal flanked by two pyramids, one small and one larger, and a stand of palm trees. He knew from elementary school that the animal wasn't really a camel; it was a one humped dromedary. But no one wanted to go into the neighborhood spa and ask for a pack of dromedaries. So the cigarettes were called *Camels*. Doherty had only seen a live camel once, as a kid at the Roger Williams Park Zoo. It was an unattractive looking beast that drooled some kind of slime from the side of its mouth. It sure didn't resemble the gallant figure on the cigarette pack.

A lot of different thoughts were spinning around in Doherty's head that afternoon. He was thinking about Poznanski and what it must feel like to live among people who had no sense of the horrors he'd seen and experienced. He was also thinking about Santiago, the old fisherman in the book he was reading - wondering how it would feel to be alone in a small boat out on the open sea and hook the biggest fish of your life. It had taken the old man nearly three days to reel in the huge marlin. It was so large he couldn't fit it in his boat so he had to lash it to the side. He then spent hours thrashing at the sharks that gathered to feed off his prized catch.

As the afternoon plodded along Doherty began to see himself as one of these men – alone, operating always in a vacuum, solving other people's problems and never having to deal with his own. His parents were dead, his sister Margaret was living out in Minnesota; his best friend was a barber who he'd never seen outside of the shop. Other than that there was Benny O'Neill, who called him every couple of months to go to the fights at the Tiogue Vista or to a Reds game up at the Arena. There was Willy Legere, the blind vet who now worked down at the water department, and of course, Gus Timilty, his old mentor, who operated out of a high-toned investigations agency in South Providence. Them plus his secretary Agnes were pretty much the full inventory of Doherty's acquaintances.

And, of course, there was Millie St. Jean, who he almost fell in love with. His relationship with her ended badly and he hadn't dated anyone since. He had to admit that right now he missed having Agnes in the office to kick things around with. He lit another Camel and continued down this path, all the while trying to understand what the mysterious woman from Providence gave Meir Pozananski that no one else could.

He was jolted out of this maudlin reverie when the phone rang. At first he delayed picking it up until he remembered that Agnes was still on her vacation.

"Doherty and Associates," he said springing back into the real world.

"Is this Doherty or one of his associates?" the female caller asked adding a snicker to her question.

"This is Doherty. How can I help you?"

"She was in here this afternoon," the still unfamiliar voice said.

"Hold on a minute. Who is this? And who was in where?"

The woman at the other end of the line laughed, "So soon you forget, eh bubbie. It's Rachel Katz. My father's been sick so I've been working at the deli after school. She came in just a little while ago. Alone, without Meir."

"What did she want?"

"She placed a large order for food. Said it was for a B'nai B'rith brunch at Temple Emmanuel. Cold cuts, breads, slaw, potato salad, pickles, the whole schmear."

"When's she coming back to pick it up?"

"That's the thing, she isn't. She wants it all delivered directly to the temple on Thursday. My mother wasn't too happy about that. She's not as accommodating about deliveries as my father, even with such big orders."

"Oh," Doherty said, not bothering to mask his disappointment.

"But fear not, Doherty. The good news is that I had her give me her address and phone number. I told her I needed them just in case there was a problem with the order. Afterwards my mother said that I didn't have to do that, but I was thinking about you the whole time."

"That's terrific. So can you give me the address?"

"Not so fast, bubbie. I'm only going to give you this information if I can come with you."

"But Rachel..."

"No buts, Mr. Private Eye. For this case I'm going to be your Gal Friday. It'll be fun, and besides, there's no way Mrs. Koplowitz is going to let you through her door if I'm not with you. So it looks like you've got a sidekick whether you want one or not."

Doherty couldn't fault her logic. He now knew the woman's name was Koplowitz and it was likely she'd be more willing to talk with him if Rachel was by his side.

"Here's the plan, Doherty. I've got to deliver some things from school to Warwick tomorrow in the late afternoon. Why don't I swing by your little town and pick you up. I'm sure I know the neighborhood where Mrs. Koplowitz lives better than you."

"You'll have to take me back to West Warwick afterwards. It could be late."

"That's okay. I'm a big girl now; I can stay up as late as I want. Besides, it'll give me a good excuse to spend less time at home with the bitch. Now where would you like me to get you?"

Doherty gave Rachel directions into Arctic and to his office on Brookside. She told him she'd be there by six.

Chapter Nine

A little after six, Rachel Katz walked right into Doherty and Associates without bothering to knock. Doherty was reading the afternoon *Providence Bulletin* when she strode through the door to his inner office.

He looked up from the paper, surprised but not displeased. "I guess you found your way all right."

"I've only been to Arctic once before, but your directions were pretty good. It's kind of easy when there's only one main street."

"Actually there are two. Main forks to the left and what you drove down to get here becomes Washington. But that's no never mind."

She perused Doherty's four empty walls. "Nice office you got here. I guess you're all about the Spartan look, huh? I suppose the lack of distractions helps you to keep your mind on your work."

"I know, I know. I should put something on the walls. I've been thinking about it for a few months now," he said feeling a little embarrassed by the austere nature of his digs.

"Well at least your secretary has some family pictures to spruce up her space out there. Anyway, we should get going since we'll probably run into some traffic getting across the city."

Rachel's car was parked at the curb. It was one of those small European jobs that were just making their way into the States. Doherty had a little trouble folding his frame into the tiny passenger seat.

"What is this tuna can anyway?" he asked once inside.

"Hey, be careful how you talk about Amelia. She's a Renault, my French mademoiselle."

"You have a name for your car."

"I do now. This is my first one. Before I got her I had to drive my father's big Ford station wagon or take the bus wherever I went. It didn't do a thing for my self-image."

Doherty took a moment to check out Rachel while she worked her way down Main toward Providence Street. She was wearing a pleated, plaid, wool skirt and a short sleeve black turtleneck sweater. She had on nylons and abbreviated high-heeled black shoes. A small necklace of gold hung around her neck. Today she wore a hint of makeup and her black hair had a glow to it that it'd lacked the other day at the deli. Doherty assumed this was one of her teacher outfits.

He instructed her to continue out Providence Street until it merged into New London Avenue. From there they headed into Cranston. Near the boys' reform school at Sockanosset, New London became Reservoir Avenue. Rachel assured him that she could find her way from this point on.

"Why a French car? American cars not good enough for you?"

She laughed and shook her head. "No, I just wanted something small to match my size, and something different. I got tired of having to sit on a phone book whenever I drove my father's station wagon. I thought about getting one of those Volkswagen Beetles, but my mother said she'd disown me if I bought a Nazi car. I guess I could see her point. The war is still pretty raw for people of her generation. What about you?"

"Are you asking about what kind of car I drive or how I feel about the war?"

"I don't know. Tell me about both since we've got a long ride ahead of us."

"Well, I used to drive a big old Packard. Most people politely referred to it as a 'shit box'." Rachel laughed at this. Her laugh at his profanity made him feel comfortable in her presence. "I finally traded it in for a '55 Chevy last year after I'd made some real money. To be honest with you, it wasn't much of a trade-in. I think the lot that took the Packard sent it to the junkyard for scrap the very next day. I tend to walk a lot so cars aren't all that important to me."

They sat in silence for a while. Once they got into Providence, where Reservoir turned into Broad Street, Rachel nosed her French roller skate toward downtown. When they passed by Classical High School from where she had graduated, she pointed it out to him.

"What about the war? Is it still too raw for you too?"

"Are you asking if I'd drive a Volkswagen?"

"I suppose so. In a roundabout way."

"Doesn't matter much to me," he said with a shrug. "A car's just a car. Though I wouldn't buy one of those Beetles mostly because I don't like they way they look. They remind me of mud pies."

"Mud pies - I like that," she said with a chuckle. "So, were you in the war?"

Doherty hesitated before answering Rachel's question. He was hoping to keep their conversation light and not too personal, but now they were about throw that out the window of her tiny Renault.

"Yeah, I was in Italy, then a little bit in Germany later on," he said trying to sound matter-of-fact about his combat experiences. It was the stock line he usually offered about his time overseas.

Once they got into downtown they got caught in some evening rush hour traffic. Rachel downshifted the little French car as they edged their way across the mall by the Biltmore Hotel, the biggest establishment of its kind in the capital city. They were only a few blocks from the office of Frank Ganetti, Jr., CPA and heir to one of Providence's more notorious crime families. Doherty had become acquainted with Ganetti last year due to circumstances surrounding the murder of Spencer Wainwright. It was an acquaintance he had no desire to renew.

"Did you see a lot of action over there?"

Doherty didn't like her use of the word *action*. He felt it reduced his wartime experiences to a movie. "Enough to last me a lifetime if you want to know the truth," he answered, purposely not offering anything more.

"Did you see any of those concentration camps we heard so much about in Hebrew school?"

Doherty shook his head. "No, not personally. We saw films of them before we got sent home. That was Eisenhower's idea. The brass said they wanted us to see what we'd been fighting against. It was pretty powerful stuff, though I still can't imagine what men like Meir Poznanski went through."

Rachel turned up College Hill and headed toward the East Side. The little Renault struggled to climb the hill at Meeting Street. She downshifted to second to help them crest the rise.

"What about you. Can you imagine being in one of those camps?"

"You know what I say, Doherty, 'there but for fortune'. Thankfully I was born on this side of the Atlantic and not over there. I wasn't even twelve yet when the war ended, but I heard about the death camps almost from the time I can remember. They would bring survivors of the Shoah to my Hebrew school and to the temple to tell us about what had happened to them. You see, by the time we got to World War Two in my high school history class it was the end of the year and everybody just wanted to get out for summer vacation. But among Jews the war and everything surrounding it were things our parents insisted we know about. Sometimes when speakers came in they'd put up big signs behind the lectern that said "Never Again." Now it's as much a part of who we Jews are as I suppose the potato famine is to the Irish."

Doherty laughed. "To be honest with you, Rachel, I don't know how many micks here in America know much about the famine these days. For us it's more about how we hated the English. I guess for the Irish, back in the old country the English were our Nazis."

"Kind of ironic wouldn't you say, given that the English helped us defeat the Nazis and win the war?"

Doherty thought about life's little ironies, such as this one of he and Rachel setting off on a quest to find a man who survived the concentration camps only to become a missing person here in America.

Rachel turned north on Hope Street then took a few turns onto smaller residential streets until they reached Camp Street. It was a narrow tree lined street with single and two family houses. They drove slowly until she found the correct address and parked in front of a nicely appointed red and white wood-framed colonial house, probably built sometime early in the century.

They got out of the Renault. He was glad to stretch his legs after being folded up in her little buggy. Rachel led him up onto a porch that ran the length of the house.

"How do you know this neighborhood so well?"

She poked his arm and said, "I live around here, silly. The deli's only three blocks away, up there on Rochambeau," she added pointing to the west. "Do

you know why they call this Camp Street?" she asked. Not waiting for a response, she explained, "General Rochambeau, the French mercenary who
helped the colonists in the Revolutionary War, camped here with his men
before striking out against the British. Rumor has it that Washington himself visited to inspect this encampment, though no historian has been able to
verify that."

Before she rang the bell Rachel turned to Doherty and said, "Let me do the
talking till we get inside. We don't want to scare Mrs. Koplowitz. Remember
these people don't have fond memories of the police."

"I'm not a cop," Doherty protested.

"I know, but you look like one in your suit. She might not see any differ-
ence between a private investigator and a policeman."

Rachel rang the bell and they waited. Eventually footsteps came to the half
glass door and a woman looked through the curtain covering it before opening up.

"Rachel," she said with a mixture of surprise and trepidation. "What are
you doing here? Is there something wrong with the B'nai B'rith order?" Mrs.
Koplowitz's accent was indeed strong, in an Eastern European fashion. The
woman then looked at Doherty and her initial smile turned to caution.

"I'm sorry to bother you, Mrs. Koplowitz. There's nothing wrong with your
deli order for Thursday. It's just that..." Rachel stammered. "My friend Mr.
Doherty here and I would like to ask you a few questions about Mr. Poznanski.
It's seems that he's missing, and some of his friends in West Warwick are worried about him. They've hired Mr. Doherty as a private investigator to find
him." She spoke very quickly giving Mrs. Koplowitz little time to respond.

The woman looked from Rachel to Doherty and back again at Rachel. A
look of resignation crossed her face. "Why don't you come in? I'll put up some
tea."

They slipped into the house, walked tentatively through a short hall and
stood nervously on the edge of a sitting room. It was neatly furnished with a
grand piano taking up a third of the room. A multitude of pictures Doherty
assumed were of family and friends covered the top of it. The furniture was old
but comfortable looking, with doilies resting on the arms of the sofa and the
easy chairs that filled most of the remaining space. A coffee table sat in front of
the sofa and it held a number of magazines, several of which were in Hebrew.

"I'll be just in," Mrs. Koplowitz shouted from the kitchen. In time she appeared with a tray carrying teacups, a teapot, bowls of milk and sugar and a plate with some sort of coffee cake cut into pieces on it. She beckoned Rachel and Doherty to sit on the sofa while she poured the tea. Mrs. Koplowitz was a striking looking woman somewhere in her mid to late-forties; she had dark brown hair edged with streaks of gray and piercing brown eyes to match. From what Doherty could tell she held her figure quite well. If Meir Poznanski was carrying on an affair with this woman Doherty could understand why after meeting his wife Edith.

Before she settled into an easy chair Mrs. Koplowitz asked if either Rachel or Doherty would like a little schnapps in their tea. Rachel begged off saying she had to teach in the morning; Doherty accepted. She added a generous amount to his tea and an equal amount to her own. Then she sat and sipped her drink.

Rachel began, "I know you're a good friend of Meir Poznanski so we were hoping you could help us find him. The men in his minyan are worried about him." She didn't add that the whole time she and Meir had been coming into Katz's Rachel thought they were husband and wife.

Mrs. Koplowitz turned to Doherty and said, "I don't suppose his wife sent you, did she?" Her words came out as a challenge.

"I'm sorry, Mrs. Koplowitz, I can't tell you who hired me."

"Please Mr. Doherty, call me 'Anna'," she said with a broad A, European style. "In Poland my name was Agnieszka, but no one here could ever spell or pronounce it correctly, so I changed it to Anna." As Rachel had indicated earlier, despite her heavy accent, Anna Koplowitz spoke with very precise diction. "And let me be clear to you two, I am also worried about my dear friend Meir."

"So you don't know where he is either? When was the last time you saw him?" Doherty asked.

Her eyes gazed at the wall above them, engrossed in thought. "The last time he came was Thursday, maybe one, two weeks ago. Yes, I believe it's been two weeks since I saw him last."

"What was his frame of mind at that time?" Doherty asked. Rachel sat demurely beside him drinking her tea, now letting Doherty take the lead.

"Oy gevalt. He was so upset. More upset that I'd ever seen him. Usually he would come here, have some tea, maybe some drinks and go home to that

wife of his. We would talk of Poland and life before the war. You see, together
we created this fantasy about our lives back then that left out all the bad parts.
We knew we were deluding ourselves but we didn't care. There is no purpose
in thinking about the war. It is too painful."

"But that night he was different?"

"Different? He was like a crazy man. I'd never seen him like that before.
He told me he had seen one of *them*. At first I didn't know who he meant by
them. I kept asking who he'd seen. I said 'sit down, tell me all about it'. But he
would not sit; he kept pacing, talking to himself. Saying he would kill him if
he could."

"Were you able to find out who he meant?"

"I think so. Eventually he calmed down. He said it was one of the men
from his old neighborhood. One of the group that turned his family in to the
Gestapo. You must understand, Mr. Doherty, many Poles welcomed the Nazis
when they first came. They worked with them because they saw a chance to
take the possessions of the Jews. Many Poles hated us as much as the Germans
did."

"Did he say anything else that might help us find him or the man he wants
to kill?"

Anna Koplowitz shook her head, "Only that he was a Pole and he was here,
here in Providence, living under a different name."

Rachel broke in, "Perhaps, Mrs. Koplowitz, you should tell us how you
know Meir in the first place."

The woman leaned forward and poured herself some more tea. She added
another healthy shot of schnapps to it.

"I was born in Bialystock, in Poland, in 1914," she began. "Sometimes we
were Poland, sometimes we were Russia; in those days; who could tell. When
the Germans first came I was twenty-five, engaged to be married to a young
man named Yankel. He was from Warsaw yet had family in Bialystock. That
was how we met. Our families thought we would be a good match. I never saw
him again after he returned to Warsaw the last time. I learned later that Yankel
was part of the uprising at the Warsaw ghetto."

"When they rounded up all the Jews from Bialystock they sent my mother,
my sister and me, first to Ravenbruck, a camp only for women. My father was
sent elsewhere. After that he disappeared from our lives. Then, in less than a

year we were transferred to the ghetto at Wierzbrik. I did not know Meir at that time. He was from Kracow, in another part of Poland. In late 1942 the ghetto was closed and we were all sent to the labor camp at Starachowice."

"I was still very pretty then so the Gestapo officers at Starachowice put me to work in their kitchen. I knew they wanted other things from me besides my cooking and…" here Anna Koplowitz stopped her story. Rachel and Doherty exchanged glances but said nothing. "You know in wartime people will sometimes do anything to stay alive. I was no different. It was at Starachowice that I first came into contact with Meir Poznanski. He was working then in the ammunition factory. I learned later that when he was first rounded up with the others in Kracow, his wife and children were sent to Treblinka. We all knew that no one survived Treblinka. It was already a death camp. Even though he was a teacher in Kracow, Meir was young and strong so he was put to hard work."

"I would watch the men everyday being marched off to the factory. If any of them faltered or fell out of line the guards would shoot them right there on the spot. To survive the men had to stay strong. Sometimes they stole whatever small amounts of food they were given from each other. I would see Meir through the wire and I could tell that he was growing weaker and weaker. One night they lined up all the men in the main yard and divided them into two groups. No one knew what this meant until they marched one set into the factory and the other into a field where they shot them all. Thank God, Meir was not among the men who were shot. After that I would pass him food through the wire – not just for him but for the other men as well to keep them strong. If I'd been caught they would have killed me. By then I didn't care if I lived or died. I felt so humiliated by what they'd made me do. I just wanted someone to survive so that our story would one day be told." Mrs. Koplowitz's expression stayed strong though her voice faltered and small tears began to gather in the corner of her eyes.

"In 1944 the camp was liquidated and we were shipped west. They didn't tell us why though we could hear the cannons and the planes at night and knew the Russians were coming from the east. We were sent to Auschwitz-Birkenau. That is where I got this," Anna said as she pushed up the sleeve of her dress to reveal the blue number tattooed on the inside of her forearm. "You know, it was only at Auschwitz that they tattooed a number on our arms. We could never figure out why, but then after the war the allied soldiers explained that it was all part of their meticulous record keeping. Germans are like that, you know."

Doherty poured Rachel another cup of tea and one for himself. Anna offered them some more schnapps. This time Rachel accepted some.

"At Birkenau I was put to work in the fields, no longer of use as a hausfrau. Meir was assigned to check in the new arrivals. His job was to take all of their worldly goods and give them to the Germans. The camp guards and the officers wanted everything except the food the people brought with them. It was suppose to be destroyed. Meir would smuggle this food into the barracks where he would share it with the other men. It was how he was able to stay healthy enough to work."

"Then one night Meir and many of the men were taken from the camp and moved west into Germany – to a camp near Stuttgart. This I only learned much later. Within weeks everyone still alive at Auschwitz and Birkenau was put on a train west into Germany. We knew the Russians were moving through Poland and were not far from Auschwitz. The German guards were so busy burning documents and all other evidence of what had been done there that the sky was as black as night even at mid-day. Those of us who were still alive were transported to Bergen-Belsen."

"There, many of the prisoners starved to death. There was so little food and what there was the Germans took for themselves. We lived like animals, devouring any scrap we could find, killing mice and rats and eating them raw. I hope to never see anything like that again in this world. I lived in one small room with five other girls; by then we were all just skin and bones. Some were so sick they lost their hair and their teeth. Between us we had just one pair of shoes. Each day a different one of us got to wear them."

"Later I learned that Meir was working at the time in a stone quarry outside of Stuttgart, hoping to stay alive, knowing that the war would soon end. When the British and Canadian soldiers finally came to Bergen-Belsen many of the prisoners were near death. At first they let the SS and their Hungarian allies continue to run the camp because there were so few allied soldiers. It was then that many of the SS fled, though not before they poisoned the camp's water supply. The British brought in fresh water and tried to feed the prisoners, but they didn't know what to give us; many died from the food that was too rich for their damaged bodies. There were other, healthier prisoners, who'd come in near the end. Some of them had been resistance fighters. Once they were liberated they turned on the traitors and the kapos in the camp. It was barbaric what was happening, and the British soldiers could not control it. Although we had been liberated many still died from starvation, and from the typhus."

"At Bergen-Belsen they made the SS who remained bury the dead. They stripped these once proud Germans down to their underwear and made them haul the corpses that were little more than skeletons into a big pit. The prisoners shouted at the Germans and spit on them when they were marched by us. I had never seen such anger. Then, because of the typhus, they burned all the bodies and everything else in the camp. After that those of us who remained were put on military trucks and taken to a Displaced Persons camp outside of Stuttgart. It was there that I was reunited with Meir, who was already at the camp. I say reunited but the truth is we had never really spoken before. We had only exchanged food and a few smiles. Yet at Stuttgart we recognized each other. We had survived."

"Later I emigrated to Boston, which was where I met my husband Herman. He was an American Jew, not from the old country. Herman had worked in intelligence in the war against the Japanese. After the war he ran an upholstering business in Framingham, Massachusetts, and later opened a factory here in Providence. We were married in 1947. I had recovered from the war and my looks, thank goodness, had more or less returned. I was not the beauty I'd been as a young girl, yet still I was attractive. My Herman used to say I was the prettiest girl he'd ever dated. He was fifteen years older than me and not so handsome in his looks. But he was a good man. He died of a heart attack just this past year. I always told him he worked too hard – that life was too short for that. You see it was just the two of us. I could never have children of my own because my health was too damaged from the camps."

"How did you meet up again with Meir?" Rachel asked.

"In Boston they created an archive of survivors who settled in New England. When we lived in Framingham I would go into the city every week to see if anyone I knew from Bialystock or the camps lived now in the area. I once hoped to find my brother though I'd been told by several people that he'd been hanged for his role in the resistance. But you know, sometimes hope springs eternal. One time I was checking the lists and I saw Meir's name. Mind you, I wasn't sure of his last name but I took a chance and wrote to him. He had an address in Providence at that time. Months passed and I didn't hear from him so I just assumed it was another Meir and that I had been mistaken about his last name. Then one day out of the blue I got a letter from him. By then he was married and living in West Warwick. He told me how he had come to Providence, met this woman Edith and married her. He told me he worked for his brother-in-law but hated his job. He asked me to write to him at The Bargain Store in the future, not at his home. I could tell reading between the lines that he had not made a good marriage."

"When my Herman took sick we moved here to Providence where he has family. That's when I contacted Meir to tell him we were now living in the same state. After my husband died Meir began to stop by on the occasional Thursday when he was in town picking up dry goods for his brother-in-law's store. We would have dinner and talk of Poland and life before the war. Soon he was here every Thursday and then he started to come for brunch on Saturday as well. That was the day he picked up the minyan breakfast food at your deli, Rachel. Don't think me wrong. We are not in love, at least not in love like in the movies. After Herman died I had no love left. But Meir will always have a piece of my heart. I guess you could say that we are comrades under the skin; comrades who dream of a Poland that never was nor ever will be again."

Anna's story had run its course and Rachel and Doherty felt that they had already overstayed their welcome. They politely finished their tea in silence. Before leaving he gave Anna Koplowitz one of his business cards and told her to call him immediately if she heard from Meir. Based on what she'd told him about Poznanski's discovery and his resultant state of mind, Doherty felt that the missing man could soon be facing a new danger.

Chapter Ten

Rachel and Doherty didn't speak for a while as they made their way back to West Warwick. He lit a cigarette and thoughtfully cranked open his window to let the smoke out.

"Can I have one of those?" Rachel asked.

"They're Camels, non-filtered."

"I don't care. I just need a smoke." He lit the second cigarette with his Zippo and handed it over to her.

Once they got south of Cranston Doherty directed Rachel back to West Warwick and into Arctic. The silence between them was a clear indication that Anna Koplowitz's story was weighing heavily on both of them.

When they reached Doherty's apartment he said, "I'd invite you in for something to eat but I don't have very much in the cupboard right now."

"Oh, damn, I almost forgot. I brought us a couple of sandwiches from the deli. I hope they're still fresh."

"That's great. I'm so hungry I could eat a horse. Come on in. I'm sure I can scratch up some drinks to go with them."

Once inside Rachel gave Doherty's digs the usual once over. It was only a mild mess today so he didn't have to do much to make it ship-shape. While he worked the place over she went into the kitchen and unwrapped the sandwiches. He then scoured the fridge for some drinks. He made sure that Rachel didn't get a look at its paltry contents.

"I've got some Coca Cola, a few cans of 'Gansett or I can make coffee if you'd prefer that," he offered as beverage choices.

"I think I'll go with the beer."

They sat at a folding card table that Doherty used for dining when he didn't eat standing at the kitchen counter or sitting in the living room reading and listening to the radio. He found a church key and popped open two cans of 'Gansett. He gave Rachel a reasonably clean glass for hers while he drank his straight from the can.

"What kind of sandwich is this? " he asked.

"I went conservative this time. I brought you roast beef on rye with some deli mustard. Is that okay?"

He looked inside the bread. The meat was pink and very lean with not a trace of fat on it.

"It's kind of rare though it sure tastes good."

"Deli beef should always be rare; otherwise you're not sure what you're eating. It's not as fine as what you'd get at a kosher deli, but if Katz's were kosher we wouldn't be able to sell cheeses or breakfast fishes. That's why my father chose not to go the kosher route. Besides, once a rebbie blesses the meat it goes up in price by 50%."

Doherty wasn't sure he fully understood what kosher meant but he was too engrossed in his sandwich to ask.

He looked at hers suspiciously. "What are you eating there?"

"I'm not sure you want to know."

"C'mon, it can't be that weird."

"It's chopped liver. Chopped chicken liver, not beef. Do you want a taste? It's sort of like liverwurst only better."

"I think I'll stick with the rare roast beef." Doherty drained his beer and went to open another can. He asked Rachel if she wanted a second beer. She reminded him that she had to drive home and also teach in the morning. It was already past nine o'clock.

When he came back she was looking at his bookshelf. "You sure have a lot of books here, Doherty." She said it in a way that made it sound like a question.

"What did you take me for, a dumb mill boy?"

"I'm sorry, I didn't mean to imply anything. It looks like you've read a lot of fiction. So what's your favorite book so far?"

Doherty weighed the question for a while, swigging his second beer as he did. "I think it's *The Grapes of Wrath.*"

"Steinbeck, huh? Why did you like that book?"

Doherty thought carefully about his answer, keeping in mind that Rachel was an English teacher and he didn't want to sound like a dummy. "I liked the people in it. They were common folks, not book smart, but world smart – and they had endurance. It's kind of like what Mrs. Koplowitz was saying earlier about how people will do damn near anything to survive no matter how bad things get. That's what the people in that book had: the will to survive during hard times."

Rachel smiled. "That's very astute. You're an interesting man, Doherty. I don't think I've ever met anyone like you."

"Why, because I'm Irish?"

"Hardly. I work in Providence remember. It's pretty hard to avoid Irish people in the city. I may live in a predominantly Jewish neighborhood, but we're just a small part of a city where the Irish and Italians pretty much run things."

"What's your favorite book, Miss English teacher?"

"It's probably *The Great Gatsby* by F. Scott Fitzgerald," she said without hesitation. "I teach it every year. I think in the end it resonates with my students though they don't like it at first because they think it's just about a bunch of rich, snobby people."

"Why do you think it's so good?"

"Well, on the surface it's a boy meets girl, boy loses girl, boy tries to win girl back kind of story. But what it's really about is the American dream: the idea that we can have anything we want in this country if we just will ourselves to have it. But, of course, life doesn't really work that way does it? In the book things turn out pretty bad by the end, especially for the main character, Gatsby. As a reader you're left both hopeful and disillusioned at the same time if that's possible. That's why I think on some level Gatsby's story is America's story. I don't think I fully realized just how innocent we Americans are until I listened to Anna tell us about her life."

"I bet your English classes are pretty interesting."

"I don't know. It's hard to get these profound messages across to kids given that they're so young and have never really experienced much of anything. I mean what do they know about life at sixteen? How could they unless they've been through something like Anna and Meir have?"

"I can see what you mean. Hell, I didn't know much about anything myself till I went into the service. Then I learned a lot of lessons I sometimes wish I could unlearn. All that killing - and afterwards you wonder what it was all for."

Rachel stood up and came around to Doherty's side of the table. At full height she wasn't much taller than he was sitting. Without hesitating she sat down on Doherty's lap and kissed him on the mouth. "You know what all that talk of death does to me? It makes me want to have sex."

Whatever was to happen next Doherty was determined to let it happen without thinking too much about it. He lifted Rachel up in his arms and carried her into his bedroom. She was as light as he expected she'd be. They fell on the bed in the darkened room. Within minutes both of them had shed their clothes and were moving toward the big deal. Rachel had the tight young body of a small girl in her twenties; she was also very enthusiastic. Her hair both on her head and down below felt wiry, like brillo. She squealed when he first went inside her, then moved rhythmically with him as he pushed deeper. As they were coming closer to the end she dug the nails of her small hands into his back. He knew she'd leave him with scratch marks and he didn't care.

Afterwards they lay beside each other in their respective pools of sweat, spent but satisfied. Doherty was dying for a cigarette yet remembered how Millie St. Jean had objected to his smoking after they made love – even suggesting it was a cliché. Soon, without prompting Rachel climbed astride his prone body and kissed him hungrily. They were at it again with the girl running the show this time. Doherty'd never engaged in lovemaking in this position, though he didn't find it at all displeasing. Her body felt clammy but taut as she moved more anxiously toward climax.

When they were done Doherty did not hesitate to reach for his cigarette this time. He asked Rachel if she wanted one. She said she needed to catch her breath first. They lay close together in Doherty's narrow bed, each breathing heavily. Finally she propped herself up on her elbow and asked, "What time is it?"

"It's a quarter past ten."

"Shit. I've got to get going. I have a class at eight tomorrow. You don't mind if I take a quick shower, do you? I don't want the bitch to smell sex all over me when I get home. I know she'll be waiting up just for spite."

Rachel walked to the bathroom in all her nudity and within seconds he could hear the shower running. He sat up trying to make sense of the evening then decided it was all too much drama for him to handle right now. When Rachel came out she dressed quickly. She hadn't bothered to wash her hair, only her body. He got up from the bed and slipped on his boxer shorts.

"Don't bother getting dressed. I can find my way out."

They stood in the living room hugging for a few seconds before she left.

"Will I see you again, bubbie?"

"I hope so. I wouldn't want to think I'm just a one night stand," he answered. Rachel kissed him deeply and then left.

After she was gone Doherty lay in bed reading a few more pages about Santiago's fruitless battle against the sharks before calling it a night.

Chapter Eleven

Doherty climbed the stairs to his office around ten the next morning. Without Agnes there the place looked the same as when he'd left it. He didn't bother to open any windows to air it out. Instead of hanging around the barren space he dropped down to Harry's for a shave and some conversation with Bill Fiore. It was a slow morning at the shop. Bill was sitting in one of the shoeshine chairs reading a men's magazine and having a smoke. Doherty plopped down in the seat next to him. Bill pretended to ignore Doherty and he did the same to his barber pal while lighting up a cigarette of his own.

"Morning Beetle," he said finally.

"Don't bother me, I'm readin' an important story here about a guy who rescued a maiden in distress after she'd been captured by some Watusi warriors in darkest Africa. It's a true story."

"Oh, yeah, I'm sure it is. As honest as the day is long. Well, let me know when you emerge from the jungle, I could use a shave." Bill put the magazine down and looked at Doherty, a smile creasing his face. "Business slow upstairs?"

"Not really. I'm working on a case and I'd like to ask your advice about it."

"What's the matter, Agnes too busy doin' her nails to give you some face time?"

"For your information Agnes is on vacation for a few weeks. Louie's ship is in port so she's acting like the good housewife while he's home."

"He still doesn't know she's been workin' for you?"

"Apparently she hasn't gotten around to telling him yet. I figure maybe I should get used to not having her in the office. It's only a matter of time before he gets her with child and she leaves Doherty and Associates for good."

"That'd be too bad. You been relyin' on her a lot lately, haven't you?"

"More than I used to. But hey, anything can happen now that the horny seaman's in town."

"Seaman is right," Bill added. "So what kind of sage advice can I give you today along with your shave?"

"I been looking for this guy who's lost and I picked up some info that leads me to believe he might be out to hurt somebody."

"Let me get this straight, it's not the person you been hired to find who's in trouble?"

"Oh, he may be in trouble all right, though it's a little more complicated than that. Seems that the missing guy told my only lead that he wanted to kill somebody. It's the main reason he's gone missing."

"Jesus, Hughie, he actually said he was gonna kill somebody? Aren't you supposed to tell the police when you get information like that?"

"Only if the person thinking of doing the killing is my client. But he isn't. He's the guy I've been hired to find."

Bill pulled on his smoke, taking a minute to dope things out. "I'd say you still gotta talk to the cops. I mean how're you gonna feel if this person you're lookin' for does somebody in before you can find him?"

"I hear what you're saying, Bill. But I got two issues with that. The first is that I don't know where this guy is so I don't even know which police department I should contact. And you know how the cops are – if it isn't in their jurisdiction, it's not their problem."

"What's your second concern?"

"Like maybe the guy he's looking for deserves to be killed."

Bill gave Doherty with a look of disbelief. "Tell me you didn't just say that."

"Look, I said it was complicated. And I'm not kidding. Based on what I've learned about this case I can't help but feel that my guy would have just cause for taking this other somebody out of this life."

"Listen Hughie, we been friends for a long time, and I think I get what you're sayin'. I know there are a lot of people in this world that deserve to die.

I can think of a few I'd like to take out myself. But then you gotta realize whoever does this could end up spendin' the rest of his life up at the ACI, or worse, swingin' from a rope in the tower. That's when you gotta step back from those kinds of thoughts. Keep somethin' else in mind, my friend. You been hired to find this guy. You find him before he shuts somebody's lights out, you'd be doin' him a big favor. That would kinda make you the hero of this story."

"I don't know, Bill. Maybe you're right. If I find my guy before he does damage to some other guy I suppose I'd be saving him from himself. I'll try to keep that in mind."

Doherty and the barber then moved to the chair where Bill gave him one of his expert shaves. Afterwards Doherty told Bill about his night with Rachel, leaving out some important details, such as how old, or rather young, she is, and how she ran the show the second time around. As usual Bill plumbed the conversation for more details than Doherty was willing to give up. In the end, though, he knew he'd made Bill Fiore's day.

Back in the office he called Edith Poznanski to see if she'd heard anything from her wayward husband. She hadn't and still didn't express much enthusiasm for Doherty's search. He had to remind himself that she wasn't the first person he'd encountered on the job who wasn't interested in being reunited with a missing spouse. He asked her about the family car. She said that Meir had taken it and she was using one of her brother's in the meantime. As with her husband she didn't sound all that concerned about the missing car either. At this point Doherty felt stymied. If Meir Poznanski didn't contact Anna Koplowitz again or didn't surface in some other way, finding him would be like looking for a needle in a haystack. Rhode Island is a small state, but it isn't that small.

Around noon, just as Doherty was about to make his daily pilgrimage up to the Arctic News for lunch, there was a small knock on the outer door. He didn't bother to get up, just yelled for the visitor to come in. He knew Agnes would have handled it in a more professional manner, but he didn't care. The next thing he knew Morris Mendelson was standing at his door.

"I've been trying to call you; nobody answered the phone," he said meekly.

"That's my fault. My secretary had to take some time off and I've been up in Providence following some leads on your friend Poznanski."

"Does that mean you've been able to locate him?" The small man's question contained a dose of enthusiasm.

"Not exactly, though I did have a conversation with that other woman we spoke about last week. If it'll ease your mind it doesn't sound like they're having an affair, least not as far as I can tell. They're old acquaintances from Poland. Unfortunately, she hasn't seen him in a couple of weeks either. That's pretty much all I can tell you right now."

"That doesn't sound too promising." Mendelson's initial enthusiasm had quickly turned to disappointment.

"No, but she's a good lead," Doherty said, not wanting to let on that she was his only lead at the moment. "I've got to ask you something important, Mr. Mendelson: Do you think Meir Poznanski is capable of violence?"

The question caught the little man off guard. "I don't know," he stammered. "Meir never struck me as that kind of person. He always seemed more of the intellectual type. But you never know. I suppose you saw men do violent things in the war that you never thought they were capable of. But with Meir, I just can't see it."

"He was in those camps, wasn't he? That kind of experience can leave a man with a terrible angry streak deep down inside."

"I suppose it could. Meir never wanted to talk about those days with any of the men in the minyan. He said when he came to America he was leaving all of that behind him. 'On the other side of the ocean', was how he put it. But I could tell from his…" Mendelson paused, searching for the right word. "From his detachment, that it was still there, somewhere inside him. How could it not be?"

"By the way, Mr. Mendelson, what was it that brought you over here?"

"The men in the minyan are getting a little restless. They wanted to know how the case was going. I knew you wouldn't come by the store because of Millie, so I decided to check in with you myself."

Doherty leaned back in his chair, trying to dope out whether Mendelson was leveling with him. "You can tell the men in the minyan that I'm working full time on their behalf. When something definite turns up I'll let them know. Tell them not to worry; I'll give them their money's worth. It's just that I've got to work this my own way, understand?"

Mendelson retreated toward the door. He hesitated and then turned back before he left. "You asked about violence before. Has Meir hurt someone?"

"No, not yet, as far as I can tell."

That night Doherty got an unexpected call at home. It was from Anna Koplowitz. She identified herself, pronouncing the w in her last name as a v, Eastern European style.

"Have you heard from Meir?" Doherty asked without hesitation.

"Yah. He came by this morning before I went shopping. He was very anxious. He asked me if I knew where he could get a gun. He wanted to know if Herman ever kept one in the house. I brought him inside and tried to calm him down. Before when he came here he was always, how do you say, always so thoughtful, careful in choosing his words. But this time he was very excitable. He kept mixing his English with Polish. I don't know how to deal with this Meir."

"What else did he say? Did he say anything about the man he wants to kill?"

"Nothing much - only that he is Polish, from the old country like us, and that he saw him again. Meir said he looked right at him but the man did not recognize him. This made Meir even greater in his anger."

"Did he say where he saw the man?"

"Yah. He saw him in one of the big department stores downtown. He said he thought the man worked in the store."

"Anything else?"

Doherty could hear Anna Koplowitz breathing heavily on the other end of the phone. "No, nothing I can remember. I told him I didn't have a gun – that Herman never owned one. I told him he had to give up this crazy idea. If he did this thing it would ruin his life."

"What did he say to that?"

"He said that his life was ruined a long time ago. That now he wanted only revenge."

"Do you have any idea where Meir is staying?"

"No. I offered to have him sleep here on my couch, but he refused. He said he did not want to involve me in this business. Meir knows no one else in Providence. He told me months ago that I was the only friend he had outside of West Warwick. I can't imagine where he's been staying. He was dressed well and clean shaven so I do not think he has been sleeping in the park or in his car."

His car, Doherty thought again. He could try to get the police to put a trace on the car, or get his wife Edith to do so, as a way of helping him locate Poznanski. However, that would involve the Providence police and he wasn't interested in going that route just yet.

"Listen, Mrs. Koplowitz, if Meir contacts you again, or if you remember anything else he said, please call me, day or night. I'm afraid if I don't find Meir soon he might commit this crime he's intent on."

Chapter Twelve

After lunch Doherty put a call in to Gus Timilty, his mentor when he was with the West Warwick police. Gus had been his shift commander and they later became good friends. Timilty'd been on the force for thirteen years before he was forced to resign due to some shady business he got mixed up in with some whores in Providence and a pimp named Jimmy Ricks. Doherty never learned the whole story and Gus never volunteered any information about it once he left the force.

Not long afterwards Timilty hooked on with a security agency in South Providence run by a guy named Johnny Briggs. Within a year the company was renamed Briggs and Timilty. Doherty suspected that it was Gus who brought in the high paying clients and did most of the real investigative work. He'd been instrumental in helping Doherty set up his own private operation, so he'd always be beholden to Gus for whatever business came his way.

For a change his old friend was in the office when Doherty clocked in with the Briggs and Timilty receptionist.

"Hey, pally," Gus said in his jocular manner when he came on the line. "What's cooking down there in old WW?"

"I'm staying busy. Good to hear your voice, Gus. How you doing these days?"

There was a pregnant pause at the other end. "Oh, I suppose I'm okay. My doc keeps telling me I've got to cut back on running around so much on account of my ticker. He also wants me to lose some weight, though that's not so easy given the number of business lunches I have to expense each week. You're working on something you need my help with, am I right?"

"I could lie to you and say this is a social call but that wouldn't be true. I've been hired to find this lost guy who my leads tell me may be thinking about committing a crime – a big crime."

"How big?"

"Like murder big."

Timilty let out a very loud "Phew." After a few seconds he said, "Have you contacted the police about this?"

"No, I can't. You see I don't know where this fellow is. He could be anywhere in the state," Doherty added as a half-truth. "I need a few favors from you to help me find him."

"I'm always here for you, pally. What can I do you for?"

"Well, first of all, if a guy is trying to maintain a low profile in Providence, but doesn't have any friends there, or a lot of cash, where would he be shacking up?"

"You asking about flop houses?"

"I guess, or cheap hotels. You know, places along those lines."

"I can give you the names of some. A few of them are soft pillow joints rented by the hour, mostly to hookers or their johns; others are flops for drunks and deadbeats. Do you think the guy you're looking for would be staying in places like that?"

Doherty considered the question carefully. He couldn't see Meir Poznanski in any of those kinds of establishments. On the other hand he didn't know what a man in his desperate circumstances would do otherwise. "I'm not sure. Any other ideas?"

"You could try the YMCA on Broad Street near downtown. Lots of men stay there when they need a short time flop. I know a few husbands who've bedded down at the Y while taking a powder from their wives. You run across that a lot in our business."

"The Y would make more sense in this case. Now I need another favor from you. Do you know anyone who works security at the Outlet Company or Shepard's downtown?"

"Yeah, I've had some dealings with a private dick who's the head of security at Shepard's. His name is Jack Moroni; he used to be a state cop. I can give him a ring to see if he'll talk to you. Don't tell me the guy you're lookin' for works at one of the department stores?"

"Not the guy I'm looking for. I have a hunch the guy he's thinking of killing might be working at one of those stores."

"Jesus, Doherty, this sounds a little balmy to me."

"Don't worry, Gus. It all kind of makes sense. I just don't want to get you involved in this any more than I need to."

"Well I appreciate your consideration, pally," Timility said, barely masking his sarcasm.

Timilty then gave him the names of a few short-term flop hotels in and around Providence that he knew of in case Poznanski was not at the Y. He also promised to call his man at Shepard's as soon as he got off the phone.

In the morning Doherty got the Chevy out of Denny Belanger's garage where he stored it when not in use and headed into Providence. It wasn't difficult finding the Y. It had a big sign that hung right out on Broad Street just outside the city center. A block before the Y was a snack joint called The Chicken Coop that Doherty had eaten at once, though he couldn't recall when or why. They were both just a stone's throw from Classical High where Rachel Katz graduated as the top girl in her class.

A large front counter greeted visitors as they entered the reception area at the Y. A few men of various ages were passing in and out of the building toting small gym bags. A heavyset guy in his thirties was manning the desk. He had dark hair, rubbery lips and a large belly. He was wearing a white, short sleeve banlon shirt with a red and blue YMCA crest over the left breast. He gave Doherty a painted-on smile.

"Hi," Doherty said in as friendly a tone as he could muster. "I'm looking for a friend of mine who I believe is staying here. I wonder if you could help me?"

The man looked at Doherty skeptically. "I'm sorry we can't give out that kind of information." The desk clerk then leaned forward and said in a low voice, "A lotta men come to stay with us to get away from their wives or jealous girlfriends. That makes us kind of a refuge if you know what I mean."

Doherty flashed his license and a picture of Meir Poznanski and said more firmly, "I've been hired to find this man. I believe he may be in danger. You wouldn't want something bad to happen to him on your watch, would you?"

The big guy backed up a foot and was clearly trying to dope out his next move. "Look, I only work the day shifts. I don't really know who's staying here or who just comes in for a workout and a steam." He waited, hoping his explanation would put Doherty off. Both men held their ground. Doherty took a five spot out of his wallet and slid it across the counter. The big man scooped it up without even looking at it.

He leaned back in toward Doherty and said, "There's a fella who lives here – been with us for a long time. He's an old Negro, name's Billy. He knows everybody and everything that goes on in this place. I don't suppose it would do any harm if you had a few words with him. He's down in room five. You'll find him there unless he's sweeping up in the gym or picking up towels by the pool." The deskman pointed Doherty in the direction of the residents' wing.

Doherty made his way down a narrow corridor and then took a left into the area where men staying overnight at the Y resided. The door to room five was closed so Doherty knocked. A voice that sounded more like a moan told him to "come on in."

The man named Billy was lying on a narrow bed in a sleeveless under-shirt that had once been white but was now a shade of gray. The only other clothes he had on were some plaid boxer shorts. He had a hangdog face, a nap of gray hair and he looked older than Methuselah. Billy's head was propped up on a pillow and he was reading a Superman comic. The room smelled of cigarette smoke and body odor. There were pictures of weight lifters and ath-letes on one wall and those of scantily clad pinup girls on another. A hot plate with a coffee pot on it sat on the only other piece of furniture in the room, a beat up, four-drawer dresser with various pieces of clothing hanging out of its open drawers.

The old black man looked up from the comic but didn't move. "You gots any cigarettes?" were the first words out of his mouth.

Doherty popped two Camels out of his pack and lit one for each of them with his Zippo. He handed a butt to the old man who took a deep drag and then punctuated it with a growling cough.

"Thanks mister." They both smoked and didn't say anything for a while.

"Do you want to know why I'm here?" Doherty finally asked.

"I s'pose so," old Billy said without much interest.

"I'm looking for somebody. The fellow at the desk said you were the man to ask."

Billy snorted, "Who, fat Bob? Why dey keep that motherfucker on the counter is a mystery to me. He ain't zactly an advertisement for physical fitness, is he?"

"I guess not."

Doherty extracted Meir Poznanski's picture from his coat pocket and handed it to Billy. "You ever see this guy around the Y?"

The old man looked at the photo and then back at Doherty. "You ain't a cop, are you? 'Cause I learnt a long time ago to never ever volunteer nothin' to the PO-lice."

"No, I'm not a cop. I'm a private investigator," Doherty said showing Billy his license. The black man sat up on his bed and studied Doherty's card very carefully.

"Ooowee, a real private eye, huh. I ain't never met one of yous before. I thought private eyes was only in the movies and on the TV. What kinda crimes you solve down dere in West Warwick?"

"Mostly I find lost people. That's why I'm here. Somebody hired me to find the guy in this picture."

Billy looked at the photo of Poznanski's again and then lifted his eyes to Doherty. "What's he done?"

"He hasn't done anything yet, but I'm afraid he might. I was hoping to find him before he did something crazy. Something he would regret later."

"You bein' kinda mysterious here, Mr. Detective. S'pose you mean dis here fella some bad business. I don't wanna be responsible for dat. You see I got a reputation around dis here Y that I gotta protect."

Doherty sat down on the edge of the bed. "I can understand that, Billy. Nobody wants to be known as a snitch - especially not in a place like this where men come to get away from things. So what'll it take for you to give me some info on the QT?"

Billy smiled for the first time and Doherty noted that he only had about eight teeth left in his mouth. "Five dollars could buy you some real information."

"How about ten and I throw in this pack of Camels?" Doherty said as he lifted the cigarettes out of his pocket and placed them on the bed.

"Damn, you ain't much for horse tradin', are you?"

"I'm just trying to protect your reputation, Billy."

Doherty pulled a sawbuck out of his billfold and placed it on the bed next to the smokes. When Billy reached for it Doherty placed his hand over the old man's wrinkled paw and said, "Not until I hear something I don't already know."

The old man laughed a guttural guffaw that quickly turned into a phlegm-laden cough. Doherty waited patiently for the hacking fit to subside.

"He bin here more dan a week now. I dint pay him no never mind at first, figurin' he just another husband the wife done throwed out. Mostly he only come in at night for to eat and sleep. Dey lock dem front doors at ten. You ain't in by ten, you sleep out on da street. Used to happen to me a lot back in de days when I was drinkin'. After dat I started goin' to the meetins dey hold here, tryin' as best I can to get myself dried out."

"I first done noticed him one day when we was in the steam. He had deese numbers tattooed on his arm. I aks him 'bout dem but he don't wanna talk wid me. Said it was none of my damn bidness. You know, you mostly see tattoos only on sailors or men bin up in the joint. Dis fella was all clean cut and shit. Dats the onliest reason I aks 'bout dem tattoos. You know I was just tryin' to make steam room talk. Wouldn't be long 'fore some of the other long timers here would aks me 'bout him and you know it's my bidness to keep check on what goes on in dis here residence wing."

"What else can you tell me about this man?"

"Ain't much else to say. He gets up every mornin', has hisself a shower and a shave and puts on his suit. Don't get too many fellas dress like dat down here. Goes off, comes back at night with a bag fulla food, goes into his room and locks the door. Don't talk to no one. Never goes down to the gym or the pool; only goes into the steam."

"And that's it? I'm not sure you earned your ten bucks yet."

"He's a Jew, ain't he?"

"What makes you say that?"

"I seen him in the steam; he's got the head of his Johnson cut off."

"Hell Billy, lots of men do that now."

"Now maybe, but not when I was a young'n. And not when you was neither, 'specially if you one of dem Catholic boys. Catholics don't believe in that prick cuttin', do they?"

"I'm pretty sure most Catholics boys get circumcised nowadays."

"But not men his age. I seen a lot of dicks in my time here at the Y, and I can always tell how old a fella is if he's had his Johnson nipped or not."

To change the subject Doherty asked, "When was the last time you saw him?"

"What's today, Friday? I ain't seen him since maybe Monday, or Tuesday. I know he dint come in last night."

"How do you know that?"

"See that ten dollars. You payin' me 'cause I know everthin' goes on in dis here buildin'. I tell you he dint come in last night, you best believe he dint."

Doherty lifted his hand from Billy's and let the old man take the ten spot. He flipped one of his business cards on the bed. "Next time you see him, you give me a call right away. My home number's on the back. You call me, I'll make it worth your while."

Billy smiled his toothless grin. "I knows you will, Mr. Detective."

When Doherty left Billy's room it was a relief to breathe something besides the fetid odor of an old man's unwashed body in a closed room.

Chapter Thirteen

After leaving the Y Doherty drove a few blocks on Webosset Street into downtown Providence and dropped the Chevy in a lot where he paid a dollar to leave it for the rest of the day. He then ducked into a greasy little diner where he forced down a cold baloney sandwich and a cup of weak coffee. He took a second refill before heading over the Shepard Company. Growing up in West Warwick with all the Arctic stores right at hand, the Doherty family had little reason to ever go into Providence to shop. Stores like Shepard's, the Outlet, Gladdings and Cherry and Webb, made the big stores of Arctic seem quaint by comparison. He had to admire the architecture of these big buildings, with their brick and stucco facades, set off by cast iron supports. There was nothing in West Warwick, not even the big Majestic Building, to match these turn-of-the-century behemoths.

Shepard's especially had a lovely archway entrance at the corner of Westminster and Union, and just a short walk away was the famous Shepard's clock, which was the most popular meeting place in the city. He was also intrigued by the Tri-Store Bridge that connected Shepard's with Gladdings and Cherry and Webb at their second floors. This bridge allowed housewives out on shopping trips in cold weather to access each of the three stores without having to venture outside.

Once he passed under the arch and into Shepard's, the first thing Doherty noticed was the elaborate terrazzo tile floor that greeted customers just inside the front door. The second thing to hit him was the strong odors from the perfume counter that confronted shoppers almost immediately. The rest of the floor behind these scents was dedicated to men's clothing in all shapes, sizes and prices. In the entire space they sold nothing but suits, shirts, slacks, topcoats, sweaters, socks, shoes, ties and accessories of all kinds. He thought St. Onge's was a big operation, but this place carried just about anything a man could want and in a wide range of prices.

Despite the grand flow of foot traffic, the aisles between the counters were set with highly polished hard wood floors. An escalator positioned in the middle of this floor escorted shoppers up to the higher levels. However, to save time Doherty opted for the elevators situated at the back of the store. Passing through the aisles to them gave him an opportunity to graze the wide variety of male offerings. After perusing the cornucopia of goods offered at each counter Doherty eventually found his way to the two elevators and checked the directory mounted between them to locate the administrative offices. They were on the fourth floor above women's fashions on the second and children's clothes and toys along with home goods on the third.

Stepping in, Doherty was the only man among the women customers in the small elevator. It was operated by a girl wearing a uniform that consisted of a white blouse, a black skirt and a red ribbon wrapped around a tight ponytail. Despite the prim outfit she was noticeably attractive. The four other passengers in the elevator were all older women. The young operator announced each floor as she slid the elevator cage open. Three got off at the second floor, which contained women's clothes and accessories. The remaining woman exited at children's and home goods on three. Doherty had already told the lift operator that he was heading to four. Once they were alone she gave him a sidelong glance accompanied by a pleasing smile. Doherty returned the favor.

Outside of the elevator the fourth floor was a beehive of activity. He figured this was where the real money transactions occurred at the Shepard Company. He asked a young clerk for the office of Mr. Moroni, who was the head of the store's security. She gave him a once over and then led him down a short corridor consisting of a warren of small offices. Doherty was glad he wore his suit. It seemed that only businessmen wore suits anymore and Doherty knew that by wearing his it gave him entrée that lesser dressed men might not enjoy.

Moroni's office was the last one on the left. When he entered the security chief was sitting in his white shirtsleeves beside an old-fashioned roll top desk.

Doherty noticed a shoulder holster with a pistol in it hanging from a coat rack in the corner. He had a licensed handgun himself though he seldom took it out of his locked desk drawer. The security chief's office was much more neatly appointed than his. Moroni rose from his chair and greeted Doherty with a smile. He was a tall man, well over six feet, and rather imposing. No longer young, he had a rounded belly that dropped over his belt and folded down the waistband of his trousers. Otherwise he was impeccably dressed with a starched shirt, a perfectly knotted print tie and well-oiled dark hair. They shook hands and he offered Doherty a seat. Moroni took out a pack of Marlboros and extended it in Doherty's direction. He waved him off and lit one of his Camels instead.

"Gus Timilty tells me you're an old friend from West Warwick PD days," Moroni said as an opener. "It's a shame what happened to him down there."

"Not according to Gus. He claims he's now making an honest living for the first time in his life."

"I don't know about that," Moroni said. "Still it's a shame that a man like Timilty should have his reputation sullied the way it was because he was trying to help some young girl get out of the hooker trade. It just doesn't seem fair." These were the first details Doherty'd ever heard as to why Gus was forced to resign from the West Warwick police. He wanted to know more but didn't think Moroni was the right person to ask. It'd be better to someday get the whole story from the horse's mouth.

"So, Mr. Doherty what can I do for you?"

"Well, it's kind of complicated. And because of the nature of my business I can't tell you everything, though I'll give you what I can."

"Fair enough. As long as I'm not breaking any laws or compromising the company in any way by helping you."

Doherty launched in. "I'm looking for a lost man, who I believe is himself looking for a man who may work here at the Shepard Company. The reason I need to find my guy and find him fast is that I have reason to believe he wants to bring great harm to this other guy."

Moroni nodded his head while maintaining an impassive expression.

"In any case, the man I'm looking for would not be without justification for taking such action. However, if he does then obviously it will have a bad effect on the lives of both men. The problem is that I've exhausted most of my resources for finding my guy. So now I'm hoping to locate the guy he's after and then work my way back from him to the one I'm searching for. That way I might be able to prevent both of them from getting hurt."

Moroni shook his head and smiled. "Sounds a little convoluted to me. I'm guessing you also don't know who this possible employee of ours is."

"No, I don't. In fact, I don't even know for sure he works here. All I know is that he works in one of the big department stores in the city. Given what I know about this man, it seemed logical to eliminate Gladdings and Cherry and Webb because they're mostly for women shoppers. That leaves either you folks or the Outlet Company. I'm here because you're the guy that Gus Timilty knows."

Moroni swung back and forth in his swivel desk chair. "Okay, tell me what you do know about our supposed employee. That will at least give me a start."

Doherty did a quick mental inventory. "I know that he's from Poland, and that he came to the U.S. as an adult. So we can assume he speaks English with a noticeable accent. I have a hunch he's a big man physically, or at least larger than average size. More than likely he's employed under an assumed name, and he might even be in the country illegally, though I don't know that for sure. And one other thing, he may be a difficult person to work with. I'm thinking he's the kind of man who has a superior attitude."

"That's not bad, Doherty. It certainly gives me a lot to go on if the person you're looking for works at the Shepard Company. Unfortunately, if he works at the Outlet you're pretty much on your own. You see, I don't get along with the security people over there so you wouldn't be able to use my name to get a foot in their door." Moroni then looked at his watch. "How much time do you have today?"

"I can stay in town as long as I need to."

"Good. Why don't you come back … let's say in two hours? That'll give me time to check our employee records. If anyone fitting the description you just gave is working in this store I'll have had time to talk with the manager of his department by then."

The two men stood and shook hands and Doherty agreed to return at around 3:30.

The same young woman was working the lift when Doherty got in to go down. They were alone this time and she didn't bother trying to hide the smile she threw his way. As they descended she asked, "Are you one of them buyers?"

"No," he said, not adding anything more.

"Are you a cop?"

Doherty laughed, "Hardly."

"But you did go up to see Mr. Moroni, didn't you?"

"How did you know that?"

She bit her lip and tossed him another coy smile. "News travels fast around here."

"What's your name?"

"Maxine. But my friends call me Max."

"You on until the end of the day?"

"Yeah, till five-thirty."

"I'm goin' out for a couple of hours and then coming back around three-thirty. Is there anything I can bring you? You know, like a coffee or a soda?"

The girl giggled nervously and then said, "Sure. How about one of them Orange Nehis? I like those."

"You bet," Doherty said as the lift hit the ground floor.

"Hey, mister, what's your name?"

"Doherty. But my friends call me Doherty." She laughed in a way that made him think this was about the funniest thing she'd heard all day.

Doherty spent most of the next two hours walking the streets of down-town Providence. He was amazed at how much action there was in the city for a weekday afternoon. Arctic wasn't ever this busy, even on the Saturday before Easter. In addition to the numerous women out shopping, there were quite a few men in suits hurrying through the city center with determined looks on their faces. Workmen were busy tarring some of the side streets or descending though manholes to attend to problems below the city's surface.

Providence had four big movie houses within a five-block radius of down-town: the Albee, the Majestic, the Strand and the largest of them all, the Loew's on Webosset Street. Each one was a palace compared to West Warwick's two small movie houses. He'd recently read that some of those new Cinerama wide-screen films were coming to Rhode Island and knew they'd come to Providence but would never make their way to his hometown. Just once he'd like to see a big-screen spectacular like the new version of *Ben-Hur*.

Doherty circled around the biggest square in the city, or The Mall, as the locals called it. It was flanked on one side by the Biltmore, Providence's finest hotel and on another side by the multi-storied Industrial Trust Building that the *Journal* had recently dubbed the "Superman building" because it looked like the one on the Superman TV show where Clark Kent and Lois Lane work at the Daily Planet. On the far side of the mall was the immense railroad station. Doherty'd only been on the New York, New Haven and Hartford train out of Providence once and that was when he shipped out overseas during the war.

After a short leave at home, his regiment was mustered up at Quonset and put on busses to Providence. Once there they took the train to Boston and were dropped off at the Charlestown Navy Yard. The next day they sailed out of Boston on a gigantic troop transport with thousands of other GIs. They went to England for further training and then were parachuted into Sicily, directly into combat. On the trip across the Atlantic many of the men were so scared their transport would be torpedoed by a German U-boat that they couldn't sleep a wink. Little did they know what waited for them in Italy would be much worse.

On his way back to Shepard's Doherty stopped in at the same greasy spoon where he'd eaten lunch and picked up an orange Nehi for the elevator operator and a coffee for himself. When he got back Maxine, the elevator operator, tried to pay him for the soda. Without making a big deal out of it Doherty said it was his treat. His watch read 3:25 when he knocked on Moroni's door. The big man opened it himself. He was still in shirtsleeves, and now accompanied by another, smaller fellow with a thick crop of red hair.

"This is Barney O'Mara," Moroni said by way of an introduction. "He works downstairs supervising the shoe departments." Doherty took a chair joining the other two men in a semi-circle.

"I'm pretty sure from what I've been able to dig up that we may have located your man," Moroni began. "His name is Stanislaw Krykowski, or at least that was the name on his social security card when he applied here."

"What about his driver's license?"

Moroni looked up from the papers he was flipping through and said, "Didn't have one; only an SS card. He told whoever interviewed him in personnel that he'd sold shoes before, first in Poland and then after he came over to the States at Florsheim in New York. That sounded good enough to her given that we don't get too many applicants at Shepard's who worked for Florsheim. Barney here put him on the day shift, first in women's shoes and later in men's."

"Why the switch?" Doherty asked.

Moroni nodded toward O'Mara and the smaller man took over. "Apparently some of the women found him to be a little … " O'Mara came to a nervous halt here. He tried again. "They said he was being fresh. At first I thought it was just his European way of doing things. You know, they can be a little abrupt sometimes with difficult customers. But later more than one woman accused him of looking up her dress while he was fitting her for shoes. Then another complained that he caressed her foot in the process of taking her size."

Doherty rolled this information around in his head and then asked, "So what happened?"

O'Mara started in again, this time even more uneasy than before. "I wasn't there. Gloria works under my supervision and runs the women's shoe department. You see I spend most of my time downstairs in men's shoes. She was the one who took the complaints. I called Stan in and told him that I was transferring him downstairs to men's shoes. I explained that we were short on qualified salesmen in men's and I needed somebody there who knew the business well. You see at Shepard's all the shoe people work on commission, and quite frankly men's shoes are more expensive than women's. I thought Stan wouldn't mind because he would be making more money downstairs with us. I did it mostly so I could keep an eye on him."

"How did he take your transfer suggestion?"

O'Mara mopped his brow and looked uncomfortably at Moroni. "He was furious. He accused me of all kinds of things. He likened me to the communist dictators in Poland. Said I was abusing him as a worker. I have to say, his behavior took me by surprise and was a little bit scary."

"Did you pass your concerns about Krykowski on to Mr. Moroni here?"

For a minute O'Mara was at a loss for words. "No, I didn't. I thought as manager of the shoe departments I should be able to handle these issues myself. I know Jack has his hands full with shoplifters and employees shuffling goods out the back door. There wasn't any theft involved and I didn't want to waste Jack's time with what I thought was basically a personality issue."

"You could have fired him."

"Oh no, that was never a consideration. Stan knows everything there is to know about shoes and I don't want to lose him. He's our best salesman. I felt that once he settled in at the men's department everything would be okay."

"And has it been?"

"More or less," O'Hara muttered. "Though I must admit that I find Krykowski to be a very formidable personality."

"You may have good reason to be concerned about his behavior," Doherty said. "If he's the man I'm looking for it's possible he's an ex-Nazi, and not the kind of person you'd want to get into a beef with." O'Mara took his handkerchief out of his pocket again and began to mop his brow.

"I think you've given us enough here, Barney," Moroni said. "Why don't you go back downstairs and Mr. Doherty and I will handle this from here on out. And whatever you do, don't let this Stanislaw fellow know that something's up. We don't want to spook him."

O'Mara shuffled out the door and Moroni turned his attention back to Doherty. "We can't really fire this employee unless someone files a formal complaint against him, or one of our store supervisors witnesses him being rude to a customer. And by that I mean really rude, not your run-of-the-mill everyday rude. And we definitely can't fire him just because you or some guy you're looking for thinks he's an ex-Nazi. I'd hazard to guess that there're a lot of former Nazis living in the U.S. by now."

Doherty nodded. "I understand. Besides, the last thing I want is for you to fire him. Right now he's the only connection I've got to my missing man, and I'm still not even sure he's the right guy. Let me put a tail on him to see where he goes. All I need from you folks is to keep this Stanislaw Krykowski employed, unless, of course, he does something way out of line."

"We can do that. What's your plan?"

"I'm not sure yet. But whatever it is I'll do whatever I can not to cause any problems for the Shepard Company. That's a promise."

"Fair enough," Moroni said. The two men shook hands and Doherty left the security chief's office.

When the elevator arrived at the fourth floor the girl named Max gave Doherty a big smile as she swung open the cage. Once the doors closed she pushed the down button. A second after the lift started to descend he reached over and pressed the 'stop' button. The lift jerked to a halt between the third and fourth floors. Maxine looked at Doherty with some concern.

"Don't worry, honey. I only want a minute of your time."

"But…" she tried to say.

He cut her off. "Do you know a guy named Stan, who works in the shoe department?"

The girl looked away, a little embarrassed. "He's a pig that one," she said without prompting. "Thinks he's God's gift or somethin'. Two different times he got into the elevator and touched my bum."

"Your bum?"

"My rear end," she said irritated. "Touched it like it was his to touch."

"What did you do?"

"I pushed his hand away and gave him a dirty look. He just stood there with that big Pollack grin on his face."

"Why didn't you report him to somebody? To your supervisor or Mr. Moroni?"

"My supervisor? That little pinprick would've said it was my own damn fault for bein' flirty. I'm not flirty, Mr. Doherty. I'm just friendly. I try to smile at people, give em a pick me up, like I done with you. I don't wanna make any trouble and lose my job."

"Don't worry, Maxine, you're not going to lose your job. But I need you to help me with something. What time does this Stan get off work?"

"Probably six o'clock like all the other salespeople."

"And you get off at five-thirty? If you can stick around till six I'll buy you some ice cream or whatever you'd like till then." Doherty looked at his watch. It was already nearly five. "All I need you to do is point out this Stan for me when he clocks out. Can you do that?" The girl agreed and Doherty let her unset the 'stop' button on the lift.

Chapter Fourteen

Instead going for ice cream Maxine convinced Doherty to take her to the elegant Shepard Tea Room across a narrow street that sided the main store. They had coffee and Maxine accompanied hers with a cheese Danish. She knew all the girls who worked there and he got the feeling she wanted to go to the Tea Room so they could see her having coffee with a man in a suit. While she chatted aimlessly Doherty occupied his time thinking about how he was going to move on Krykowski. Whenever his name came up in the conversation Maxine got a worried look on her face. He suspected that the Pole might have done a little more to this girl than touch her 'bum'. Her girlfriend that waited on them didn't charge for the drinks or the Danish so Doherty left her a nice tip.

At five to six Maxine took Doherty around the main building to the corner of Westminster and Union Streets and pointed to the doorway where the store's salespeople exited at the end of the day. Promptly at six a tide of humanity began to flow out of the side door of Shepard's. Many of the men loosened their ties as soon as they hit the streets. The saleswomen tended to cluster together in small groups and emitted loud chatter as they headed away from the store. A few sashayed up the street on the arms of male sales clerks. Krykowski was one of the last to leave. After Maxine pointed him out to Doherty she quickly slunk back around the corner not wanting the Pole to see her.

As Doherty expected he was a big man with broad shoulders, had blondish hair and wore what looked like a permanent sneer on his face. Krykowski did not interact with his coworkers nor did he offer a parting remark to any of them as he walked by himself down Union. Doherty squeezed Maxine's hand and whispered a 'thank you', then followed after his prey. He made sure to keep a safe distance so as not to attract his attention. Krykowski continued on Union to Washington where he took a left and headed in the direction of the public library. A half block later he crossed the street and stopped. There were a few other people standing there and Doherty realized they were all waiting for a bus.

He had to make a quick decision. He could follow the Pole on the bus or try to get his car out of hock before the bus arrived. He concluded that the latter was too great a gamble so he crossed the street and stood at the bus stop alongside the others. The only problem was that he looked a little out of place wearing a nice suit. He loosened his tie, removed his jacket and let out an audible sigh. The woman standing next to him gave Doherty a knowing look: the end of another hard workday in the city. Luckily Krykowski never turned in his direction.

When the bus arrived Doherty hung back, not knowing what the bus fare in Providence was. The people in front of him all dropped a collection of coins in the slot as they passed by the driver. When it was his turn he handed the bus jockey a buck and the driver squeezed four quarters out of the change dispenser hanging by his seat. Doherty dropped a quarter into the slot and moved on. Krykowski was sitting by himself toward the rear, smoking a cigarette and looking out the window. Doherty sat where he wouldn't be in his direct sight line. The bus lumbered through rush hour traffic up Washington. It stopped several times before Krykowski pulled himself out of his seat and moved toward the rear door. When the bus came to a halt he stepped down slowly. Doherty waited a few counts and then slipped through the front door, barely exiting before it squeezed shut.

Krykowski ambled down the street and then planted himself at another bus stop. This time Doherty couldn't hang back, though once again there were a number of other people waiting for their ride so he wasn't all that conspicuous. When the second bus arrived most of the passengers handed the driver a transfer slip. Doherty was caught off guard for a moment. Once aboard he dropped another quarter in the slot and that did the trick. This bus crossed from Providence along Armistice Boulevard into Pawtucket. Doherty was getting further and further away from familiar territory. The vehicle turned left up Newport Avenue and passed through the center of Pawtucket. Quite a few riders exited along Newport leaving Doherty and Krykowski with only a few other remaining passengers. Still, nothing in the Pole's demeanor was sending any caution signals in his direction.

Finally the big man got up from his seat and stepped down at the next stop. Doherty again waited before stepping through the exit door a second before it closed. By the time he hit the sidewalk Krykowski was a good half block ahead of him. He followed discreetly, keeping his head down so the Pole couldn't get a good look at his face. Two blocks up Krykowski crossed the street and turned down a smaller side street. A block and a half later he ducked into a storefront doorway. Doherty moved to the other side of the street and walked by at a normal pace. When he was directly across from where Krykowski had turned in he saw a sign on a plain wooden door that said "Polish-American Citizens Club." The place had two large windows facing the street blocked by heavy curtains. The door Krykowski had passed through fronted right onto the street. There was no way for Doherty, as a non-member of the club, to continue to follow Krykowski without stepping into a potentially hostile setting.

Instead he took out his note pad and tried to recreate the route he'd taken on the two busses. Newport was a pretty big street running through the center of Pawtucket so he assumed he'd be able to find his way back to where the club was located on Annie Street if or when he needed to. He then retraced his steps back to where he'd gotten off the Pawtucket bus and found a stop on the opposite side of Newport. When a bus finally pulled to the curb he asked the driver if this line would take him back to the downtown Providence connection. The bus driver assured him it would. This time Doherty paid a quarter and got a transfer slip. Once he got down from the first ride it took nearly ten minutes before the downtown bus pulled in. Back in Providence Doherty hustled to the lot where he'd dropped the Chevy. The carhop told him if he'd come back fifteen minutes later it would've cost him another fifty cents. Doherty flipped the kid a half-dollar coin anyway and headed back to West Warwick.

Chapter Fifteen

On Monday afternoon he found himself once again on the East Side of Providence, this time sitting in his Chevy having a smoke in the faculty parking lot across from Hope High School. It was a warm spring day so he had the window rolled down while he sucked on his Camel. He admired the old brick building that housed the school with its decorative double columns on the second floor façade. A large white tower, resembling a bell tower dominated the roof on the right hand side of the structure. Hope High was a much grander structure than Deering High in West Warwick where Doherty had attended. At two-thirty a loud bell rang and the students poured out of the main entrance onto the sidewalk. Within minutes most of them scattered away from the building in a myriad of directions. From the scramble that ensued it looked as if the kids couldn't get away from the school fast enough. Doherty was surprised at the number of Hope High students who were Negroes. During his time at high school in West Warwick he couldn't remember any Negroes ever in attendance - or living in the town for that matter.

The faculty lot was filled with vehicles not much better than his own four-year old Chevy. There were a number of station wagons with fake wood on the sides as well other Ford, Chevy and Mercury sedans of various ages. Rachel Katz's miniscule Renault stuck out among the large American cars like a sore thumb. It was parked next to a two-toned Country Squire that was twice its size. A little after three the petite, dark-skinned English teacher crossed Hope Street to the lot. She was wearing a lightweight tan trench coat and was carrying a raft of file folders in her arms. In addition she was hauling a large briefcase that weighed down her left side, causing her to walk in a listing fashion. Once she got closer Doherty gave her a soft tap on his horn. Rachel shielded her eyes and looked his way. When she saw who it was her face lit up with her characteristic smile. She dropped her goods on the hood of her French roller skate and walked his way.

"It's been a long time since a boy picked me up after school in his car," she said.

Doherty stubbed out his Camel and smiled back at her. She wasn't as short as usual today given that she was wearing a pair of black high heels. "I didn't know how to get in touch with you except by hanging around the deli counter or coming here."

"I can give you my home phone number, but you've got to promise me you won't talk to the bitch if she answers. She'll give you the third degree about what's none of her business."

"Would you like to go for a ride?"

Rachel looked up at the perfectly blue sky. "How about a walk instead? It's such a beautiful day."

"That sounds good."

"Let me put this stuff in my car, then we can drive over to Thayer Street and walk around by the colleges. I don't want to walk here; I might bump into some of my students."

Rachel got into the Chevy after disposing of her teacher goods and directed Doherty the few blocks back to the university district. They parked near the Avon Cinema and Rachel took off her coat and tossed it in the back seat. She was wearing a woman's dark suit with a jacket and skirt. Beneath it was a white ruffle fronted blouse buttoned to the neck. She looked like the quintessential young schoolteacher.

The theater was playing an Italian movie called *La Strada*, accompanied by another foreign film. Doherty looked up at the marquee and asked, "Doesn't this place ever play any American movies?"

"They do sometimes; mostly old ones like *Citizen Kane* or *Casablanca*," Rachel answered. "You got something against foreign movies?"

"To tell you the truth, I've never seen one. How do you know what's going on in them if all the actors're speaking a foreign language?"

Rachel laughed and softly punched his arm. "They have subtitles, silly. They wouldn't expect you to be able to understand all the foreign languages that play here. A few weeks ago I came here to see *The Seventh Seal*. That one was in Swedish. Except for the few native Swedes I doubt too many people in Providence understand Swedish."

"How do subtitles work?" he asked having never seen or heard of such a device.

"It's simple. They just flash the English words at the bottom of the screen while the actors are speaking in whatever language the film's in. I'll take you to one sometime. Some of these foreign movies are really good and they often have more sex in them than American movies, especially the Italian ones. Do you like movies?"

"Yeah, I do. I don't own a TV so I go to the movies a lot in West Warwick. They don't show any foreign movies at my regular theater, the Palace."

Rachel looked at him with a funny grin. "You don't own a TV. What kind of American are you? I ought to report you to the House Un-American Activities Committee."

"From what I can tell, most of what's on TV is junk."

"A vast wasteland," Rachel said echoing his comment.

They began to walk up Thayer away from the Avon. "You got me there. Most of what we watch at home is pretty awful. My parents keep the boob tube on all the time when they're home. My father says it takes his mind off the deli. I think he really keeps it on so he doesn't have to listen to my mother."

They turned at the next corner and headed in the direction of the Brown Quadrangle. When they passed by the ivy-covered walls of the Brown dorms Rachel said, "I could've gone to Pembroke you know. That's the girls' part of Brown. I got accepted no problem."

"Why didn't you?"

"My father said we couldn't afford it. I always knew it was my mother who didn't want to spend the money to send me here. She said, 'Why should we spend all that money when you're just going to end up as a teacher or a secretary?' So I went at RIC instead. But I would've liked to have gone here. It would've been so exciting. How about you? Did you ever want to go to college?"

They walked down a tree-lined street with beautiful nineteenth century houses on either side. Doherty had to slow his usual gait to let the smaller woman in high heels keep up with him. "I went to Bryant for a semester. Thought I might want to start my own business. You know, there was a lot of GI Bill money around for college after the war."

"So what happened?"

Doherty shrugged. "My father died and I needed to go to work to help my mother make the payments on our house. She wanted to stay in the place where we grew up."

"Does she still live there?"

"No, she passed away a while back. My sister and I sold the old house after she was gone."

"Ah, so you have a sister?"

"Yeah, Margaret. She's my only sibling. She lives out in Minnesota now. I don't see her much since she moved. Every Christmas I send her a card and she sends me a card and a box of candy. I keep promising myself to go out to visit her and see her kids, but I haven't gotten around to it yet. What about you? Do you have any brothers or sisters?"

Rachel looked away. She bit her lip and didn't say anything for a while. "I had a brother; an older brother, Larry. He died in the polio epidemic when he was eight. Sometimes I think it's why my mother is so nasty toward me. She loved that boy so much. I can't help but feel that she resents the fact that he died and I lived."

They walked on, each trying to put thoughts of their families aside for a while. Rachel reached out and took his hand. Doherty hadn't walked down the street holding a girl's hand since high school.

"Do you ever think about going back to school?"

"Do you mean like college? Not really. When I was there it all seemed so pointless after being in the war. Besides I kind of like what I do now. It doesn't take a college education to be a good PI."

"That reminds me. How's your search for Meir Poznanski going?"

Doherty considered what he could share with Rachel without compromising his agreement with the men from the minyan. Since she'd gotten him in the door at Mrs. Koplowitz's he guessed she was part of the deal now. Plus with Agnes on vacation he could use Rachel's feedback.

"I think I found the guy Meir's been after. The Nazi he told Mrs. Koplowitz about."

"Really?" Rachel said excited now. "You saw a real Nazi - right here in Providence?"

"I'm not a hundred percent certain it's him yet, though he seems to fit the bill. Still, it doesn't put me any closer to Meir."

"What will you do now?"

"I don't know exactly. At some point I'll have to tell this guy that somebody's out to do him harm. I feel obligated to at least do that."

"You're going to save the life of some Nazi while you put Meir Poznanski in trouble with the law?" she said angrily.

"Calm down, Rachel. I don't care about this Nazi guy any more than you do. From what I've been told he's still something of a bastard. But killing him wouldn't put Meir in a very good place. And I didn't say anything about going to the cops. I'm hoping I can get to Meir myself before he does something stupid. Maybe this other guy deserves what's coming to him, but I don't see what good it would do for Meir to spend the rest of his life in prison."

Rachel let go of Doherty's hand and walked quickly on ahead. When he caught up to her, she stopped and looked up at him. "I suppose you're right. It's just that when I think about some Nazi, any Nazi, here in Providence right under our noses all I want to do is kill him myself. Can't you understand how we Jews feel?"

"Of course I understand. But you should keep something else in mind: I'm the one who's actually killed Nazis – a lot of them during the war. So *you* have no right to be telling me how I should feel or act."

Rachel wrapped her arms around him and said, "I'm sorry, Doherty. I guess I saw too many of those concentration camp movies in Hebrew school not to get emotional about this. You're right. Your job is to find Meir, not to go on a Nazi hunt."

Their walk had taken them back down to Thayer. Rachel took his hand again and said, "Take a little walk with me. I want to show you one of my favorite places here in the city." They crossed Thayer, walked down a block, took a left and then a right at the next intersection. A half block down Rachel pointed to a set of stairs that led down to what looked like a cellar. A small sign over the door said Café Medici.

"What is this place?" he asked.

Rachel smiled up at him. "It's a coffee house. It's a beatnik kind of place where they serve European style coffees and teas and have live music on the weekends. Maybe we can come here together sometime. You like coffee don't you?"

Doherty laughed and then without thinking wrapped Rachel up in a hug and gave her a big smooch, right there out in public. This girl was like no one he'd ever met before, certainly like no girl in West Warwick. He was starting to feel the thrill of being in her company.

They walked back to the car arm in arm and Doherty drove Rachel to her Renault at the high school. The faculty parking lot was almost empty when they arrived. They sat quietly for a few minutes.

"What are you doing this weekend?" Rachel asked.

"I have no plans. Why do you ask?"

"You're not going to make this easy, are you? I was hoping to take you to the Café Medici. That coffee house I showed you."

Doherty smiled at the girl. "I would do that. Will I have to grow a beard and wear a beret to get in?"

She punched him in the arm. "No, silly. But I wouldn't wear your suit. The people there might take you for a cop. They get nervous around *straight* people. I've heard that some of the regulars often blow reefer in the back room."

"Real reefer, like marijuana?"

"That's what they tell me."

"Have you ever tried it?"

"Not yet," Rachel said not even trying to mask her sheepish grin.

"You said they play music there. What kind of music are we talking about?"

"Sometimes jazz, sometimes folk. You like music, don't you?"

"Yeah, I like music. I'm more of a Sinatra type, but I like jazz too. Count Basie, Ellington, stuff like that."

"What about progressive jazz?"

"I'm not sure what that is."

"You know, musicians like Dave Brubeck, Miles Davis, John Coltrane."

"I can listen to that. I'm not sure about the folk music though."

Rachel smiled at Doherty. "Come on, it'll be fun. Here's my number in case you change your mind," she said as she wrote on a slip of paper she pulled from her bag. "Otherwise I'll meet you at the Medici Friday night, around nine. I wrote down the address in case you get lost. You saw it's only two blocks away from Thayer. Look carefully for the stairs. It's easy to miss them at night. And remember it's underground so you have to go down to get in."

"You don't want me to pick you up at home?"

"No. I think it's better if we meet this way for now," she said without further explanation. Rachel then gave him a very sweet kiss before leaving.

Chapter Sixteen

Nothing turned up that whole week regarding the Poznanski case. The only thing Doherty discovered was that Meir Poznanski had surreptitiously returned the family car to his wife. How the man had come and gone from his home without being spotted was a mystery in itself. Doherty suspected that Meir was clever enough to drop the car at a time when he knew his wife would be out of the house. He wondered how Poznanski got transported out of West Warwick. He must've taken one of the infrequent busses that went from Arctic into downtown Providence. It was reassuring to know that the missing man wasn't entirely missing. With Poznanski still moving below the radar, Doherty knew that for the moment Krykowski would have to be the key to unlocking the case.

On Friday Doherty was prepping himself for his meet up with Rachel at the Café Medici when his phone rang. At first he thought it was her calling to cancel their date. However, the voice at the other end was about as far from Rachel's as one could be. He couldn't make out what the caller was saying because his words were so garbled. He asked the man to repeat himself.

"It's Billy James, man. You know, from the Y."

It took Doherty a moment to remember who Billy James was. "Oh yeah, Billy. How're you doing?"

"Oh, I be doin' jus fine, Mr. Doherty. But you done aks me to call you when your man come in. And well, he in his room right now."

"You're sure about that?" Doherty said as he looked at his watch. It was almost eight, time to leave to meet Rachel.

"Yessir, he come in 'bout twenty minute ago. Ain't left his room since."

"And you're sure he's still in there?"

"I jus tolt you he was, dint I? But you gotta come right away. Dey won't let you into the residence after eight lessen I meet you at the front desk."

Doherty looked at his watch again and said, "I'll be there in half an hour. If he tries to leave see if you can delay him."

"I dunno bout dat, but you best be comin' soon if you wanna to talk wid him."

"Thanks, Billy. I'll be there as soon as I can."

"Oh, and Mr. Doherty," the man said in a whispering voice. "You best bring Mr. Green 'long wid you."

It was clear sailing north out of West Warwick and up through Cranston. It took him almost a half hour to get onto Broad Street and even with the Friday evening traffic Doherty still made it to the Providence Y by a quarter to nine. He parked right out front and as expected the old Negro was waiting for him by the reception desk.

"You late, Mr. Doherty."

"I underestimated how long it would take. Is he still in his room?"

"I ain't seen him leave. You lookin' mighty casual tonight, young fella," Billy said referring to Doherty's sport shirt, slacks and cardigan sweater. "You got a date or somethin'?"

"As a matter of fact I do. Is there a pay phone nearby where I can make a quick call?"

Billy pointed at a set of booths that lined the opposite wall. Only one was occupied. "You makes yer call while I keeps a lookout on yer man."

Doherty dialed the home number Rachel had given him. A woman's sharp voice answered instead of Rachel's. When he asked to speak with her the woman barked, "She's not here. Who is this?"

"My name is Doherty. I was suppose to meet Rachel at nine, but it looks like I'm going to be late so ... "

"This is the first I've heard of you," she said. "That daughter of mine goes out and stays out till all hours and never tells us where she's going or who's she meeting up with. What did you say your name was?"

"Doherty."

"What is that, Irish?"

"Look, Mrs. Katz, if she calls home could you please tell her I got delayed and I'll catch up to her later."

"What am I, my daughter's answering service now? Is there a number I can give her?"

" 'Fraid not. I'm on a job and I'm not near a phone."

"You're on one right now, aren't you?"

"Yeah, but it's a pay phone. Just tell her I called if she phones home."

"What kind of date calls my daughter from a pay phone?"

"Thanks for your help," he said and hung up.

The old Negro was nervously scratching at his arm when Doherty returned from his call. "Okay Billy, can you take me to see my man now."

"Not 'fore you gimme a little grease," he said smiling his toothless grin.

"How much you want?"

"How much you got?"

"Don't try to play me for a sucker, Billy. How about another five?"

"Make that ten and we got ourselves a deal." Doherty handed the old man two fives. It still left him with another ten when, or if, he caught up with Rachel.

Billy led Doherty down to the residents' wing. At this hour the corridor was dimly lit. Along the way the old fellow greeted several other residents by name. At the end of the hall were two rooms facing each other. One had its door wide open and a middle-aged man in his underwear was inside watching a small TV while smoking a thin cigar. The door to the room across the hall was shut. Billy pointed at that door and then withdrew a few paces. Doherty knocked. There was no answer, though he did hear some stirring inside. He carefully tried the knob but it was locked. Doherty knocked again. In the meantime, the man from across the hall got up and kicked his own door shut.

In a quiet voice Doherty said, "Mr. Poznanski, I know you're in there. My name is Doherty. I'm a private investigator. I've been hired by your friends in West Warwick to find you. Please open the door. All I want to do is talk. I mean you no harm."

He heard some muttered words that sounded like, "Go away."

Doherty tried again. "Your friends are worried about you. I've even spoken to Anna Koplowitz and she's concerned for you too." Still no response. It was time for Doherty to play his trump card. Billy James had backed down the hallway clearly not wanting Poznanski to know it was he who led Doherty to his door. But he was not leaving the scene entirely until he saw how it played out.

"Mr. Poznanski, I suggest you talk with me before I get the police involved." That did it. The door opened a slit and a shadow stood on the other side. There was only muted light coming from the room. In the dimly lit corridor Doherty had a hard time making out the man's features. From the direction of his voice he could tell that Poznanski was taller than he.

"I've broken no law," the voice said with the trace of an accent.

"Your wife might not see it that way."

"My wife, what does she know?" the voice spit out with disdain.

"Please Mr. Poznanski, just let me in for a few minutes for a friendly chat. I'm causing quite a stir out here and you don't want your neighbors to get suspicious, do you?"

The door opened a little wider and Poznanski's head peered out and looked down the hallway. He was a tall man with soft, sensitive facial features. Some snatches of gray crept out around the temples of his light colored hair. Poznanski was handsome in a European sort of way.

"May I see your license?" he asked in an officious voice. Doherty flashed his card and Poznanski looked at it carefully. He then swung the door open and said, "You may come in, though you can only stay for a short while."

The room was barely lit by a small bedside lamp and it smelled of fried food. An open book lay atop the neatly made bed. Otherwise Pozananski's temporary flop looked barely lived in. A small suitcase sat on the room's only chair, opened with a few articles of men's clothing inside. A white shirt and suit jacket hung on a hook on the back of the door. Pozananski was dressed in slacks that matched the jacket, a sleeveless undershirt and stocking feet. He was, as Doherty would have predicted, well groomed and clean-shaven. Doherty clocked the numbered tattoo that ran up the inside of Poznanski's left forearm. His host placed the small suitcase on the floor and offered Doherty the chair.

"Who sent you to find me?" he asked in a voice devoid of accusation.

Doherty knew that he didn't have to tell Poznanski who his client, or in this case, clients, were though thought he would anyway to help break the ice. "The men from your synagogue minyan. It was a group decision."

"How much are they paying you?"

"I'm afraid I can't tell you that. They're the clients, not you."

Poznanski made a dismissive sound that was somewhere between a snort and a whistle.

"I've been hired to find you and convince you to go back to West Warwick. You don't have to go if you don't want to. Personally I think it would be in everyone's best interest if you did."

"And why is that, Mr. Doherty?" Poznanski asked with an edge in his voice.

He gave the runaway man a stern look. "Because I know what you're planning on doing, and I know who you're planning on doing it to. And I don't think that would be a very wise decision. You're a family man, Mr. Poznanski, not a killer. Go back to your family and leave the past alone."

The man got up from the bed and began pacing the small room. Then he turned on Doherty. "My family. Have you met my family?"

"Only your wife and brother-in-law."

"My wife, you know what I call her?" Doherty didn't respond. "I call her the horse. You see what she looks like. An uglier woman you couldn't find. And my brother-in-law, that gonif." Doherty still didn't know what a 'gonif' was, though from Meir's tone knew it clearly wasn't a compliment.

"Why did you marry Edith if you find her so repulsive?"

"I took pity on her. We were at this dance at the community center and all the girls were being asked to dance but not her." Poznanski shrugged, "I felt sorry for her."

"Are you telling me you married your wife because you felt sorry for her?"

Poznanski looked away and let out a sardonic laugh. "No, of course not. I married her so I could stay in this country. You see my immigration papers were, shall we say, somewhat irregular. If I were to be arrested for something the authorities could've made trouble for me. They might have even sent me back to Poland. After I married Edith and found work at The Bargain Store, I could obtain a green card and stay here permanently. I could even become a citizen if I chose to. You see it was a marriage of convenience for both of us. She made me legal and I gave her my sperm so she could have our children. Once that was done we no longer had any use for one another."

"What about Mrs. Koplowitz?"

Poznanski hesitated. He looked wistfully at the far wall and said, "Agnieszka? She will always be dear to my soul. We were in hell together and she saved my life. For this I am eternally in her debt. You have spoken with her?"

Doherty nodded. "Yes, she was the one who told me about your plan to kill Stanislaw Krykowski. She's very worried about you."

"Krykowski? Is this the name he is using now? Stanislaw Krykowski?"

"It is if he's the man you're intending to kill."

"In Poland he was Antonin Bradz. He was one of the many young men who joined the Nazi movement long before the Germans came to Kracow. They were bullyboys, all of them. In the school they were always the stupid ones, the ones the teachers mocked because they could never do their lessons correctly. They hated the smart boys like me. Antonin lived on my same street; his father was the barber, Kristik Bradz. At night Antonin and his gang of toughs would walk the streets beating anyone they suspected of being a Jew. Then they started to smash the windows of the Jewish shops, and later the synagogue. They were preparing the way for the Nazis, you see."

Doherty asked Poznanski if he could smoke and his host agreed.

"Even before the Germans came they began to pass laws telling us Jews what we could and could not do. I was a young teacher at the time, just out of university. I taught in the Kracow Limited Upper School for boys. I taught mathematics. But soon word spread through the school that I was a Jew. I never hid it and there were other Jewish teachers at the Limited as well, but things were changing. First they reduced me to only two classes, mostly of the stupid or retarded boys. Then they told me I must also clean the gymnasium and the eating hall, like a common laborer. On some days I would come into my classroom and the boys had written nasty remarks about Jews on the chalkboard. I tried to soldier on but I was young and still insecure about my skills as a teacher. I had just married so I needed the position. It wasn't long before the headmaster called me in to tell me my services were no longer required at the school. He said to me it was because so many boys were leaving the school for military training. I knew what was happening. He was a decent man, yet weak in the face of this new Poland that was emerging."

"What happened between you and Bradz?"

"Ah, when the Germans came to Kracow the people were divided. Many welcomed them because they still feared the Russians and thought the Nazis would protect them. Others, like Bradz, saw a chance to take what the Jews had: not just their belongings, their places in society as well. Don't get me wrong, Mr. Doherty, there were many Poles, Jews and Gentiles alike, who joined the resistance against the Germans. Unfortunately, in the end, that only made it worse for us. With the help of young Nazi sympathizers like Bradz and his bullyboys, many Polish men and women were taken from their homes and shot right out in the street for being part of the resistance. Most of them were not on either side, just people from the town that these young boys resented for one reason or another. Someone who caught them stealing from his shop, or who reprimanded them for hurting animals. Everyone was now fair game to these young monsters."

"Soon the Gestapo came to round up all the Jews in our neighborhood. By then Bradz and his friends were in special uniforms. They called themselves the Granatowa Policja, the blue police as you would say in English. They helped to identify who the Jews were. My wife and I now had two small children. They took my wife, my little ones, my mother, my father, aunts, uncles, cousins, all of us. Took us from our homes and our shops never to return again. And there was Bradz, standing right next to these German officials, pointing out who the dangerous ones were. Some were shot right there on the spot while the others were sent off to camps. My wife and children were sent to Treblinka, where everyone went to die. I never saw them again. There was no word as to what happened to my parents or any of my other relatives. Only one of my uncles and I survived. He is now in Israel, and I am here at the YMCA."

Poznanski sat down, exhausted from relating so much of his past. He lit a cigarette of his own and stared aimlessly into space. They could hear noises from TVs and laughter coming from down the hall. There was no laughter in this room, only raw memories.

Finally Poznanski looked up at Doherty and said, "So you see why I must kill this man. I have waited almost twenty years to wipe the ugly grin from his face. I have seen him in my sleep every night since that day."

"Look, I can sympathize with your feelings. I won't belittle them by saying I know how you feel, because frankly there's no way I can. But you have come here to make a new life. You have a wife, children, friends who care about you, a job – things to live for. If you do this, if you kill this man, no matter how much satisfaction you think it will bring, it will also be the end of your life as you know it. Why do such a thing now?"

Poznanski was looking down at the floor. He raised his head and said, "How can I not after what he has done to me?"

"You could try going to the police. If what I've uncovered is true, then this Bradz may be in the country under false pretenses. That alone is a criminal violation. If he's carrying fake identification he could be arrested and possibly deported."

Poznanski laughed. "You Americans have such faith in the police. Where I come from the police were always the enemy, the ones to be avoided. Do you honestly think if I go to the Providence police or some other government police and tell them about Antonin Bradz that they will give a damn? How many former Nazis do you think are living the good life here in America today? I'll tell you, the number is in the thousands. No one cares anymore about those who were Nazis. The Germans are our friends; now it's the Russians everyone must fear."

Doherty stood and looked at his watch. It was already nine-thirty and he was late for his date with Rachel.

"In that case I may have to go to the police myself to warn them about you and what you intend to do."

Poznanski laughed again. "And what will you tell them? That I ran away from home and am living at the YMCA. That I plan to kill a man whose name I don't even know. They will mock you more than they would mock me if I told them my story."

"I'm asking you one last time: Are you willing to go back to West Warwick and forget this vengeance that you hold so dear?"

Poznanski glared down at Doherty. "You can tell my wife and the men in the minyan that I am well and have no immediate plans to come home. The men, they may ask for their money back. You know, Jews used to be people of the book, now they are people only of the pocketbook."

"That's not fair. There are many Jews working as doctors, lawyers, and teachers right here in Rhode Island. Not all Jews are interested only in money."

"Maybe so," Poznanski said with a sigh. "But the ones I know in West Warwick are. There are too many men now like my brother-in-law Milton. Always chasing the dollar. It is all they care about anymore."

Doherty left the Y quickly. As he did he brusquely passed by Billy James without exchanging a word with the old Negro.

Chapter Seventeen

Doherty wasn't sure what his next move would be. One thing was certain though, Rachel Katz would not be happy with him being an hour late. Thayer Street was jam-packed on a Friday night, so he had to park a couple of blocks away on a side street. It took him a while to locate the Café Medici. The street it was on was dark and there was only a faint red light above the coffeehouse sign. As a result he nearly stumbled down the steep steps that led to the underground club. He could hear music even before he pushed open the red entrance door. There was a small alcove inside that was separated from the main area by a hanging beaded curtain.

On the other side of the curtain was an open space filled with small tables and a low ceiling. A thick cloud of cigarette smoke hung in the air. The café area was dark except for some bright spotlights that lit a small stage on which two men were performing. One of them was tall and angular and sported an Abe Lincoln style beard. He wore a blue work shirt and black pants and was playing a guitar. The other was shorter and stouter with thinning long hair. He rested a banjo against his substantial belly while they played and sang out the lyrics to an old Irish ballad about a boy named Roddy McCorley who was hanged for his role in one of their many uprisings against the English. Doherty was familiar with the tune, as he'd heard it sung many times by drunken Irishmen in taprooms in West Warwick on St. Patrick's Day. He'd never heard it accompanied by stringed instruments before and liked the rendition the two young men on the stage were performing.

He scanned the dark room hoping to locate Rachel. A waitress sauntered in his direction. She was a tall and thin and had straight blond hair that hung almost to her waist. She was wearing black tights and a sweater that came down just far enough to cover her backside. She was carrying a small round tray holding a coffee drink with some foam on top and a magenta colored substance in a tall glass with ice.

"Can I help you?" she said in a flat tone.

Doherty continued to scan the room. "I'm looking for a small woman; dark hair, dark skin, in her twenties. I'm suppose to meet her here."

The waitress did a nice pirouette without spilling any of the drinks. "I believe she's at that table over by the wall talking to Tango." Doherty got the general drift of where she meant and slipped between the tables in that direction. By now the Irish boy in the song had been hanged on the bridge at Troon and the players were belting out another song about crack corn and a blue tail fly.

Rachel was indeed sitting at a table with an older black man who sported a goatee and a dark pork pie hat. They were having a very animated conversation until Doherty came into view. Rachel gave him a less than welcoming look as he took a seat at the small table with the two of them.

The black man held out his hand and said, "Hi, I'm Dave Tancrene. You can call me Tango; everyone else does. And I believe you know my friend Rachel. I think she'd all but given you up for lost." Doherty smiled but Rachel did not return one of her own. Sensing the tension Tango stood and said, "I gotta get ready for my set. Maybe I'll see you two later." He then leaned over and kissed Rachel on the cheek. Doherty had never seen a black man kiss a white woman before.

Rachel turned toward the stage and purposely ignored Doherty as she stirred her coffee. The folksingers had launched into a version of "Goodnight Irene," which Doherty recalled singing at summer camp. He didn't, however, remember the campers singing the last verse where the singer threatens to take morphine and die because his woman has left him.

The waitress eased over to their table and asked Doherty if he'd like something to drink. He asked if they had coffee and she cracked up saying, "We are a coffee house, are we not?"

Rachel then turned in her chair and said, "I recommend the café au lait. It's really good here. You know what café au lait is, don't you?"

"Yes, Rachel, I know what it is. I had some when I was in Paris," he said snidely. Doherty ordered the café au lait and a piece of cinnamon cake to go with it.

"Are you talking to me now or are you just telling me what to order?"

Rachel looked at him and then at her watch. "You're an hour late. I wasn't sure you were going to show at all. I thought maybe you got cold feet."

"Well it was nice that you had Tango to keep you company."

"He likes to sit with me because he thinks I'm part Negro."

"Are you?"

"No, asshole. I'm part Sephardim."

"What does that mean?"

"Sephardim were originally Jews who lived in North Africa and Spain. My mother would never admit it, but my father told me that her grandfather was an African Jew – North African, not black African. More like an Arab. That's where she and I get our black hair from. Some Sephardim have dark skin and kinky hair like me. Some European Jews think of Sephardic Jews as being like Negroes, but many of us are direct descendants of the Moors who ruled Spain before the Catholics kicked us out. Most of Sephardim went back to Africa though some ended up in Europe and the Middle East. Many of the earliest Jewish settlers in Palestine were Sephardim. Which still doesn't answer my question of where the hell have you been?"

Doherty smiled at Rachel. "I was wondering when you'd get around to asking. Right before I was about to leave to meet you I got a call from a guy I met at the Providence YMCA the other day. You see I had a hunch Meir Poznanski was staying there. Well, it turned out my hunch was right and this guy called to tell me Meir was in his room. I had to go right away otherwise I might not've been able to catch up with him. I called your house; your mother answered the phone."

"You talked to the bitch?"

"Only briefly."

"What did she say?"

"She wanted to know if I was Irish."

"Figures. What else did she say?"

"Nothing much. Just that her daughter stays out to all hours of the night without telling her where she's going or who she's with. You know, stuff like that."

"Stuff that's none of her damn business."

"Maybe she's just worried about you."

"Oh bullshit."

The folksingers had left the stage to tepid applause. Doherty assumed that audiences in a coffee house were not expected to show too much enthusiasm for the performers. The waitress arrived with his coffee au lait, which was quite good. He then spent the quiet time while the jazz group was setting up on stage telling Rachel about his conversation with Meir Poznanski.

"Sounds like he's not going back to West Warwick."

"Not for the time being anyway."

"So what're you going to do? Will you have to return the money the minyan gave you to find him?"

"No, my job was only to find Meir, which I've done. My standard agreement clearly states that if the missing person doesn't want to return home I can't compel him to do so. I thought about going to the Providence police, but I don't have any concrete proof that Meir will really attempt to kill this Polish guy. Right now I'd like to see what I can do to keep Meir out of trouble. For the moment the only card I have to play is with this Krykowski character. But I've got to be careful how I play him to make sure that Meir remains safe. In the end it would be best if both men stayed alive."

The jazz group began its set. There were three Negroes, a drummer, guitar player, and Tango on upright bass, and a white guy who played the flute. The music was more pleasing to Doherty than that of the folksingers. It was also soft enough that he and Rachel could continue talking.

"What are you going to do about this Nazi guy?" she asked.

"I don't know. Far as I can tell he may be in the country illegally with phony immigration papers. That's if he really is the person Meir thinks he is. There's always the possibility that Poznanski has misidentified him. Maybe he wants him to be this Bradz character because he's thought about the guy so deeply and for so long that Bradz has come to haunt him. If that's the case he might end up killing the wrong man. Unless I can prevent him from doing so."

"But what if he is Bradz? From what Meir told you he sounds like the kind of person who deserves to die."

Doherty shook his head. "I can't think that way. I know there are a lot of people in this world who deserve to die. Hell, we're all going to die someday, but we can't go around playing God saying this person deserves to live and this person deserves to die."

"Why not? That's what the Nazis did during the war, didn't they?"

Doherty took a sip of his coffee and checked out the jazz combo for a few beats. "That's exactly what they did, and that's why we had to defeat them. So that people or governments can't make those kind of arbitrary decisions anymore. Jeez, Rachel, that's what the whole fucking war was about." Doherty immediately felt ashamed for letting his temper get the better of him. He'd never used the F word in front of a woman before.

After a few long numbers the combo took a break. There was still tension in the air between the two of them and Doherty selfishly didn't want Tango to join them again. They sat in silence for a while as Doherty smoked and tried to figure out how to make things right between them.

"Let's get out of here," Rachel said breaking the silence.

Once out on the street they stood looking away from each other but still not talking.

"Take me home with you," she said after a few minutes.

"To my place? It's a long drive. I don't know if I can take you back home later." He looked at his watch. It was almost midnight.

"I'm not going home. I'm going to spend the night with you."

"What?"

"You heard me. We just had our first fight. Now we have to have some make-up sex."

"Are you sure?"

Rachel took his hand. "Let's go before I change my mind. Where's your car?"

On the ride down to West Warwick they talked about the Café Medici, the music, Meir Poznanski and anything else they could think of except what had happened between them at the coffee house. Once in the apartment Doherty straightened up the various messes around the place while Rachel poured each of them four fingers of Jameson. She slugged hers down faster than she should have.

They undressed each other quickly, though Doherty had some trouble freeing Rachel from her girdle. She giggled as he struggled. When they were naked in bed she slid down and did something to him he'd never experienced outside of a French whorehouse. He thought about stopping her, but before he could it was too late.

When she was finished she flopped over to her back and said, "Now screw me, screw me hard."

"I'm not sure I can. I'm kind of spent."

"Oh, I think you can. I got faith in your stamina, Doherty." He did as she wanted though it took so long that he was thoroughly exhausted by the time they were through.

Doherty was on the verge of falling sleep when Rachel hopped out of bed and headed toward the living room.

"Where're you going?"

"I have to call home to tell my folks I'll be out all night."

"Jesus, Rachel. It's almost one-thirty."

"Doesn't matter. It's part of the deal we have." Doherty watched as Rachel's dark little bottom moved through the doorway. He forced himself to stay awake until she returned.

"Everything okay?"

"Not really," she said. "My father answered the phone. When I told him I wasn't coming home he sounded hurt and disappointed. It's better when she answers because then I don't feel so guilty."

Chapter Eighteen

In the morning they lazed in bed until almost ten. They made love again, but without the ferocity of the night before. Doherty smoked afterwards while Rachel propped herself up on her elbow and watched him. He tried to ignore her, except there was nothing else to look at.

"Why are you staring at me?"

"You're kind of traditional, aren't you?"

"By traditional do you mean prudish?"

Rachel giggled. "Maybe. I'm not sure yet."

"It could be the Irish in me. You know what they say about sex for the Irish: it's ten minutes of action and twenty minutes in the confessional booth."

Rachel smiled. "That's something I never understood. How can you go into a confessional booth and tell some sexless priest that you screwed some girl or jerked off to a dirty magazine? I could never do that."

"I didn't much like it myself," Doherty said. "Most of the time I would go in and lie about what I'd done. You know, I'd say stuff about how I swore a lot or showed disrespect for my mother. I couldn't very well tell the priest I jacked off."

"What does the priest say after you confess?"

"Not much. He asks you if you're sorry and if you repent for your sins. Then he tells you to say some Hail Marys and you're absolved."

"That's pretty sweet. But why do you have to confess to a priest in the first place. Why can't you just tell God you're sorry? That's what we do."

Doherty pulled on his smoke and said, "Because Catholics don't believe they have the right to talk directly to God except in prayer. If you've sinned then you have to be absolved by a priest. The rejection of that tenet of the church was part of what the Protestant Reformation was all about. Luther and some of the other Protestants argued that Christians should be able to talk directly to God and that they didn't need to tell all their affairs to a clergyman unless they wanted to. And worst of all as far as the clergy were concerned, they no longer had to pay off a priest to exonerate them, as was often the case in the old days. What about Jews? Where do they come down on all this?"

Rachel took some time to consider the question. "We talk to God through our prayers all the time. But our sins, if there are such things, are more about how we've treated others rather than how we treat ourselves. That's why rabbis don't make a big deal about masturbation or having impure thoughts about someone of the opposite sex. You're guilty, or sinful, based more on what you do to others rather than what you think or do to yourself."

"But isn't 'Thou shalt not covet they neighbor's wife' one of your Ten Commandments too?"

"Of course it is, but so is 'taking the lord's name in vain', and we do that every time we hit our thumb with a hammer. And don't get me started on 'honoring thy father and thy mother'. For God's sake, Doherty, half the Ten Commandments aren't even illegal any more"

"Speaking of honoring thy mother, don't you have to work in the deli today?"

"It's okay if I get there a little late. It'll do the bitch some good trying to handle the crowds without me for a while. Maybe it'll make her appreciate me a little more, though I doubt it. Anyway, it's the least I can do to her for being so rude to you on the phone last night."

Rachel slid out of bed and stood with her hands on her hips fully naked facing Doherty. He furtively looked her up and down. She could tell he was embarrassed and thought it was humorous.

"I'm sorry, Rachel, sometimes I feel like you're a little too fast for me." Although he had to admit he liked looking at her nudity in the full light of day.

"I'm going to take a shower. You got something I can put on afterwards?"

Doherty climbed out of bed, fully naked himself, and took his threadbare terry cloth robe off its hook in the closet. Rachel threw it over her shoulder and headed toward the bathroom.

While she showered Doherty ducked out to Belanger's and picked up some milk, a dozen eggs and a rasher of bacon. He put up some coffee and was whipping the eggs when she came out of the bathroom.

"You left me here all by myself, didn't you? I could've been raped while you were gone."

"I locked the door. You were perfectly safe. The only one you have to worry about raping you is me. By the way, do you eat bacon?"

Rachel laughed out loud. "I'm Jewish, Doherty, not kosher. Yes, I eat bacon. I especially like it after a full night of sex." Again she succeeded in embarrassing him.

When they sat down to their breakfast of scrambles eggs, bacon and toast both of them attacked their food ravenously. Apparently the night of sex was good for his appetite as well.

Rachel sipped her coffee and then said out of the blue, "Tell me about your first time."

"My first time at what?"

"You know, the first time you got laid, or went all the way, did it or whatever you Irish liked to call it."

"You got an awfully smart mouth, Miss Katz."

"I've heard that before. Afraid to fess up? It's not like I'm a priest."

"No, I'm not afraid," he said trying to recall his memory of that first experience. "I was nineteen, just out of high school, working my first year at Quonset. There was this girl, a secretary in the office of my division. Whenever I'd go in with a requisition slip she'd kind of flirt with me. I was young and inexperienced so I didn't think anything of it. We all knew she was married."

"How old was she?"

"I don't know. Maybe twenty-three. Older than me anyway. One day there was this party for one of the office guys who was leaving. Everyone in our division was invited, including the stiffs who worked on the line like me. Well, I guess I got pretty drunk because near the end of the party she told me I was too loaded to drive and that she'd take me home. I was still living with my mother and my sister at the time."

"What happened next?"

"I'm getting to that," he said trying to recall the details as best he could. "She took me home all right, but to her place not mine. Turns out her husband was out of town, and well …"

"Come on, Doherty. Let's have some details."

"Why do you want to know all this?"

"Maybe it turns me on," she said with a smirk.

"I'll tell you the rest, but in return you got to tell me your story after I'm done."

Rachel considered the proposition for a few seconds and said, "Okay. It's a deal." She stuck out her hand and they shook on it.

Doherty started in again, "We went back to her place. We started kissing and stuff, and the next thing I knew we were in her bed. But you see I didn't really know what to do. I mean I'd never seen a woman's privates before except in pictures, let alone touched them. Anyway one thing led to another, and I guess you could say nature took its course. Like I said, she was already married and older than me so she knew her way around the bedroom. And she did what she could to make it easier for me."

"What did you think once the deed was done?"

"I'm not going to sit here and say I didn't like it. I mean it was a hell of a lot better than doing it with myself. It probably would've been nicer if I was going steady with her or if I wasn't so drunk. At least after that I knew what to do with a girl."

"Were you with a lot of girls after her?"

"Not so many. Mostly whores when I was in the army. Those times I was more worried about getting the clap than having a good time."

"What happened to the girl from the office?"

"I don't know. We stayed kind of friendly for a while, though neither of us ever talked about that night. A few months later she got transferred to another division at Quonset. After that I never saw her again."

Rachel smiled at Doherty. "That's kind of a sad story."

"Not really. What would've been sad is if the first time I did it was with one those whores. At least Connie was a real woman, somebody with a name. And the fact that she was married meant there were no strings attached. Now it's your turn little Miss Noseybody."

Rachel began, "I was fifteen. He was my boyfriend at the time. He was seventeen and had a car so he thought he was King Shit. He was Jewish, rich, and good-looking. All the girls thought he was a catch, but I was the one who caught him. We went to a temple dance on the East Side one night; he brought along a little flask filled with some scotch he'd pilfered from his parents' liquor cabinet. I'd never drunk liquor before, only the occasional glass of wine my father'd let me have on holidays or other special occasions. Never enough to get high on. That night was different. When nobody was watching my boyfriend would mix some in with our ginger ales."

"When it got late, and by late I mean around ten, we left in his car. It was actually his father's car. Only then did he tell me his parents were in Miami Beach for the week and he wanted me to come back to his house with him. They lived in this beautiful, gigantic house off Blackstone Boulevard. You see his father owned a chain of drug stores. I'd like to be able to say I was too drunk to know what I was doing, like in your story, but I wasn't. I was a little high so I let him do what he wanted with me. He was so cool and popular, I felt lucky that he wanted me. Plus, you know, I was curious too. I mean, a girl's got to lose it sometime, so why not that night with a guy I thought I was in love with."

"Was it as good as you hoped it would be?"

"I suppose. Up to a point anyway, but I was still a virgin and he didn't know that. He took me into his parents' bedroom to have sex in their big king sized bed, not on the little bed in his room. I guess that made us feel like adults, or as close as I was going to feel at fifteen."

"How did it turn out?"

Rachel laughed. "Not so good. I wasn't prepared for how much it was going to hurt, and neither was he. That kind of took some of the romance out of it. But that wasn't the worst of it. The worst part was that I bled on his parents' silk sheets. Steve, his name was Steve, kind of threw a fit when he saw what had happened. You see, he didn't know how to work the washing machine. So our romantic night ended with me washing the sheets and showing him how to put them in the dryer and back on the bed."

"And that was it?"

"No, not at all. We went out for a few more months and in that time all he ever wanted to do was have sex with me. I smartened up pretty quick and made sure he always used a rubber, especially since he was like a dog in heat all the time. To pacify me he stole a box of them from one of his father's stores. In the fall he went off to college and we broke up, but not before he told all his friends that I 'put out'. I got something of a reputation after that, though I didn't really care because I knew that most of the other girls were jealous I'd 'done it' with a guy like Steve and they hadn't. They were all still virgins. And I suppose you could say that I never looked back with any regrets. In case you haven't noticed, I like having sex. And I like having sex with you, even if you are my first Catholic boy."

Chapter Nineteen

When Doherty dropped Rachel off at her car on College Hill she was happy to see that there wasn't a parking ticket tucked under one of her windshield wipers. They sat for a minute waiting to see what would happen next. Then Doherty leaned over to give her a goodbye kiss.

"Listen, I'm going home to change before I go to work. Why don't you come by the deli a little later and I'll make you one of my special sandwiches? It's the least I can do in return for the trafe you fed me this morning."

"Trafe? What's trafe?"

"Bacon, bubbie. If something's not kosher it's trafe – especially if it's pork."

"But you said you weren't kosher," he protested.

"I know. I'm just teasing. It's so much fun throwing these Jewish words at you. I think I like doing it mostly because you make your living as a private investigator. I'm trying to show you what you don't know."

Doherty laughed. "Don't worry about that. The older I get the more I realize what I don't know."

Rachel leaned over and kissed him hard on the mouth despite the passersby who could see them through the car window. "I'll see you in a bit my Irish beau."

Doherty killed some time milling around Thayer Street. He was fast becoming familiar with this intellectual center of Providence. Not that he was an intellectual himself by any measure. But he did like being around people who read books and cared about what was in them – people like Rachel and others who'd been to college. Doherty liked the stories in books and movies that brought imagined people and places to life for him. Though he had a hard time admitting it, they transported him out of West Warwick and out of Rhode Island to a bigger world. The army had done that for him even if it did involve a lot of fighting and killing and watching good men die in heinous ways. As bad as it was, it was real - more real than wasting his life working on the line at Quonset or in the mills in West Warwick. Sometimes he wished he was one of the characters in the books he read, like the Joads heading out to California to start their new lives, or Santiago out on the open sea trying to reel in the huge marlin.

When he got to the deli he waited in the car to make sure Rachel was at her post behind the counter before he went in. The last thing he wanted to do was deal with her mother. When he finally spotted her through the milling crowd he crossed Rochambeau and ducked inside the crowded food store.

Katz's was as busy as it had been when he first made Rachel's acquaintance. Being there today made him realize how much had happened between them in such a short time. She was wearing the same dirty white apron that hung around her neck and tied at the waist. Amongst the women who were obviously regulars at Katz's were a few men ordering sandwiches either to take back to work or home because their wives were out Saturday shopping. He took his number and waited patiently. Rachel caught his eye and gave him one of her sly suggestive smiles. Her mother was too busy with another customer to notice this exchange.

When his number came up Rachel didn't bother asking him what he wanted and went right to work on a hefty sandwich. She wrapped the sandwich in wax paper along with a thick dill pickle. Without his asking she added a bottle of Dr. Brown's Cream Soda. Doherty reached in his pocket for his wallet but Rachel waved him off. This caught the mother's attention. As Doherty backed away from the counter he could hear the mother asking Rachel, "Who is that man?" To add insult to injury Rachel blew him a kiss as he moved toward the exit.

It was two o'clock and Doherty was hoping to pay a visit to the Polish-American Citizens Club in Pawtucket before he returned to West Warwick. As he sat in his car eating his sandwich he wondered how he was going to kill the next few hours. Rachel told him the sandwich was hot pastrami, a meat Doherty wasn't familiar with. It was warm and salty like the corned beef, but stringier and tastier. She'd slathered the rye bread with some dark mustard to add to the flavor. The pickle was large and sour and went perfectly with the pastrami. Doherty'd only had a cream soda once before in his life so the Dr. Brown's was a real treat.

He kept glancing at the deli every time someone went through the front door. He needed some time to figure out what was going on between Rachel and him. He knew they were at best an odd match. She was in her twenties and he was nearly forty. She was Jewish and he Catholic, though neither of them was particularly religious. She was a college grad, first girl in her class at Classical, and he, well, he did graduate from high school, and although he was not at the bottom of his class, he was not a great student by any stretch of the imagination. He also had to admit there were moments when Rachel seemed a little too *progressive* for him. Maybe that's what girls of her generation were like nowadays, at least here in Providence. Girls who acted like Rachel in West Warwick would be considered *easy or slutty*. Still, if she was fast even for this age he was more than willing to try to catch up to her.

After finishing his sandwich Doherty lit a smoke and walked down to the nearest drug store where he picked up a copy of the afternoon *Bulletin*. He took it back to the car and scanned the Providence movie ads. A movie called *North by Northwest* starring Cary Grant and directed by Alfred Hitchcock was playing at the Majestic downtown. He figured this would be a good way to kill the rest of the afternoon. He'd seen *The Man Who Knew Too Much* a few years ago and enjoyed Hitchcock's movie making quite a bit. Another picture called *The Best of Everything* was on the double bill. He drove around downtown until he located the Majestic, dropped the car by the curb, bought a ticket at the kiosk and went in. He assumed there wouldn't be any noisy kids at this Saturday matinee.

When he was young his mother used to give him and Margaret money to go to the Palace almost every Saturday afternoon. The show was a dime back then for kids. The Saturday matinees were usually some combination of a full-length cartoon like *Cinderella* or *Snow White and the Seven Dwarfs* along with another kids' movie. If not that, then there might be a Laurel and Hardy or Bowery Boys comedy double feature playing. Whatever was being shown didn't much matter because Saturday afternoon at the Palace was pure mayhem. All the kids talked and shouted at one another throughout the movies and some even yelled at the actors on the screen. They'd buy popcorn for a nickel in one of those rectangular boxes and when the snack was all eaten or dropped on the floor they'd flatten out the boxes and hurl them like coasters at the screen. Soon the ushers would escort the rowdier kids out of the theater and on a few occasions they even had to call in the police to restore order. Sometimes Doherty would join in with the hijinks, though when he did it upset his sister. At other times he would be just as annoyed as she because he wanted to watch the picture.

The Majestic was only half full, mostly because the theater was palatial compared to the ones in West Warwick. The walls were decorated with beautiful gold filigree designs and the ceiling was a mural of blue sky and birds in flight. The screen was twice the size of the one at the Palace and the audience was relatively quiet. The only signs of spectators in the theater were the small dots of light that came from their cigarettes. *The Best of Everything* was already playing when Doherty took his seat. It was in color, which made it seem that much brighter because of the size of the screen. The story had something to do with the cutthroat publishing industry in New York and it starred a bunch of young actresses he'd never seen before. One of the bosses was Joan Crawford, who was an ambitious and ruthless boss. Doherty'd remembered her from *Mildred Pierce*, in which she played a mother sacrificing everything for her spoiled daughter. He recalled that he'd seen that movie at the Palace right after he came home from the army. He decided he preferred her in this movie where she was the heartless one. It fit her tough looks better.

When the newsreels came on after the first movie Doherty took the opportunity to use the men's room and to buy some popcorn. It came in the same square boxes as it did at the Palace. For a split second after finishing his popcorn he thought of crushing the box flat and tossing it at the screen. This juvenile remembrance caused him to laugh out loud. A few people sitting nearby looked at Doherty with peculiar glances given that nothing going on in *North by Northwest* at that point was the least bit amusing.

That movie starred Cary Grant, one of Doherty's favorite actors, as a sophisticated ad executive who gets mixed up with a woman played by Eva Marie Saint, who may or may not be playing him for a sucker. This was a very different role for her than the goody two-shoes she played opposite Marlon Brando in *On the Waterfront*. There was a curious scene early in the film that hinted she and Grant might have slept together on an overnight train to Chicago. It made him think of last night with Rachel.

As the movie went on it became clear that Saint's character was either being chased by some bad men or was in cahoots with them. Against his better judgment and because he is the victim of mistaken identity, Grant gets hooked into a complicated series of events that he doesn't fully understand. At one point, as a result of her instructions, he is dropped off by a bus in the middle of a flat arid field somewhere in the Midwest. Soon a crop duster plane appears out of the blue and tries to run him down. It's a terrific scene made even more dramatic by the Majestic's large screen.

The real stunner, however, is a scene near the end when Grant and Eva Marie Saint have to climb and then crawl across the faces of the presidents on Mt. Rushmore while being pursued by the bad guys. Unfortunately for Doherty, when James Mason turns up as the lead villain it throws him back to last fall when he accompanied Millie St. Jean to a movie starring Mason at the Palace. As it turned out, that was their first and nearly last date. Despite the unpleasant memory, he had to admit that Mason made a very good villain in this picture. In the end the whole mystery had to do with foreign spies being chased by a U.S. government agency that was using Grant and Saint as decoys to track them down.

The movie was long, over two hours, and by the time it ended Doherty had killed the afternoon in a thoroughly enjoyable fashion. There were some previews being shown before *The Best of Everything* came back on, but he felt he'd already spent enough time in the dark. He was feeling tired and knew he had to have his wits about him for his next move.

Chapter Twenty

It was still too early for him to expect Stanislaw Krykowski to be at the Polish-American club in Pawtucket, so Doherty dropped into a bar near the theater to knock down a shot of Jameson. He thought he'd need it to steel up his courage. The place had the usual bar smell of stale beer and piss. Still, it was a nice quiet respite after the high stakes drama of the movie. There were only a few other patrons in the place as it was the dinner hour. Doherty drank in peace while Dean Martin sang, "That's Amore," on the jukebox.

Once back in the car he tried as best he could to retrace the bus route he'd taken to Pawtucket. He got lost briefly, but had no trouble getting directions to Newport Avenue from a pedestrian. It was like asking someone in West Warwick where Washington Street was. In time he found the Polish-American Citizens Club on the small street that ran parallel to Newport. He parked a half block away and took some time to plan his strategy. He recalled how strangers wandering into the Hibernian Club or the Irish-American Hall in West Warwick were greeted rudely. He didn't expect any warmer welcome from the Polish crowd. Doherty had no idea how the ethnic lines were drawn in Pawtucket, though he assumed that the Poles were not one of the larger groups in this burgh, and therefore were probably somewhat clannish.

The wooden door was closed as tightly as it had been when he tracked Krykowski there a week before. Without hesitation Doherty pushed his way in. The entrance opened into a large hall that was brightly lit and was filled with a number of long tables and a few smaller, round ones. There were about twenty men and a few women scattered about the room. A few looked his way with curiosity then went back to their dinners, their card games or their private conversations. Doherty took a minute to case the place. Large portraits of famous Poles festooned the beige colored walls. The only one he recognized was that of Thaddeus Kosciusko, a Polish mercenary who'd fought with the Colonial army during the American Revolution. He'd seen the same portrait in a history textbook years ago. The rest of the mostly mustachioed faces were unfamiliar to him. A large Polish flag flanked by an American one covered much of the facing wall.

Some music was playing in the background and although it had a polka beat to it no one in the hall was dancing. A woman was singing along with it in a language Doherty'd never heard before that he figured must be Polish. The hall smelled of fried meat being cooked in a kitchen somewhere. Many of the men had bottles and glasses of beer in front of them. Doherty took a seat at an unoccupied table and lit up a smoke. A few minutes later two men from another table got up and came over to sit across from him. At first no one said anything though Doherty did give them a friendly nod.

Finally one of the men said in a thick accent, "Can ve help you?"

Doherty carefully considered his new companions. The one who spoke was of average size, had dark hair combed sideways across his head and a dark, bushy, old world style mustache. Doherty took him to be in his thirties. The other guy was about the same age, had blond hair that he wore in a modified pompadour and was large all over. When he smiled Doherty could see a couple of gold teeth flashing on his choppers.

"I'm looking for someone. A man named Stanislaw Krykowski. I understand he comes here regularly."

The two men looked amused. The bigger one said, "You're not Polish are you?" Doherty shook his head.

"It don't matter," the same guy added. "Anyone can come in for dinner or a drink. We welcome all people." He didn't speak with an accent. "Would you like some kielbasa?"

"I'm not sure what that is," Doherty said. Strange dishes were becoming a regular part of his palate these days.

"It's sausage. Thick Polish sausage."

"You mean like Italian sausage?"

"Yeah, only bigger and better," the man said proudly.

"Maybe I'll try some then." The big guy whistled loudly and a women appeared out of what Doherty assumed was the kitchen. She was stout and older than his two new companions.

"Franciscka, a kielbasa for our friend here and three more beers, please." The woman smiled kindly at them and left. After she did the two exchanged some Polish with each other.

"Vat is your name?" the one with the accent asked.

"Doherty," he said reaching out a hand to shake.

"I am Jerzy. This is Tomasz. Vy is it that you vant to talk vit Stanie?"

Doherty weighed his answer. "I came to warn him. I believe someone wants to hurt him." Both men burst out laughing. Doherty waited patiently for the moment of mirth to pass.

"Am I missing some joke here?"

"No, my friend," the big one replied. "We are laughing because many people would like to hurt Stanie Krykowski."

"Why's that?"

"Because he is not a nice man. He is, as you say in English, a bastard. He comes here all the time but has few friends."

"Are you police?" the smaller man asked with a hopeful note in his voice.

"No, I'm not the police. I'm a private investigator. I've been searching for a man who I think wants to do harm to Stanislaw."

"Then he will have to stand in line," the big man said without humor.

The waitress interrupted them by delivering a steaming plate of large brown sausage and boiled potatoes covered in butter and parsley. It was accompanied by beers all around. Doherty dug into the sausage; it was tasty but so hot that he had to fill his mouth with beer before chewing it.

"Be careful, my friend. You will burn the top of your mouth. First cut the Kielbasa open to let the heat out."

The three men poured some beer into their glasses and waited for the head to settle. It was some kind of Polish beer Doherty had never seen in Rhode Island before. As they waited Doherty noticed out of the corner of his eye two other men at a nearby table shooting glances in their direction. He made it a point to clock their faces for future reference.

"Can you tell me what you know about Stanislaw?" Doherty asked his two new friends.

"Vat's to know?" the little man responded. "He comes here to the club, maybe tree nights to a veek. He eats, he drinks too much and he insults the womens. He complains about everything: the food, the music, the pictures on the walls. Everyone is happy ven he takes to leave."

"Do you know where he works or where he lives?"

The two men looked at each other and shrugged. "I hear he works down in Providence in one of the department stores," the one named Tomasz said. "I don't know where he lives. Do you, Jerzy?"

"I don't know and I don't vant to know. I don't like some of the tings he says."

"Like what?" Doherty asked.

"He says bad tings about America. I say to him vy you come here if you hate it so much. Then he gives me that nasty look of his and says that Americans are veak, veak like the Poles vere ven the Germans came. He say all the Poles in U.S. have lost their vay – they have lost their pride. I tell him if the Americans are so veak how come they vin the var. He say the Russians vin var – Americans only came along at the end to take all the glory ven the Germans was already lost. I say to him forget the var. Ve are in America now, ve have to learn to love this country."

"Are you originally from Poland?"

The little man smiled. "Can't you tell from my accent? I come here only four year ago. I come because the Communists are no better for Polish people than the Nazis vere. In America ve are more free."

"Free to be anything but Polish," the big man added. "Tell me Mr. Doherty, where are you from?"

"I was born in West Warwick. And I still live there."

"That is south near Warwick."

"Yeah, right next door."

"In this West Warwick, do they make Polack jokes?"

Doherty considered the question. He had heard some of these jokes, though like most ethnic humor he tended not to pay them much mind. They were as stupid to him as the new *moron* jokes that were currently going around.

"Yeah, I've heard those Polish jokes," he said.

"We hear them all the time. Because of them everyone in America thinks Polacks are ignorant. What are you Doherty? Irish, Italian?"

"I'm Irish."

"And what is it about the Irish that jokes make fun of?"

"Drinking. We're all drunks. That's our stereotype."

"Not so bad as Polish," the little man said. "Better to be a drunk than stupid, no?"

Doherty smirked. "I don't think either stereotype does much to advance the cause of civilization."

Doherty finished most of his kielbasa and the three of them had another round of beers. He checked his watch; it was almost nine.

"It doesn't look like Stanislaw is going to make it to the club tonight, gentlemen."

"No; it's better. He make trouble ven he come here. Insults all the members. Dey should trow him out."

The other man spoke. "We can't do that, Jerzy. We can only expel him if he gets into a fight or fails to pay his dues. The women he insults are afraid to complain about him because they don't want more trouble. Sometimes I think someone should take him outside and teach him a lesson."

'Yaw, someone like you, Tomasz," Jerzy said.

The big man shook his head. "I don't want no more trouble. I had enough to last my lifetime over in Korea."

"You were in the army?" Doherty asked.

"Oh, yeah. Don't you know that dumb Polacks make the best soldiers? They don't know enough to duck when they hear a shell coming in. That's what my lieutenant used to say – before he had his own head blown off." Doherty wanted to tell these men that he'd been in the big war himself, but didn't think it would add anything to their conversation.

He handed Jerzy and Tomasz each one of his business cards and suggested that they call him the next time Stanislaw Krykowski came in. Or if they felt like it, to tell Krykowski to call him. Then he pulled some bills out of his wallet, but Tomasz stayed his hand. "The kielbasa and beer are on us. Think of it as Polish hospitality."

Doherty thanked them and dropped two bucks on the table and said, "This is for the woman in the kitchen."

It was dark when he left the club. He had a full head of beer and had to remind himself where he'd parked the Chevy. As he walked to his car he heard footsteps behind him. He picked up his gait without looking back. He had the car door half closed when a hand braced it from the outside. It belonged to one of the men from the other table who'd been eyeballing him in the club. Doherty looked at the intruder along with his companion who stood a few steps back near the trunk.

"What can I do for you, gents?" Doherty asked while he assessed the situation. The man leaned in the window. Doherty could smell the mixture of kielbasa and beer coming off his breath. He was tall and thin and not very menacing looking. He was wearing a sport coat with a shirt underneath buttoned to the neck. The other man was larger though Doherty couldn't get a good look at him because he was out of eyeshot.

The one leaning on the door smiled and said, "Stay away from Stanislaw if you know what's good for you." He spoke with a mild accent, not thick like that of the fellow named Jerzy.

Doherty gave him a level gaze and replied, "And if I don't know what's good for me?"

The man smiled again and Doherty took in his crooked teeth. "Then someone's gonna get hurt."

"I came to help Stanislaw not to hurt him."

The tall man leaned in again and said, "Take my advice and stay out of what's not your business."

The other man began to move slowly up the length of the Chevy. Before he could get any closer Doherty quickly swung the door open and smashed it hard against the tall man's knees. He fell to the ground in pain. In the split second that his companion went to his aid, Doherty slipped behind him and put a hammerlock on his neck. His left forearm slid across the guy's throat as his right locked behind his head and gripped the bicep of his other arm. It was a killer hold he'd learned during hand-to-hand combat training in the army. One that could easily break a man's neck if that was your intention.

The one who'd fallen to his knees slowly worked himself back up to his feet. Seeing the hold Doherty had on his friend he was at a loss as to what to do. Doherty helped things along. "Either tell me what this is all about or I break your buddy's neck right here and now." He then tightened his grip. Everyone was breathing hard. While his adversary looked confused and helpless, Doherty tightened the pressure.

The guy in his grip wheezed, "Gustav, please, say something – or he will kill me."

The other man stood motionless by the car door as Doherty continued to feel his forearm grind into the bones of his captive's neck.

The thin one then spoke rapidly, "In Poland during the war we were part of a group called the Granatowa Policija. The English called us the Blue Police. Some of us have continued to meet here since we came to America. We thought it was just to make political talk, you know. But Stanie, he is different." The man was visibly nervous about giving out this information. Doherty didn't know if it was him that he was fearful of or Krykowski.

"Talk about what? The good old days of the Fuhrer? Tell me, how is Stanislaw different?"

"He still hates the Jews. He thinks they're out to get him. He say they follow him here from New York."

"Who are *they*?"

The man in Doherty's grip began to struggle so he tightened his hold, knowing that if he stiffened it too much his prisoner would soon pass out.

"The Nazi hunters from Israel."

It was Doherty who was now confused. "He thinks there are Nazi hunters following him here in America?"

"That's what Stanie say. He say they come to America to kidnap people like us to take to Israel for trial. Stanie is the only one I know who believes this." A few seconds passed before he added, "We heard you asking questions about him in the club and thought maybe he was right and that you are one of them."

The man Doherty was holding suddenly went limp. He knew he was not dead, just out cold. He let the dead weight slide down to the sidewalk. The other man stepped back as Doherty approached him. He handed the man one of his business cards.

"Tell Stanislaw that I'm not a Nazi hunter. That I came to warn him that someone is intent on doing him great harm. Someone who knew him back in Poland. It's in everybody's interests that it not happen. Tell him that's the only reason I'm looking for him and it's important that he and I talk."

The man squatted down to administer to his friend who was beginning to regain consciousness. Doherty reached down and grabbed the thin man by the hair and pulled his head back. "The next time you two come up on me in the dark like you did tonight I might have my .38 with me. If that's the case I won't think twice about blowing your brains out. And that, my friend, would not be good for anyone."

Chapter Twenty-One

With nothing else to do, Doherty went into the office on Sunday to try to dope things out. He could've used Agnes to throw some ideas at, but her husband Louie was still in town and she was playing housewife for the time being. One thing Doherty knew he'd have to do was pass on to the men in the minyan that he'd located Meir Poznanski and that the missing man had no desire to return home to West Warwick. Doherty wondered if the men would believe him. He suspected some might even want their money back. With little else to occupy his mind he spent some time thinking about what was happening between him and Rachel Katz. He concluded that perhaps he shouldn't look that gift horse in the mouth too closely.

On Monday Doherty wandered over to The Bargain Store to pass on what he knew to Meir's brother-in-law Milton. He would've preferred to approach Morris Mendelson first, but that would've required him to go to into Francine's where he might run into Millie St. Jean. He definitely didn't want to do that now that things were percolating with Rachel.

There were few customers in The Bargain Store. Orlovsky was working a man with a joke about Moses and golf. Doherty hung back, not wanting to even hear the punch line. The store's proprietor was tapping the client's belly with his cigar hand as he finished up the joke. When he was done Orlovsky laughed loudly while his listener merely smiled politely. Whatever his intentions, Orlovsky did not look pleased when the customer left the store empty-handed.

"Schmuck can't even take a joke," Orlovsky said bitterly as he approached Doherty.

"No sale?"

"Sale? That one's my landlord. He wants to raise our rent another ten dollars. Like I don't have enough troubles with my brother-in-law being missing and my business in the toilet on account of the mills closing. There are already too many men in West Warwick outta work. Can't that putz see what's happening to the businesses here in Arctic?"

"Actually it's because of your brother-in-law that I'm here," Doherty said.

Orlovsky stuck what was left of his cigar in the corner of his mouth and looked hard at Doherty. No service with a smile for the PI today. "Have you found him? Is he okay?" He asked only vaguely interested.

Doherty nodded. "I've found him all right and spoke with him. As of now he has no intentions of coming back home."

Orlovsky shook his head. "I'm not surprised. Where is he? Keeping house with some other tootsie?"

"I wish that was the case. The situation is a little more complicated than I thought it would be. Maybe I should speak with Mr. Mendelson first."

"What am I, lunchmeat? He's married to my sister and he works in my store for chrisssake. Don't I have a right to know where he is? I put thirty bucks of my own money in the kitty we put up to hire you."

Doherty tried to remain calm despite the fact that Orlovsky and his cigar were getting on his nerves. "Could you tell Mr. Mendelson to come by my office as soon as he can so I can fill him in?"

Orlovsky pulled the cigar out of his mouth and said scornfully, "Tell him yourself, Mr. Bigshot. His shop is right up the street. It's a women's store; the one called Francine's."

"I know where Francine's is, but I have a good reason why I don't want to go in there. So I'd appreciate it if you'd pass on my request to Mr. Mendelson."

Orlovsky was already mumbling under his breath as Doherty turned to leave. "Hey, Mr. Private Eye, have you told my sister yet that you found her *lost survivor*?"

"No, I haven't. Meir didn't think she'd care one way or the other. Besides, she's not my client, you and the other men in the minyan are."

Doherty stopped at the Arctic News and had a quick lunch before return-ing to the office. The baloney and cheese he ate was a pale imitation of a sand-wich compared to the overstuffed ones Rachel had been whipping up for him. All that Jewish lunchmeat was beginning to spoil him. He knew he'd never get a sandwich that good or that thick anywhere in West Warwick.

He wasn't back at the office for long before Morris Mendelson meekly en-tered through the open door. Doherty ushered him into his inner office and offered the little man a chair. As usual Mendelson was fidgeting with his hat. This time Doherty didn't bother to relieve him of his lid.

"Milton tells me you've found Meir. Is that true?"

Doherty rocked back in his swivel chair as he considered how much he could or would tell the spokesman for the minyan. "Yeah, I found him. As of Friday he was alive and well and has no desire to come back to West Warwick."

Mendelson looked genuinely disappointed. "That's too bad. Is there some reason why he wishes to stay away? Is it because of Edith?"

"I think that's part of it," Doherty said remaining tightlipped.

"What's the rest of it?" Mendelson asked.

"Well, it appears that your friend Meir is intent upon killing someone."

"Oh my God! You can't be serious? Meir is not capable of such a thing. Who in God's name does he want to kill?" His questions came out fast and furiously, all but spilling over one another.

Doherty swung around slowly in his chair. Then he casually lit a cigarette. "I said he's intent upon killing someone, not that he's capable of it, or that he necessarily will."

"I don't understand."

"Neither do I, not entirely anyway. Apparently the person he wishes to harm is someone he knew back in Poland. Someone who was instrumental in him and his family being sent off to the camps. Meir believes he saw this man in Providence. That's about all I know at this point," he added as a half-truth.

"You can't let this happen. You have to contact the police or someone to stop him."

"Right now I'm hoping I can intervene myself before Meir does something foolish. I'm afraid if I get the police involved, they'll either arrest Meir, or more likely tell me they can't do anything until he shows that he's a real threat. It's not like he has a history of violence or even a weapon as far as I can tell. For everyone's sake, I'd first like to see what I can do to prevent this crime from happening."

Mendelson let out a deep sigh. "Will that put you in danger?"

"I don't know. I hope not," Doherty replied. "Meir has no reason to harm me, and I know a little more about these kind of things than he does. If he won't listen to reason, I have other, more persuasive means I can use."

Now Mendelson looked frightened. "You wouldn't hurt Meir, would you?"

"Not really hurt him. However, I might have to use force to prevent him from doing what he's intent upon. Whatever I do, it will be for his own good."

"What about the man he wants to kill? What do you know about him?"

"All I know is that he may be the man Meir thinks he is, or he may not be. If he is, he's using a different name than the one he had back in Poland when Meir knew him. It could be that he's in this country illegally. That's one angle I can play right now if I need to. But first I've got to establish that he is who Meir thinks he is. If he is then he's a former Nazi. I don't know if that means anything anymore to the police or the immigration authorities. There could be some statute of limitations where certain crimes from the war are concerned. On top of that I don't know if what this Pole did would still be considered a crime this long after the war. Hell, for all I know he could have every right to live and work here in America."

"Even if he was a Nazi? Someone who did what Meir says he did gets to live here like nothing happened?"

Doherty got up from his desk and walked over to where Mendelson was sitting. He put a hand on the little man's shoulder and said, "There're a lot of things left over from the war that don't seem right these days. But time goes on and people forget. Kids nowadays, the only thing they know about the war is what gets taught to them in school. The concentration camps, the exterminations, someday there'll all be forgotten. There will even be people who'll say they never happened. Look at Germany today. They're our allies. We give them lots of money so they won't side with the Communists."

Mendelson dropped his head and said softly, "Perhaps that's why Meir feels like he has to do this thing himself. Maybe he's right."

"I've thought about that, Mr. Mendelson. But I also know sometimes we just have to move on with our lives. Don't get me wrong, I saw plenty of killing over there, and once you've seen that, it's hard not to hate the other guys. But carrying that hatred around for the rest of your life? That, my friend, is very heavy burden."

Mendelson rose, still nervously fingering his hat. "Please, Mr. Doherty. Don't let Meir do this. I don't care if this Nazi deserves to die or not, I only care that Meir not do it. He's a good man who's had too much pain in his life already. Please don't let him get hurt or be put in jail."

"I'll do what I can. I promise you that."

Chapter Twenty-Two

That night Doherty was heating up some canned beef stew when his phone rang. Initially he hoped it would be Rachel. He was disappointed when it was Billy James from the Y instead. This time he recognized the man's deep guttural voice immediately.

"Your boy bin here and gone," Billy said, slobbering his words through his toothless mouth.

"Gone where?"

"Now how in the hell would I know dat?"

"Then how do you know he's gone?"

"I knows 'cause he ain't been here since Saturday night."

"You're sure of that?"

"Sure I'm sure. He could be he shackin' up wid some woman or gone home; he sure ain't here no more."

"Are you gonna be there for a while?"

Billy laughed hard enough that Doherty could hear the phlegmy cough at the other end. "Course I be here. Where the hell else I gonna be on a Monday night?"

"I'll be down there in less than an hour."

"I be waitin' fer ya at the desk like I done before."

Doherty threw down a few spoonfuls of stew and left the rest on the stove. He then grabbed his coat and hustled down to Belanger's garage to get the Chevy. He drove as fast as he could and this time got to the Providence Y in less than forty minutes. As promised, Billy James was waiting by the main desk. After they shook hands, Doherty pulled out his Camels, lit one and gave Billy the rest of the pack. The old Negro flashed his toothless grin. Doherty hoped that would be enough of a payoff tonight.

"I got Jessie, the night man, to open the room fer us," Billy said as he led Doherty down the dark corridor. Most of the other tenants had already closed their doors or did so as Billy and Doherty walked along the hallway. Doherty suspected they thought he was some kind of cop. He didn't want to disabuse them of that notion since it would keep them out of his business. At the end of the hallway Doherty flung Meir Poznanski's door open without first knocking and flipped on the light. The shirt and suit jacket were gone from the back of the door. His suitcase still sat open on the chair and a book rested atop the bed. Otherwise everything was pretty much as it had been when they spoke the other day except that Poznanski wasn't there. Doherty turned on Billy James and said, "I don't understand. It looks like he's still living here. You said he was gone."

"I tolt you he was gone, and now you see for youself he ain't here."

"But most of his clothes and everything else are here just as they were the other day."

"Dat's what I been tryin' to tell you, man. He gone but all his stuff still be here. I knows he ain't been here since Saturday. Before he always be back come nighttime. You ain't inside by ten o'clock, dey lock you out; make you sleep in the cold."

"He could be staying with someone else, a friend or someone. Maybe even a woman."

"Yeah, suh. He could be but he ain't."

"And how do you know that?"

"Cause I seen him leavin' wid two men and he dint look too happy 'bout it neither. If you aks me, it look like he was goin' wid dem 'gainst his will."

"Jesus, Billy. Why didn't you tell me that right off the bat? You made it sound like he went out to the movies or something and didn't come back."

Billy smiled his old toothless grin. "You dint aks me, that's why."

Doherty shook his head while Billy took the occasion to make himself comfortable on Meir Pozananski's bed.

"What did these men look like?"

"Sorry, man, but that there information is gonna cost you some."

Doherty shrugged. "You know something, Billy, you're becoming a very expensive habit." The Negro man smiled and let out a throaty chuckle. Doherty slipped him a fin and said, "That's all I got on me tonight."

Billy James looked disappointed. "I gots to put a little butter on Jessie's toast for lettin' me and you come on in here," he said.

"That comes out of the five I just gave you. Now tell me about these men before I lose my patience," Doherty said trying to sound menacing.

"Dey looked like cops but dey wasn't."

"How do you know they weren't?"

" 'Cause I heard dem talkin' while dey was takin' your boy out. Both of dem had haccents."

"What kind of accents?"

"Damn, man. Now how would I know what kindsa haccents dey had. Alls I can tell you is dat dey was white men wearing suits – older, you know, like thirties or forties. Both had on suits like plain clothes cops wear and was talkin' wid dese haccents. Off hand, I'd say dey was Europe men. Dey sure wasn't speakin' no spic or Chinese."

"Do you have any idea where they went?"

"Sure as shootin' I do," Billy said with a grin. "Dey walked out da front door and got into a black car. Big sedan – an old one. Nothin' fancy like dem new cars wid big fins and two colors. Dis one looked like a PO-lice car, but it weren't one."

"How could you tell?"

Billy chuckled until it turned into a ragged cough. "Shit, man. I bin in plenty o' PO-lice cars in my time and I run from a few a dem too. I can tell a PO-lice car from a reg'lar car any day o' the week. And that there wasn't no PO-lice car. It just looked like it coulda bin."

Doherty was wondering what this all added up to. His worst fear was that Stanislaw Kykowski and his buddies got wind of where Meir was staying and picked him up. Somehow Meir must've tipped his hand as to what his intentions were. Or maybe it was really Doherty's fault that Poznanski was now in the wrong hands. If that were the case then he would now have to confront Krykowski directly. It no longer mattered that the two guys he'd roughed up outside the Polish-American club knew who he was. Now his fear was that he might not find Meir Poznanski before it was too late.

Doherty thanked Billy James and shook his shriveled, boney hand before leaving the Y. He asked the old Negro to give him a call if Meir returned or if anyone else showed up looking for him. He assured Billy he would make it worth his while.

Chapter Twenty-Three

It was time for Doherty to look the demon in the eye. He drove into Providence late Tuesday afternoon and dropped his car at the same lot where he'd left it the first time he went to the Shepard store. This time he didn't bother checking in with Jack Moroni or anyone else from the store's security staff. His plan was to simply act like a regular customer looking to buy a new pair of shoes.

There wasn't much business in the men's shoe department when Doherty first spotted Stanislaw Krykowski. The former Nazi was standing by the register in shirtsleeves wearing a red striped tie that hung about halfway to his belt and a sneer on his face. Krykowski was a big man who wore his blond hair combed back in a series of waves that looked like a yellowed ocean. Doherty scoured a rack of brogues, carefully handling each one as if he were in the throes of a deep decision. In a short time Krykowski wandered over.

"Can I help you," he said with a trace of a European accent. Nothing in his demeanor indicated he recognized Doherty from the bus rides the other day. As a result Doherty saw an opportunity to engage the big Pole in conversation.

"I'm looking for some new dress shoes; perhaps something in oxblood."

Krykowski picked up a shoe and said, "I recommend these Bostonians. You can't buy a better shoe outside of Florsheim's." Doherty thought it curious that Krykowski would mention a shoe brand Shepard's didn't carry as a point of comparison.

"I don't know. They look a little pricey to me."

Krykowski waved his arm and said, "Please sit, try them on. I guarantee once they are on your feet you will change your mind about the price." Doherty took a seat in one of the chairs lined up for shoe fittings. Krykowski grabbed a metal sizing plate and placed it on the floor in front of Doherty.

"Please to remove your shoes and stand," he said sounding more foreign now. "I will take the measure of your foot and we will see." Doherty removed his right shoe and stood on the plate. Krykowski moved a metal slide on the plate down to his toe to get his size. He then moved another plate from the side to measure the width of his foot.

"You are a size ten, but will need a wide width. Might be problem. Bostonians tend to be narrower than other brands. We will see."

Krykowski then disappeared into the back room to retrieve some shoeboxes. While he was gone Doherty lit a cigarette and rolled a stand-up ashtray over next to his chair. Within minutes Krykowski returned carrying four different boxes.

"I bring some other brands so you can compare with Bostonian. Please to check for size and comfort."

"You sound European. Are you from over there?"

"Yes, from Poland. I come here almost twelve years ago."

"I was in Europe during the war," Doherty said. "You look about the same age as me. Were you in the war?"

Krykowski ignored his question and took a pair of shoes out of a box. "Please to try these on. Very good Bostonians."

Doherty did not move to put the shoes on even though Krykowski was kneeling in front of him brandishing a metal shoehorn. "You didn't answer my question. I asked if you were in the war."

"What matter does it make? The war was long time ago. I live in America now." Krykowski was purposely avoiding eye contact. It was time for Doherty to stir the pot.

"Maybe you were on the side of those krauts we were fighting. I heard a lot of Poles were Nazi collaborators. I believe some were part of the Blue Police. Is that true?"

"I was with the resistance," Krykowski said without conviction. "Are you here to buy shoes or talk of war?"

"I was just making conversation," Doherty said as he blew some smoke in the Pole's direction.

Krykowski looked up. The patented sneer was now on his face. "I sell shoes. I don't make conversation. You want to talk, go to the women's department. Women like to talk all the time."

"Hey, you don't have to get sore. I was thinking, though, that selling shoes must be a little demeaning for a man of your background."

Now Krykowski was looking straight at Doherty with his piercing blue eyes. If looks could kill Doherty would've been be a corpse already.

"Are you a policeman?"

"No, I'm a private investigator. I came here to talk with you, not to buy a pair of shoes."

Krykowski looked nervously around the shoe department. There was no one else in sight save for the two of them. "I don't understand what this private investigator thing is. You are not from the police?"

Doherty slowly pulled on his cigarette while Krykowski returned the metal shoehorn to his back pocket and stood. He was towering over Doherty. He rose to meet the big Pole's gaze. "I've been hired to find a man who went missing. My information is that he may be intent upon hurting you. I'm here to warn you that your life could be in danger."

Krykowski shook his head and laughed. It was a forced and mirthless laugh that hinted at some unease underneath. "So you are here to make me afraid. I am not so easy to make afraid, Mr. Investigator." He pounded his fist on his chest and added, "Stanislaw Krykowski can take care of himself." His bravado had a false ring to it.

Doherty slid his foot into his shoe never once taking his eyes off Krykowski. He wondered why he had any interest at all in protecting this man. By all accounts he was the kind of person who took liberties with women, was a nuisance to everyone at the Polish-American Club and was an anti-Semite and ex-Nazi. On top of that, Doherty didn't particularly like his looks either. Still, he had to remind himself that his mission was to insure that Meir Poznanski remained safe and not instigate some needless act of violence.

"Does the name Antonin Bradz mean anything to you?"

Krykowski's look hardened but otherwise he showed no sign of recognition at the mention of what his real name might be.

"What about Kristik Bradz?" he asked throwing the father's name into the mix. For a second he thought Krykowski flinched at the mention of his father, now possibly dead and buried somewhere back in Poland.

"I do not know these names. Is one of them the man you are looking to find?"

Doherty took a step closer to Krykowski and even though the Pole was a couple of inches taller he gave him his best dead-eyed smile. "No, I believe one of them is you. And I also believe you may be in this country illegally. I think the immigration authorities would have a field day with someone of your background. An illegal alien living in the U.S. with invalid papers - and an ex-Nazi to boot. Working as a shoe salesman right here at Shepard's. You certainly would make for a great story in the Providence papers."

Krykowski drew himself up to his full height. "My name is Stanislaw Krykowski and I have been living in America since 1947. My papers are all in order and I work selling shoes, first in New York and now here in Providence. I know nothing of these other people that you speak of. If you have no wish to buy shoes then I suggest you leave the store and stop wasting my time."

Doherty pulled out one of his business cards and stuck it in Krykowski's shirt pocket. "Here's my card in case you find yourself in trouble or are approached by someone who wishes to hurt you. If so, feel free to give me a call." He then patted the place where he'd placed the card and said, "Perhaps we will meet again."

He was sweating as he strode out of the Shepard building. The confrontation with Krykowski hadn't exactly gone as planned. But at least now he had rattled the big Pole's cage. He spent the next hour walking around the city until hunger overtook him. He stopped to get some eats at the Haven Brothers Diner truck that parked alongside City Hall. He had two hot dogs with the works and a bottle of Coke. Sitting on the steps of the Hall Doherty was trying to figure out what his next move would be. Whatever he did he had to find Meir Poznanski. He wasn't sure who the men were that escorted him from the Y. He hoped that they weren't associated with Stanislaw Krykowski and his crew of ex-Nazis. If they were then what he'd just done at the Shepard store would do nothing to insure Poznanski's safety. Whatever trouble Poznanski had gotten himself into, Doherty now felt responsible for getting him out of it.

Chapter Twenty-Four

It was dark by the time he returned to the lot where he'd left the Chevy. He slipped the car jockey a buck and drove back to West Warwick deep in thought, so deep that he never saw the dark green panel truck that followed him all the way from the city. Doherty was just closing the doors to Belanger's garage when two men in trench coats stepped up behind him. Sensing their presence he whirled around in a defensive stance only to find himself staring down the barrels of two revolvers, each pointed at his midsection.

"We would like you to come with us," one of the men said. He was neatly dressed, bald headed and clean-shaven. Like everyone else Doherty seemed to be meeting these days, he too spoke with a European accent.

"I'm not going anywhere until you tell me who you are."

The other man stepped forward. He had longish black hair sticking out from under his hat and was younger and slightly larger than the first. "This gun says otherwise."

"Please Jozef," the first man said. "Do not threaten Mr. Doherty." By inadvertently using a name the speaker indicated either they were not going to harm him if he cooperated with them or they were going to kill him. He turned to Doherty and said, "We will not hurt you if you would please come with us. If you refuse I will instruct Jozef to shoot you right here. Believe me, Mr. Doherty, we are not unfamiliar with killing."

"Then why should I come with you? Why shouldn't I just make you shoot me here?"

"Because we have Meir Poznanski. And he is who his friends hired you to find, is he not?"

Doherty looked at the men and realized he had but a pair of deuces to play against their full house. "Is Meir okay?" was all he could think to say.

"He is fine. We are only holding him for his own protection."

"I don't understand."

"You will in time. Please come with us and I will explain everything when we get there." He didn't bother to tell him where *there* was. The two men then ushered Doherty into the back of a panel truck. There were no seats so he and the spokesman sat on the floor with a third man. The other gunman slid behind the wheel. The first man held out a strip of black cloth and said, "We request that you put this blindfold on. You may do it yourself as long as it is tight enough to block your vision."

"Why?"

"Please do as I say if you ever wish to see Meir Poznanski alive again." Doherty didn't know how to take this last remark so he did as he was told.

The spokesman for the three men leaned in to speak quietly to Doherty. He could smell the scent of tobacco on the man's breath. It made Doherty wish he could spark up a cigarette of his own.

"My name is Avraham. You don't need to know my surname. We are taking you to a safe house. It is where we are holding Meir Poznanski. When we get there everything will be explained to you. You may smoke if you wish. Give me your cigarettes and I will light one for you." Doherty pulled a fresh pack of Camels out of his inside pocket and the man unwrapped it and lit a smoke. He handed it to Doherty and then returned the pack to his pocket. He did not speak to Doherty again though he did speak to the other men in a language Doherty thought was Yiddish based on what he'd heard among the women who crowded the counter at Katz's.

They drove for about a half hour; Doherty had no idea which direction they traveled in. Finally the truck stopped, made a pivot and then backed up slowly. When the engine was turned off Doherty was maneuvered out of the rear doors. He could tell from the lack of fresh air and the smell of oil that they were in a garage. He was then hustled into what he assumed was a house. Once inside he was roughly pushed into a chair and the blindfold was removed. A strong beam from a desk lamp was focused directly on his face so that he could not see the faces, only the images, of three men arrayed against the far wall. Doherty was seated behind a desk. A man sat down across from him and spoke. He was not one of the men from the crew that had grabbed him outside of Belanger's garage.

"Mr. Doherty, my name is Janisz," the new voice said. "Do you know why you are here?"

"Apparently to insure that you don't kill Meir Poznanski."

The man spoke in a soft but clear voice. "We understand that you have been pursuing a man who goes by the name of Stanislaw Krykowski. Is that correct?" Doherty nodded adding nothing more.

"We would like you to stop this quest." The accent was foreign, but his English was very precise. His diction reminded him of that of Anna Koplowitz.

"And why's that?"

The man turned and spoke quietly to one of the other men. Doherty couldn't understand what they were saying. Although they were whispering he was pretty sure they were speaking in Yiddish.

"We have been following Mr. Krykowski for some time now. He is, as a hunter would say, our prey. We would like it if you did not interfere."

"Sorry Janisz, you're going to have to give me more than that."

The man chuckled. "Mr. Doherty, under the present circumstances I do not think you are in a position to make demands on us. If you do not do as we ask, I'm afraid it will not be good for you or for Meir Poznanski."

"I don't get it. What the hell does Meir have to do with all this cloak and dagger business?"

The man on the other side of the desk adjusted the light to strengthen the beam on Doherty's face. It was so painful that Doherty had to divert his eyes. Meanwhile his captor consulted once again with the men behind him.

"I will be frank with you, Mr. Doherty. Our mission is to track down men like Stanislaw Krykowski, or Antonin Bradz, as he was known in Poland, and bring them to justice. It is our understanding that Meir Poznanski wished to take the law into his own hands by killing Bradz. We could not let that happen."

"How did you know Meir was intent upon killing Krykowski?"

"We were informed of this by Mrs. Koplowitz. She has been serving our cause for some time now."

"And what exactly is your cause?"

"To take such men as Bradz out of this country to Israel. There he will receive the retribution he so richly deserves."

"What if he refuses to go with you?"

"Then he will receive his retribution here."

"Now who's taking the law into their own hands? Why don't you just contact the police or immigration? Let them take care of Krykowski."

"I am afraid we cannot depend on the American authorities anymore. They are at war with the Russians and do not wish to do anything that would upset the West Germans. And by upset I mean they no longer care about former Nazis living here or in South America. Many of them now serve America's Cold War purposes and live here in comfort. Can you imagine what that means to us? To see things like that. When we tried to approach these Americans they said to us, 'the war is over, forget the Nazis'. For us there can be no forgetting and no forgiving. Can you understand that?"

"Of course I can. I was in the war myself. I fought against the Germans. What are you planning to do with Meir Poznanski in the meantime?"

"Since he too refuses to see our point of view, we are forced to hold him until we have dealt with Bradz. Once the Nazi is in our possession we will set Poznanski free. As for now we cannot take the chance that he will do something to interfere with our operation. Neither can we take that chance with you."

"Are you planning on keeping me captive as well?"

"That depends on how persuasive you are in explaining why we should set you free."

Doherty considered what he could say to convince his captors that he posed no danger to their plans of kidnapping Krykowski. "Look I don't know who you guys are, nor do I care. I was hired to find Poznanski. If he's okay and you're willing to let him go once you've snatched up Krykowski, then it's no skin off my nose. I was hired to find Meir and hopefully convince him to go back home. I see no reason why he won't give up his foolish quest once you have the man he is pursuing. As for me I've got no personal interest in this ex-Nazi. I was only following him to protect Meir. As far as I'm concerned Kykowski is all yours."

The man behind the desk conferred once again with his colleagues. Doherty waited patiently. "I am glad you are a man of reason, Mr. Doherty. I see no cause for you to remain with us. I assume you will not be reporting any of our conversation to the police."

"I have no reason to go to the cops. I do have one request, though."

"What is that, Mr. Doherty?" the voice of Janisz asked.

"I would like to see Meir to make sure he is in good health. Maybe if *I* explain the situation to him he will be more cooperative with you people."

More Yiddish was slung around. Eventually a man strode from the light and stepped behind Doherty. He reattached the blindfold and took him by the arm. They moved slowly through the house and then up a flight of stairs. At the top they turned to the right and then rose up another, narrower flight. When they reached the next floor a door above their heads was pushed open and what sounded to Doherty like a retractable stairway was lowered. He was instructed to ascend and watch his step as he did. Upon reaching the top he noticed that the air smelled musty and close. He assumed they were now in the attic of the house. Once they'd safely reached that level Doherty's blindfold was removed and the trapdoor behind him was refastened.

Meir Poznanski sat on the edge of a small bed, a cot really, holding a book. He looked surprised to see Doherty. The two men who had escorted him up the stairs stood near the exit with their arms crossed. They were big men, not to be trifled with. Each wore a sidearm attached to his belt. Doherty walked over and shook hands with Poznanski who rose to greet him.

"We meet again, Mr. Doherty. What brings you to my humble abode?" he said with a trace of a smile.

"I suppose it's the acquaintance we have in common: Stanislaw Krykowski, or Antonin Bradz as you know him." Mentioning Bradz quickly removed the smile from Poznanski's face.

"I had him in my sights and was formulating a plan when..."

"When this bunch snatched you up. It appears they are determined to mete out their own form of justice on your old friend Bradz. To be honest with you, I think that would be better than whatever ideas you had cooked up."

Pozananski looked perplexed. "Why do you say that?"

"It's simple, Meir. These men apparently know how to deal with people like Bradz professionally, while you are a rank amateur. I'll say to you what I said before: go home to West Warwick, to your family and your minyan and forget about Stanislaw Krykowski. Leave it to these people to take care of him in their own way."

"How can you say that after what he did to me and my family? This I can never forget," he said in a louder voice. Loud enough to cause one of their guards to step away from the trap door and move in their direction.

Doherty raised his hand to indicate to the man that everything was jake. "I'm sorry, I didn't mean that you should forget him. I know you will never be able to do that. How can you? But you're not a killer, Meir. If you continue to pursue this Krykowski, who's to say he wouldn't kill you first. I can never know how you feel, but I do know what could happen if you had stayed on the path you were taking. Look at it this way: the people downstairs will take care of Krykowski for you. You will get a measure of justice without putting blood on your own hands."

"You must stop calling him by that name. He will always be Antonin Bradz to me."

"Whatever his name is, I have a feeling he's not long for this world."

Poznanski sat back on the cot and rested his head between his hands. "I suppose you are right," he said softly. "Still I do not understand how they found out I was after Bradz. You didn't tell them did you?"

"That would've been impossible given that I didn't make their acquaintance until earlier this evening, long after they'd taken you from the Y." At this point Doherty could've given up Anna Koplowitz but saw no reason for that. She was Poznanski's best friend. She must have informed someone among the Nazi hunters in order to save Meir from himself. She was a better friend to him than he'd ever know.

"I'm leaving now, Meir. Hopefully the next time I see you will be at The Bargain Store in West Warwick. Whatever you do, I suggest you cooperate with these people. They are trying to do the right thing by saving you from doing the wrong thing."

Once he indicated he was ready to leave his two keepers blindfolded Doherty and escorted him down to the first floor. After some conversation that was carried on again in Yiddish he was whisked back into the panel truck. He could've lifted the blindfold at various times to see what the route was they'd taken but he chose not to. If they were Nazi hunters as they said they were, then who was he to interfere with their work. A half hour later he found himself standing outside of his apartment at the corner of Crossen and Main.

Chapter Twenty-Five

With Meir Poznanski in the hands of Janisz and his gang, Doherty felt he'd done all he could to fulfill his obligation to the men in the minyan. He didn't know if Meir would return to West Warwick once the Nazi hunters picked up Krykowski. If he didn't then his pals back in town would just have to find someone else to pick up their bagels and fish at Katz's. In the end, Meir's decision would rest on whether or not he wanted to return to his loveless marriage and thankless job. The case wasn't as neatly tucked away as Doherty would've liked, though now at least he could move on to other jobs, assuming some came along.

Agnes had called that morning to tell him she'd be in the following Monday. Apparently Louie had grown restless being in dry dock and was heading down to Norfolk, Virginia on Monday to ship out on an oil tanker to the Mediterranean. Agnes hinted that she wouldn't be all that sad to see him go. With nothing on the docket Doherty decided to walk down to the water department office to pay a long overdue visit to his old buddy, Willy Legere.

Willy was a navy veteran from the war whose destroyer was sunk by some Japanese bombers on its second trip across the Pacific. Most of his crewmates lost their lives in the attack or to sharks after their ship sank. Willy was luckier – he'd only lost his eyesight. For more than ten years after he came home Willy sat on a chair outside of the Arctic News selling pencils as a licensed disabled vet. This begging helped him supplement the meager amount he received in monthly disability checks from the government.

Last fall Doherty had used some leverage with Judge DeCenza to secure Willy a legitimate job. DeCenza had arranged for Legere to be hired on in the office of the town's water department under the Judge's number one man, Angel Touhy. Doherty'd only seen the blind vet intermittently since then, though he heard Willy was getting on just fine working for the town.

The department office was a short distance from Doherty's apartment down in Centreville on the other side of the mill bridge. The walk gave Doherty a chance to think about his next moves, or if he even had any, relative to the Poznanski case. He assumed it was only a matter of time before the Nazi hunters picked up Stanislaw Krykowski. One way or another they would see to it that the big Pole got what was coming to him. In any event, for the time being Poznanski was on ice and out of harm's way. So it didn't seem that Krykowski and Poznanski would ever have their long overdue reunion.

A secretary was sitting at a desk behind a counter at the water department office when Doherty entered. She was close to middle-aged, wore her graying hair up in a bun along with horned-rim glasses that rose up at the corners. She quickly came to the counter when Doherty entered and asked him if he was there to pay a bill.

"No, this is a social call. I'm here to see Willy Legere," he replied. The woman smiled and then raised part of the counter to let Doherty through to the inner sanctum. He figured the smile was because Willy didn't get too many visitors at the department office. Legere had his own little office and was fingering some Braille sheets as Doherty slid into his space.

"You have a visitor, Mr. Legere," the woman said politely. Willy looked up. Despite wearing his dark glasses, his face showed confusion.

"Hey, Willy boy, how's it going?"

"Why Mr. D. ain't you a voice from the past."

"Sorry I haven't been by sooner. I guess it was easier for me to stop and chat when you were outside the News everyday." He immediately wished he hadn't reminded his blind friend of his street corner days.

"Ah, forgetaboutit. To tell you the truth I kinda miss bein' out there talkin' with folks everyday. Don't get me wrong, I appreciate havin' this here job and all. I mean it's a real job. I come in everyday and I make plenty of dough. That's helped me and mom fix up the old house some. It's just that it can be a little lonely sittin' here by myself all day."

"Your secretary seems nice enough."

"Who, Elaine? Oh, she's a peach. She's more Mr. Touhy's secretary than mine. She don't help me much 'cause she can't read Braille or nothin'. She does the best she can to make my work easier though."

"Speaking of Angel Touhy, is the big man around?"

Willy smiled at this question. "He ain't never around, Mr. D. I don't know where he goes and I don't ask. I just keep my head down and do my job. I did hear that the Judge is considerin' runnin' Mr. Touhy for state rep next year. Whaddya think of that?"

Doherty didn't know what to think. When he was on the police force Angel Touhy was always at the station telling the cops what the Judge wanted and what the Judge didn't want. Back then Touhy was just a cheap goon doing heavy lifting for the machine. Since then he's graduated to expensive suits and put on thirty pounds of public pork. Lately he's become the Judge's right-hand man and mouthpiece. But state rep? That might be pushing things a little too far.

"I'm sure he'd do his best representing the interests of the town and the party in the legislature if he's elected," Doherty said as diplomatically as he could.

"You mean the DeCenza machine, don't you?"

"If you say so, Willy."

Legere turned in his chair and stretched out his legs. "I've wised up some since I been down here. It don't take long before you figure out what side of the bread the butter's on in this town."

"Enough of this political talk, Willy. What do you have to say about the Red Sox this year?"

Willy shook his head sadly. "I dunno, Mr. D., it don't look too good – not with Williams hurt like he is. He ain't been the same since he got dinged on the elbow down in Florida. Plus they got no pitchin'. I hate to say it, but it'll probably be the Yankees again this season."

Doherty sensed that Willy was still sore about last year's World Series when he bet on the Braves, who had the Yankees down three games to two going home for the final two. He and Willy had made a small bet on the Series and the New Yorkers took both games in Milwaukee to close it out. Poor Willy still felt some devotion to the National League team who'd been the Boston Braves not so long ago.

"You're probably right. The Indians and the White Sox look pretty good too this year. They both have a lot of promising young players. On the flip side it seems like the Sox are going in the other direction." They both knew that without Ted Williams there wouldn't be much rooting interest for the Boston team. Thank God for the Washington Senators because minus Williams' bat the Red Sox could be headed toward the cellar.

"Do you think Teddy is done?" Willy asked.

"Hard to say. They didn't think he'd come back after Korea like he did. If he isn't hurt too bad, he'll be okay. At least now they can't walk him every time he comes up. Not with Jensen batting behind him. But except for those two, Runnels and Malzone, they don't appear to have much else. With all the other teams loading up with Negro players, the Sox are going to find themselves behind the eight ball if they don't sign up some black talent."

"I hear they're gonna bring up this Pumpsie Green to be their first Negro player. But he ain't no Willie Mays from what I can tell."

"Leave it to the Sox to bring up a Negro boy who's not much better than mediocre. Even the Yankees are adding some good black players. They say this Howard kid is going to take Yogi's place in a year or two. You can't be successful in baseball any more with an all white team. Those days are over."

Willy and Doherty talked baseball for another half hour. Somewhere in that space Elaine, the secretary, brought them both a cup of coffee. She gave Doherty a nice smile, clearly indicating how much she appreciated him visiting with Willy Legere. Before he left Doherty promised he'd come by more often, and he meant it. Gabbing with Willy about baseball made him realize how much he missed their regular conversations. It also helped take his mind off Meir Poznanski and the ex-Nazi.

Doherty walked back into town and opened the office for the day. Not having Agnes around or any new cases to work on he was looking at a boring afternoon. Fortunately the nice bankroll he'd gotten last fall doing jobs for Judge DeCenza and later Frank Ganetti on the Wainwright case would keep Doherty and Associates in the black for some time to come. Around three there was a loud knock on the outer door – loud enough to rouse Doherty from his daydreams. Before he could get to it the knock grew louder.

"Coming, coming," he shouted as he moved through the outer office. When he opened the door two men in suits were there to greet him. The smaller of the two he recognized as Sgt. Gerald Squillante of the Providence Police Department. The other guy was unfamiliar. They both flashed their badges and he invited them into his back office. Squillante sat on the visitor's side and lit a smoke. Doherty slid the large glass ashtray in his direction. The other plain-clothes cop stood against the wall. Doherty had had dealings with Squillante the previous fall around the Wainwright murder. Back then he was the junior officer who stood against the wall while his boss, Lt. Brian Halloran, had been the sitter.

"Where's your boyfriend Halloran?" Doherty asked. The young cop against the wall shot him a look that indicated he thought Doherty was cracking wise.

"He slipped a disk in his back. He'll be riding a desk for a coupla months, 'less he decides to take an early retirement."

"I would say it's a pleasure to see you again, Sgt. Squillante, but I got a feeling this isn't a social call."

"Did that broad Wainwright was running around with ever show up?"

"Annette Patrullo? Not that I know of. Is that why you're here – to talk about some old murder case?"

The lady in question had been the mistress of the Kent County Republican Committee chairman who was murdered last October in a case involving a crooked land deal and some members of the Ganetti crime family. The guy who killed Wainwright was himself shot right in front of Doherty, but there was more to the case than the Providence cops would ever be able to unravel without Doherty's help or that of the Patrullo girl. Doherty knew the full extent of the story, but the influence it afforded him, especially over Judge DeCenza, gave him no reason to help the police any more than he already had. Plus, he knew it wouldn't be a smart move to cross anyone from the Ganetti operation and put his own life in danger.

"No, we're not here about that. As far as we're concerned that's a cold case until that broad turns up. For all we know she could be dead herself by now. We'd like to know about your dealings with an old nigger named Billy James who lived at the Y downtown. And don't start out by denying you know him. We got two witnesses who say they saw a man matching your description meeting this James a coupla times up there. That along with one of your business cards prominently displayed on the late Mr. James' bureau is enough cause for us to pay you a visit."

"The late Mr. James?"

"Yeah, your dark skinned friend was found with his throat cut in an alley near some low rent gin joint in downtown Providence last night. You wouldn't happen to know who'd want the dinge done like that, would you?"

Squillante unbuttoned his suit jacket and slouched down in his chair waiting for Doherty to spin out one of his tall tales. It was only then that Doherty noted that the cut of the cop's suit was noticeably nicer than the Robert Hall off-the-rack job he wore on their previous meetings. The young cop leaning on the wall now wore the cheapo Robert Hall. He also featured the kind of military buzz cut that went out of style for guys his age ten years ago.

Doherty decided to play it straight, or at least partially so. "I met Billy James while I was looking for a lost guy I was hired to find. I had a hunch my guy was flopping at the Y on account of him having left his wife without taking much dough with him. I was told men often take up temporary residence there when they don't want to be found. The place is pretty discreet about who's in residence, unless you grease a few palms."

"And whose palms did you grease?" Squillante asked without bothering to give Doherty the benefit of the doubt.

"A heavyset guy at the desk who sent me to Billy James. Told me Billy knew everything about everybody staying at the Y. Then I greased Billy's hand a few times to get the lowdown on my guy."

"Did you ever find him?"

"Yeah, I did eventually thanks to Billy. Talked to the guy for a while, but he didn't have any interest in going back home. And that was pretty much it as far as my case went."

"Any reason to believe this guy you were looking for would've killed the old nigger?" Doherty cringed a little at Squillante's use of that word. He never liked its use though he'd certainly heard it hundreds of times. "Like maybe he was pissed off this James finked on him to you?"

Doherty shrugged and eyed the wall hanger who had perked up at this last question. Doherty wondered if this guy was offended by Squillante's use of the word *nigger*, or if he used it himself on a regular basis.

"He didn't seem like the killing type," Doherty said not bothering to mention Stanislaw Krykowski and Poznanski's vendetta against him. "To me he looked like every other guy in an unhappy marriage who needed to get away from his wife. I tried talking him into going back home but he wasn't interested. Problem is he works for the wife's brother here in Arctic, so without any real cash I figured he'd head back home sooner or later."

"And you'll have closed another big case, eh Doherty," Squillante said with a nasty grin. "Would you mind giving us this mook's name?" Squillante signaled his partner to start writing things down.

With Poznanski in the hands of the Nazi hunters Doherty didn't see any reason why he couldn't give him up to the cops. They would look in all the usual places for him, including the Y, and for now anyway would find nothing. His only concern was that their trail might lead to Anna Koplowitz. He'd prefer to keep her out of things at least until Krykowski was disposed of. Doherty couldn't help but feel that Krykowski had something to do with Billy's death, though for the time being it was just a hunch. For all he knew the old Negro might've been the victim of a bar brawl or one of his monetary scams that had gone awry.

He had to spell Poznanski's name twice before the wall hanger got it down correctly. Once the cops had all the particulars on Meir Poznanski they seemed satisfied for the time being. Of course, they asked Doherty if he knew anyone who'd want Billy James dead. He told them that he didn't know the old man well enough to answer that question. He did add that from all appearances Billy James was a habitual, cut-rate snitch at the Y, so he could have alienated any number of men along the way.

Squillante and his partner seemed satisfied with Doherty's explanation, or as satisfied as the sergeant would be with anything he told them. After the Wainwright murder, he knew the Providence cops would always suspect Doherty of holding some information back. In any case, that was fine by him. He had no reason to be fully truthful with the police, never knowing exactly how they would use it against him in the future. It was part of the hangover Doherty still had from his days on the force in West Warwick.

Chapter Twenty-Six

In the morning Doherty dragged the Chevy out of the garage and made the trip once more to the Providence YMCA. This time a different, shorter guy was at the main desk, wearing the same logo shirt as Fat Bob. Doherty slipped him a five and told him he was there to visit a friend in the residence. The desk clerk was too transfixed by Lincoln's portrait to pay him any further attention. He walked slowly down the hall, past Billy James' room where someone had taped a cardboard tombstone to the door with RIP printed on it. Doherty didn't know if this was a sincere tribute or someone was mocking the dead man. Below it was an official notice from the Providence police telling everyone that the room was off limits due to police business. Needless to say when Doherty tried the knob the door was locked. But it wasn't Billy's room he was interested in. It was the one at the end of the hall across from Meir's old digs.

The fleshy guy was sitting on his bed in a sleeveless tee shirt and dark slacks. He had neither his shoes nor socks on and was reading a girly magazine. A thin, half smoked cigar protruded from the corner of his mouth. When he saw Doherty he got up quickly to shut the door, but not quickly enough before Doherty kicked it back open.

"Hey," was all he said as the cigar fell from his mouth. Doherty quietly closed the door and told the man to sit down. His host did so reluctantly.

"You can't just barge in here like that," he protested in a voice rising almost to a squeal.

"Oh but I can - and I just did."

The man sat down but did not hide his disgruntlement. "I told the police everythin' I knew." Doherty just glared at him. "If you ask me that darkie got what he deserved, always stickin' his big flat nose where it dint belong," he continued. "Billy'd do damn near anythin' for a pack of cigarettes. I don't haveta tell you that though, do I? I seen you two go into the room across the hall when that foreign guy wasn't there. That ain't right. We're entitled to our privacy here."

The man's voice was shaky throughout his diatribe. He then lay back on his bed trying to look relaxed. He folded up the dirty magazine to hide the naked girls he'd been visiting with.

Doherty took the only chair in the room and turned it around and straddled it facing the occupant. "Have you seen the fellow from across the hall lately? And don't lie to me like you did with the cops. I don't have to play by the rules like them."

"Are you threatenin' me?" the man asked as a worried look creased his face.

"Threaten? Why not at all. I'm just looking for some straight answers. Have you seen the Polish man from across the hall?"

"Polish, huh. Don't think I ever met no one from Poland before. Is that in Europe someplace?"

"Yeah, as a matter of fact it is. It's where World War Two started."

"Really? I thought it started when the Japs bombed Pearl Harbor. But hey, what do I know. I ain't no history man," he said with a shrug, apparently comfortable with his ignorance. "No, I ain't seen the man from across the hall since last week. That's the God's honest truth. He ain't been here since before you and Billy went snoopin' around in his room," he added, resentment creeping back into his voice.

"Okay. That sounds about right. Now tell me about Billy. Any idea who would've killed him – and don't give me any of that 'I don't know nothing' crap you gave the police."

The man looked annoyed and a little scared. He began fingering the girlie magazine again, hoping it would bring him some relief. Doherty figured the guy couldn't wait for his uninvited guest to leave so he could start fingering himself. He leaned forward to put slightly more pressure on his host.

"There was a man here," he began with some hesitation. "A big man with blond hair. He was arguin' with Billy down in his room. I saw the two of them when I walked by. His door was open so I could hear everythin' they was sayin'. Not that it was any of my business or nothin'. I guess I was just curious after you were here and all. The big guy kept askin' Billy 'bout the man from across the hall just like you done. I knew Billy hadn't seen him 'cause I hadn't and I almost always keep my door open. You see, I need the air for my asthma." Yeah open, Doherty thought, except when you're busy making the scene with a magazine.

"From what he was sayin' I could tell he was gettin' upset with Billy. Sayin' if Billy couldn't tell him where this other man was then he wanted his money back. I could hear Billy tryin' to play one of his jive games on this guy. Problem was this fellow sounded really mad, and scary. If it was me I woulda been too afraid to keep his money. But Billy was bein' the stupid nigger he always was. We all knew he was sick so maybe he dint have nothin' left to be ascared of. After a while I backed up down the hall not wantin' them to see me. I could still hear what they was sayin' the whole time."

"This big guy, did he have a foreign accent?"

"Yeah, yeah, just like the guy from across the hall. This one Billy was arguin' with, he wasn't no American neither. Is there some trouble between them two foreigners?"

"That's none of your concern," Doherty said knowing his answer disappointed Mr. Snoopy. "So tell me, how did they leave it?"

The man nervously fingered his magazine again. "Billy kept tellin' him he dint know where the guy was. He kept usin' his name, Myron or Meyer, somethin' like that. He wouldn't give the big blond guy his money back neither. Said he was the one takin' the risk. Billy was always like that – squealin' on people for a pack of cigarettes or some chump change. If you ask me the men stayin' here are better off without him."

Doherty wanted to ask the fleshy man if he was the one who put the cardboard tombstone on Billy's door. Instead he said, "How did their conversation end?"

"The big guy left all angry and stuff. He told Billy he wasn't through with him yet."

"Those were the exact words he used?"

"Those or thereabouts."

"And you didn't relate any of this to the police?"

The man now looked sheepish, as if all he wanted to do was get back to his two-dimensional naked girlfriends. "I dint wanna get involved. I came here to get away from all that kinda shit. I dint have no use for that nigger anyway, so why would I care if the police caught who killed him?"

Doherty stood and turned the chair back around. He flipped a couple of bucks onto the bed and thanked the man for his help. From now on he figured the guy would keep his door shut despite his asthma.

Chapter Twenty-Seven

This time he parked directly across the street from the Polish-American Citizens Club in case he had to make a clean getaway. If Stanislaw Krykowski was in the club Doherty knew things could get ugly real fast. It was later than the last time he'd been there and tonight the place was more crowded and noisier. He spotted Jerzy and Tomasz from his earlier visit. They were playing checkers at a table where a number of other pairs were likewise engaged in board games. When he saw him Jerzy gave Doherty a friendly wave. He nodded back at the man even as his eyes were scanning the rest of the big room. It wasn't long before they focused on another table where Stanislaw Krykowski was holding court with the two men Doherty'd had the run-in with at his car.

He made a beeline in their direction and sat down on the opposite side of a round table from Krykowski and his cohorts. The other two men sat on either side of the big Pole. A large collection of beer bottles rested on the table in front of the three men and they looked like they were well into their cups. Doherty glared at Krykowski, who looked up through bleary eyes and met Doherty's stare with his patented sneer. Neither said anything as Krykowski tried to clear his mind enough to recall where he knew Doherty from.

"Well, if it isn't the private investigations man," Krykowski said finally, his voice heavy with alcohol and derision. "Come to my club to ask me more questions about the war, eh mister?"

Doherty leaned forward and said, "No, I came to tell you there will be payback for the murder of Billy James."

Krykowski shook his head. Doherty wasn't sure if it was because he was trying to clear it or because the dead man's name didn't mean anything to him.

"He's the old Negro from the Y you murdered because he couldn't or wouldn't give up Meir Poznanski."

Krykowski shook his big head again. "All these names; I do not know these men you speak of. I think maybe it is you who needs some beer, eh Gustav," he said nudging one his companions. The other man was not amused. He was the one whose knees Doherty had smashed with his car door. The thin man kept looking intently at Doherty with a crooked grin on his flushed face. Krykowski called a waitress over and asked for four more beers. This girl was younger and prettier than the stout woman who'd waited on Doherty the last time. When she turned toward the kitchen Krykowski gave her behind a good squeeze and laughed uproariously. Only his two pals joined in his merriment. No one else, least of all the waitress, seemed amused.

"Big Polish asses. There is nothing like them, eh my friend. You should try one sometime. Oh, my mistake. I think maybe you prefer Jewish asses instead. Yeah, Jew touchises. Isn't that how they call them?"

Doherty half rose from his chair and said loudly, "You rotten sonofabitch!"

His outburst caught the attention of people at the neighboring tables. Krykowski only met his accusation with another sneer. Doherty sat back and added, also loudly, "I wonder how many of your fellow Poles in here know that you were part of the Granatowa Policja during the war. What would they say if they knew you three helped the Nazi round up your fellow countrymen?" He had done his best to pronounce the Polish words as accurately as he could. Suddenly there was a noticeable hush in the room.

Krykowski's mouth smiled but his eyes bored into Doherty's skull. "I don't know of what you talk. You come into the club of my people, I buy you a beer and you insult me in front of my friends. You accuse me of killing some *czarnuch* I don't even know. To me you are nothing but a big asshole."

The waitress arrived with the beer bottles and a glass for Doherty. She placed a bottle in front of each man, leaning across the table to serve Krykowski while carefully staying out of her unwanted reach. Stanislaw poured some beer and hoisted his glass in a Polish toast. Doherty lifted his glass slowly and then threw its content in Krykowski's face. A loud gasp swept through the room. Krykowski stood up abruptly causing his chair to fall over backwards and clatter to the floor. Doherty rose to meet his challenge. Before anything more could happen a strong arm grabbed Doherty's shoulder. It belonged to Thomaz, the big man with the gold teeth he'd drunk with on his earlier visit.

He leaned in and said forcefully, "Please my friend, I think you'd better leave now before something very bad happens." Reluctantly Doherty allowed Thomaz to escort him toward the door. On the way he continued to look over his shoulder at Krykowski, who sneered at him as he toweled the beer off his face and shoulders. Halfway to the door Doherty and Thomaz were joined by Thomaz's pal Jerzy.

Once outside the small man said, "Please sir, do not come here again. It is not safe; you only make trouble for us all. Ve are a peace loving people – Ve don't vant any trouble vit the police. You understand?"

Doherty nodded. "I understand. I just want you fellows to know what kind of people you've allowed into your *citizens* club. Stanislaw, or should I say Antonin Bradz, which is his real name, was a Nazi collaborator back in Poland; a member of what you people called the Blue Police. I have good reason to believe that he and his friends recently murdered a helpless old Negro."

"Den you should talk vit the police. Please, mister, do not tink to make the law vit your own hands. Not on a man like Stanie Krykowski. He is a bad man, yes – and a dangerous one too."

Doherty appealed to Tomaz but the larger man shook his head in agreement with his friend. Doherty knew that he would have to go this one alone, at least until Janisz and his boys showed up. He could take his suspicions about Krykowski killing Billy James to the police, but that plus a nickel would buy him a cup of coffee in Providence. A dead Negro with his throat slashed outside a low rent bar in Providence wouldn't even make it into the *Journal*. Without corroboration from Billy's fleshy neighbor at the Y, Doherty's suspicion of Krykowski would amount to only that in the eyes of Sgt. Squillante and the city cops. More likely anything Doherty said would only bring him grief with Squillante. The cop already suspected that Doherty wasn't on the level because of his role in the Wainwright case.

He was still sweating when he climbed into the Chevy. He lit a smoke and saw that his hand was shaking when he sparked his Zippo. The kind of confrontation he precipitated in the club was not his style and it left Krykowski with a decided advantage. The best thing for him to do now was to let the Nazi hunters pick up Krykowski before things got any hotter between him and the big Pole. Still Doherty had an overriding urge to punch the self-satisfied sneer off Krykowski's face.

He started to pull away then changed his mind. He made a quick u-turn and parked a half block down the street keeping a keen eye on the door of the citizens club all the while. He sat quietly and smoked, living inside his thoughts while he waited. It was over an hour before Krykowski and his pals stumbled out the front door. They were drunk enough that they staggered in a wayward fashion as they tried to make their way to a car parked nearby. It was an old blue Ford with a passenger side door painted a color that did not match the rest of the car. Fortunately they drove away in the same direction Doherty was facing. He followed them at a discreet distance, carefully watching as the Ford swerved all over the road on its way through the center of Pawtucket.

On the other side of the city's business district they turned off Newport onto a side street. After another turn they parked in front of a shabby gray house, but not before knocking over a metal garbage can that was sitting on the curb. When they did lights went on in a few adjacent houses. A man came out of one in his undershirt and yelled at the three drunks. Doherty could hear Krykowski return the shouts with some of his own, only they were in Polish. The three men then laughed drunkenly and clumsily bumped into one another on their way into the house. One of them even fell on his face as he tried to climb the front steps.

Doherty sat patiently in his car watching and waiting. Soon a series of lights went on in the gray house. That was followed by a lot of yelling back and forth among the men. All of it was in a language he assumed was Polish. They were making such a racket Doherty was sure one of the neighbors would soon call the police to complain. He took this as a sign that it was time for him to exit the scene. Before leaving he carefully wrote down the house number and its location.

It was an uneasy trip back to West Warwick as Doherty tried to figure out what his next move would be, or even if he had a move to make at all. He was wondering where Janisz and his Nazi hunting crew were. Doherty assumed that he was still a few steps ahead of them - unless they were secretly following him. However, experience and careful scrutiny told him that no one had been tailing him the last couple of days. So he knew he still had a chance to make a move on Krykowski before they did. The only question was why he wanted to. Even if Krykowski and his pals had killed Billy James, what concern was that of his? The old Negro was a snitch and a two-bit grifter. He'd put the bite on Doherty and no doubt many others in exchange for information about people hiding out at the Y. Men stayed at the YMCA to be out of sight and Billy had knowingly violated their privacy for money and cigarettes. It would've only been a matter of time before his little con game came back to bite him on the ass. And maybe that was exactly what happened to Billy. Still, Doherty could not dismiss the notion that Krykowski was responsible for the man's recent demise. It would be too big a coincidence for it to have happened any other way.

No, it wasn't the murder of Billy that bothered Doherty so much. It was the fact that an ex-Nazi like Krykowski could come to live and work in America with impunity. He felt for Poznanski and his tragic story, but Krykowski being a former Nazi stuck in Doherty's craw as well. Here this bastard was right in front of his eyes, laughing and drinking with his pals as if the millions the Nazis had slaughtered and the men in his unit who'd died fighting them meant nothing. Whether Doherty liked it or not, seeing Krykowski in the flesh made Meir's cause and that of the Nazi hunters his cause as well. He couldn't fully explain it to himself; he just knew it was there staring him in the face, and he wouldn't be at peace until Stanislaw Krykowski was no longer part of this world.

Chapter Twenty-Eight

On Thursday afternoon Rachel called to see if he'd like to meet her for dinner on Friday night. Doherty felt funny about her calling him for a date. Yet with Rachel living at home and not wishing him to call her there, he was stuck waiting until she took the initiative. Maybe this was the new way of doing things, though it still didn't sit right with Doherty. Perhaps he was too traditional as Rachel had indicated. After some fencing back and forth, they agreed to meet at a restaurant on Federal Hill called The Old Canteen. Doherty'd never been there though he knew the place by reputation. Rachel asked about Meir Poznanski and Doherty gave her only a brief rundown of the latest developments in the case, leaving out both the Nazi hunters and Billy James' murder. He told her he'd fill her in more when they met on Friday.

With no new clients and Agnes still on leave, Doherty was at a loss as to what to do with himself. He spent the balance of the day taking a long walk through town and looping back along the river to his apartment. While out he dropped off one of his suits at Sunshine Cleaners for a pressing so that he'd look his best come Friday night.

Later that evening he finished reading *The Old Man and the Sea*. The fisherman, Santiago, worn down by the sharks attacking the giant marlin he'd lashed to the side of his small boat, eventually fell into a deep sleep. When he finally made landfall all that was left was the bony skeleton of his once gigantic catch. Feeling defeated he returned to his small hut, too fatigued to think about his bad fortune.

In the morning the young boy who had been his helper brought him some coffee and food and promised the old man he would once again go out to fish with him. Later, when Santiago wandered down to the docks to check on his boat many of the villagers were gathered around it admiring the size of the fish skeleton the old man had returned with. Because of this catch Santiago was now perceived in the village as a hero rather than a useless old man. Doherty fell asleep wondering if he had any heroic acts left in his own life. Perhaps bringing down Stanislaw Krykowski would be one.

As he entered The Old Canteen, Doherty was struck by the pink walls and tablecloths that decorated the place to such a degree that it was almost overwhelming. A large mural of St. Mark's Square in Venice, Italy covered most of the right hand wall of the restaurant. The place was smaller than he expected. A rather flamboyant maitre d' seated him at a table by one of the large front windows that looked out over Atwells Avenue. The windows were trimmed with heavy brocaded curtains that added to the old world flavor of the place. Except for the occasional lunches he'd eaten with Gus Timilty at Ballard's down in the financial district, this place was about the fanciest restaurant he'd ever eaten in. Gus always expensed those lunches off on his clients. Tonight's meal would be entirely on Doherty's tab. Soon he'd have to learn again to economize as those big fees he'd collected last fall doing jobs for Judge DeCenza and Frank Ganetti, Jr. were rapidly evaporating.

Rachel wasn't there yet so he nursed a glass of Jameson while he waited. She arrived about ten minutes later and was ushered to their table by the same maitre d'. As she made her way through the dining room he was struck by how exceptionally attractive she looked tonight. She was wearing a close fitting black dress set off by a string of white pearls. The darkness of the dress accentuated her black hair and deep brown eyes. Doherty stood when she reached the table and they kissed each other softly on the cheek as the maitre d' pulled her chair out with great ceremony.

"You look beautiful tonight," was the first thing out of his mouth.

"Does that mean I only look ordinary on other occasions?" she replied.

"I didn't mean…"

"I'm only kidding, Doherty," she said softly poking him in the ribs. "You look pretty handsome yourself. Got yourself a haircut and a shave just for me, huh?"

A waiter in a white tuxedo shirt, a bow tie and black trousers came to the table to ask if Rachel would like something to drink. She ordered a Chivas Regal on the rocks.

"I didn't take you for a Scotch drinker."

"I'm not usually, but it's been a rough week at work. And please, whatever you do, don't let me get started talking about school. All I want to do now is enjoy this night. And then think about how much fun it'll be working the deli counter with my mother tomorrow," she added with a chuckle. "So, what's new with you? Any success changing Meir Poznanski's mind about going back home? I have to admit I'm beginning to miss his Saturday visits to the deli."

Doherty didn't know how or if to bring Rachel up to date. Whatever he chose to share with her he was definitely not going to drop Billy James' murder into the conversation. The last time he dated a girl and a murder came into his life she'd beaten a hasty exit. He wasn't going to make that same mistake twice.

"Despite my powers of persuasion, it doesn't look like Meir wants to go back home to West Warwick. And, it turns out that I'm not the only one who's been interested in finding him. I met a group of men who've been trailing the same man that Poznanski's been after. They represented themselves to me as Nazi hunters working for the Israelis."

Rachel looked shocked. "You're kidding me! Real live Nazi hunters, here in the U.S.?"

"Please keep your voice down," he said while communicating the same message with his hand. Fortunately her Scotch arrived and they took a break in their conversation while the waiter set it down. He also unfolded two large menus and handed them over with a flourish.

"You know, there's always been a lot of talk within the Jewish community about people hunting down Nazis here in America. Mostly I've written that off as wishful thinking. Occasionally we'd read in *The Jewish Exponent* about how some important Nazi was picked up by the Israeli secret police in a place like Paraguay or Argentina but never in the U.S. Of course, nothing of that sort would ever find its way into the Providence papers."

"Look, Rachel, I can't talk about this too much. My suspicion is that these people, whoever they are, are operating here illegally. What I can tell you is that they have Meir and are holding him at a safe house until they get their hands on the man he was intent on killing. I saw him at this house with my own eyes and he's in good health and being well taken care of."

Rachel seemed puzzled. "I don't understand. How did they know Meir was out to kill this Nazi?"

Doherty hesitated, not sure what else he should share with Rachel. She gave him a hard stare while waiting for an answer. "Apparently Mrs. Koplowitz has been working with these men for some time now. That's all I can tell you at this point. I've probably said too much already. The last thing I want to do is implicate you in any of this."

"How did you find Meir? I mean how did you know where he was being held?"

Doherty took a swig of Jameson. "I didn't find him. These Nazi hunters found me and took me to see him. I wasn't taken against my will, though it wasn't exactly my idea either. I went mostly to make sure that Meir was okay and in safe hands." He decided not to mention that the Nazi hunters initially greeted him at gunpoint.

"Just one final question then we can eat: What do you think will happen to Meir?"

Doherty took another sip of his whiskey. "Once they've swooped in and caught this Nazi guy, they said they'd set Meir free. He can go back to West Warwick and resume his old life, which he says he has no desire to do. Or he can do whatever else he wants to with himself. At least then he won't have a murder on his hands."

"And what about you?"

"Me? Hell, my job is finished. I found Meir like I was hired to. I told the men in the minyan that he was alive and well and didn't want to come home. As far as I'm concerned, this case is closed," he said in a tone he hoped would put Rachel at ease.

The waiter returned and they ordered their meals. They agreed to split a large antipasto platter as an appetizer. Rachel ordered lasagna and Doherty opted for the spaghetti with sausage and green peppers. They chose a bottle of Chianti to accompany the food. When the wine arrived it was in one of those basket-enclosed bottles. As with everything else connected to the meal the waiter opened it in a highly ritualized fashion. Doherty peaked at Rachel as he did; she was doing her best to suppress a giggle. The alcohol was doing a good job of putting them both in relaxed moods.

Despite the pink décor, The Old Canteen had a certain coziness to it. All of the tables were taken and the room was full boisterous conversation. Happy diners out on a Friday night, celebrating the end of a workweek. For the two of them, the wine on top of the liquor increased their enjoyment of each other's company. Federal Hill was the most famous Italian section in a city now dominated to a great degree by Italians. It was also the headquarters of the New England mob, which according to Doherty's old friend Gus, operated out of a vending machine company located in a modest storefront just a few blocks up Atwells Avenue from the restaurant.

As they ate and drank Rachel and Doherty flirted shamelessly. She made no bones about the fact that she wanted him to take her back to his place after dinner. He'd already cleaned up his apartment with that expectation in mind. Doherty was not only getting used to Rachel's forward manner, he was beginning to enjoy it. He liked the fact that she didn't play coy or leave things undefined. It was a new experience for him and one he was getting comfortable with. Although they both admitted to being stuffed, they ordered a cannoli to split for dessert along with some Italian coffees. All in all it turned out to be a grand meal. When the bill came Rachel insisted upon paying half. Although Doherty was a little light on cash at the moment, he politely refused her offer and handled the check himself. It was the least he could do given how he expected the night to end.

Rachel was a little unsteady on her feet when they left the restaurant. Doherty had drunk as much as she, but he had a bigger vessel to put it in. Plus he was more used to hard liquor. She told him that her car was parked a little ways up Atwells. They thought it best to leave it there and have him drive them both to West Warwick. There were a number of young Italian guys with greasy pompadours, tight black pants and shiny shirts hanging out on street. Many of them had cigarettes dangling from their lips, though it didn't prevent them from whistling at Rachel as she and Doherty walked by. One of them even made a sucking sound with his mouth. Under some circumstances Doherty might've been offended, but tonight he appreciated the fact that these young men found his date so attractive.

They turned down the side street where he'd parked the Chevy and he put his arm around her. She pressed her head against his chest. He steadied her while she stumbled along beside him. He was so charmed by her and consumed by thoughts of how the rest of the night would play out that he didn't hear the sound of the men who came up quickly behind them. When he turned he saw a red faced Stanislaw Krykowski wrap one of his meaty paws around the Rachel's mouth before she could let out more than a quick yelp. Just as Doherty stepped toward her assailant something hard hit him on the back of the head. He was out cold before he hit the ground.

Chapter Twenty-Nine

When he awoke he was lying in a bed somewhere. The room was faintly lit but Doherty couldn't tell if it was from a lamp or daylight streaming in. He tried to prop himself up on his pillow; the effort only increased the terrible pain he felt in the back of his head. He slid back against the pillow and was about to conk out again. Before he did he reached up and felt his head. The whole thing was swaddled in soft cotton cloth.

The next time Doherty came to he was immediately aware that someone else was in the room with him. He turned his head slightly to the left and saw a stern looking woman in a nurse's uniform pouring some water from a pitcher into a glass on the table by his bed.

"Where?" was all he could get out.

The nurse looked down at him and smiled. "So, we're finally awake, are we?" she said. He thought her voice had the trace of an Irish brogue in it, though he wasn't quite sure. He also wondered why she referred to him as *we*.

"Where am I?" he asked through the marbles in his mouth.

She reached over and adjusted one of the pillows behind his head. It was then that he felt the tube attached to his member that ran down his leg and off the end of bed.

"You're at Our Lady of Fatima Hospital. You've had a serious blow to the head. The doctor says you're suffering from a severe head injury."

"Rachel? Where's Rachel?" he blubbered.

The nurse looked confused. "I don't know about any Rachel. I wasn't on duty when they brought you in last night. When I came on I was told to monitor your condition, and if you woke up to give you two of these," she said as she picked up a small vial of pills.

"What are they?"

"Painkillers mainly – with a little sedative to help you sleep."

"I don't wanna sleep," Doherty mumbled. The scrambled thoughts running around inside his head seemed to fall over one another. "I need to know about Rachel," he said again.

"I'm sorry, you'll have to ask the doctor about this person. All I know is that you were brought in by ambulance around nine-thirty last night." She fluffed up his pillows and went to leave. Doherty called after her.

"Has anyone been in to visit me?" She picked up his chart and looked at a note attached to it.

"I can't read the doctor's writing very well though it looks like a Sgt. Squillaney came by. It says here we should call him as soon as you wake up."

"Squillante."

"What?"

"His name is Squillante. He's a Providence police detective."

She gave him half a smile and said, "I see. I'll ask the doctor on duty if it's safe for you to have any visitors. Is there anything else I can do for you right now Mr.…." The nurse checked the chart and then smiled when she realized Doherty was a fellow product of the Emerald Isle. "Mr. Doherty?"

"Yes, could you please find out what happened to Rachel. Her full name is Rachel Katz. She was with me when I was attacked."

Because the pain in his head was so excruciating, Doherty took two pills from the little vial. Within minutes he was asleep again.

When he woke the third time he had some unexpected visitors. His old pal Gus Timilty was standing by the door in a tan trench coat sucking on an unlit cigarette. Sitting in a chair by his bed was his secretary Agnes Benvenutti. Doherty was puzzled by their presence.

"I think he's awake, Mr. Timilty," Agnes said anxiously. Timilty lumbered over and leaned down toward Doherty.

"You look like death warmed over, pally," was Gus' first comment.

"You don't look so hot yourself. You're starting to get fat, Gus."

Timilty patted his stomach and said, "Whaddya mean starting to? I been working on this paunch for a coupla years now."

"What are you two doing here?"

Agnes went to speak but Gus interrupted her. "Me and Agnes came up here for the food. You know how these hospital serve only the best cuisine."

"Gus heard about your assault on his police scanner. Soon as your name came across he called me at home. It was almost midnight," Agnes explained.

"What about Louie?"

Agnes smiled. "I told him it was my sister Lucille having one of her nightmares. She always calls me when she wakes up from one of them. Louie just rolled over and went back to his snoring."

Doherty looked up at Timilty. His head still ached something awful yet his thoughts were starting to fall into some kind of order. "What did you hear, Gus?"

"I heard that you and some girl were attacked up on Federal Hill. The cops think it was a random assault and larceny. Your wallet and the girl's purse were left at the scene but neither had any money in them."

"Is that all you know?"

"Well I looked at your chart and saw that officer Squillante came by to pay you a visit. That tells me the Providence cops think this could be more than an A and B with a purse snatching attached."

"Do me a favor, Gus. Can you find out what happened to the girl who was with me? Her name is Rachel Katz. I don't know if she's here at Our Lady. She Jewish so…"

Gus smiled. "Don't sweat it, pally. This hospital is a pretty ecumenical place. They serve all kinds of sick people regardless of race, color or creed. All you need is the money to pay the bill when you're discharged." Gus patted him on the shoulder. "I'll look into it. Agnes, why don't you keep our injured warrior company while I go scratch up what I can about his girlfriend."

After Gus left Doherty spent some time filling Agnes in on the Poznanski case, leaving out most of the juicier parts. She asked insightful questions, but was careful not to push him for too many details in his present condition. After a while he grew tired again. Before he nodded off he asked Agnes if she had a mirror. She rummaged through her purse and came out with a small make-up mirror. He took a good look at himself in the hand glass. His head was wrapped in a cloth bandage that made him look like a turbaned Arab. Deep purple markings covered the area below each of his eyes.

The next time Doherty came to Agnes and Gus were gone, replaced by Squillante's junior partner with the bad haircut who was in the room keeping him company. As Doherty stirred back to consciousness the young guy slid out of the door. When he returned he had Sgt. Squillante in tow. The Providence cop was carrying a cardboard coffee cup.

Squillante stepped close to the bed to get a good gander at Doherty's injuries. He was near enough that Doherty could smell tobacco smoke on his breath. It made him crave a cigarette of his own.

"Looks like you took quite a hit there, buddy," Squillante said once he was convinced Doherty was back among the living.

Doherty didn't bother replying so the two men just stared at each other. Finally he mumbled, "Why are you here?"

An uncertain look crossed Squillante's face. To put on a more casual air, he hooked one of his thumbs inside the waistband of his trousers and leaned back in the chair. "We're here because we're cops. Investigating crimes is what we do."

"I know that – but this was just a snatch and run. Why would someone of your *stature* be involved in a petty crime like this?"

Squillante bit his lower lip and looked at his partner. Something was going on that Doherty couldn't sort out in his current mental state.

"I just figured I'd come by because me and you are like old friends. Besides I find it interesting that your name keeps popping up on our crime blotter. For some reason I'm getting this funny feeling it's not just a coincidence. First some nigger gets slashed who has one of your business cards on his dresser at the Y, and now a few days later, you and some dolly are attacked up on Federal Hill. So, why don't you tell me what you remember about last night and then maybe I can put two and two together?" Squillante turned to his junior partner. "Henry, can you write this down?"

"Yeah, sure Sarge," the young guy said, pulling a small note pad and a pencil out of his pocket. He put the tip of the pencil in his mouth. Doherty guessed the young guy never heard of lead poisoning.

Doherty told them of how he and Rachel had left The Old Canteen, walked in the direction of his car and been jumped before they got there. Squillante asked if he'd gotten a look at any of the *assailants*. Doherty told him he only got a quick glimpse of the one that muzzled Rachel before he was knocked out. He didn't tell the cop that he could identify the man as Stanislaw Krykowski. The last thing he wanted was for the police to pick up the big Pole and put him in jail. Either he or Janisz and his gang would take care of Krykowski, not the police. Instead he gave Squillante a vague general description of the man who grabbed Rachel.

When Doherty asked the cops about Rachel he saw the quick glance pass between them. They told him that she was alive and that she too was being treated at Our Lady. Otherwise that was all they knew. By their expressions Doherty could tell that wasn't all by a long shot. Squillante told him he'd have to ask the docs himself about her condition. Whatever they were hiding he decided he didn't want to hear it from their mouths anyway. Squillante dropped one of his business cards on the bedside table before he left. He asked Doherty to get in touch if he remembered anything else about the attack.

The pain in Doherty's head hadn't diminished any, though he was determined not to take any more knockout drops before Gus returned. It was nearly an hour before his old buddy came back. Gus had a grave look on his face. Doherty delayed the bad news by giving him a rundown of Squillante's visit. Gus' responses indicated he thought even less of Jeru Squillante as a cop than Doherty did.

"So what's the verdict on Rachel, Gus?"

"It ain't good, pally."

"Give it to me straight."

Timilty parked his sizable weight on the chair by the bed. "She's busted up pretty bad, though not nearly as bad as you. Her face is kinda swollen up and she may have a coupla cracked ribs." Gus stopped there though Doherty knew there was more to come.

"Goddamnit, Gus, gimme the whole package."

"It looks like at least one of them had his way with her. The nurses couldn't come right out and say it, but I eyeballed her chart when they weren't looking and saw that they'd done a rape test on her." Timilty reached up and patted Doherty's knee over the covers. "Hey, pally, I'm really sorry about this. I sure hope the cops catch up to these bastards. You know how they treat rapists in the joint."

"I don't want the cops to catch them."

"What're you talking' about kid?"

"These guys're gonna be all mine."

Gus shook his head. "You sonofabitch. You know who did this, don't you?"

"I'm not saying anything more. I'm just telling you that when I get out of here, if it's not too late, I'm going to settle this my own way."

Timilty nodded his head and smiled. "You know you're one crazy bastard." After a few beats his old pal added, "If you need some backup, gimme a ring." Doherty then popped two more pills and in no time was back in dreamland.

Chapter Thirty

The next day the doctor came in early and ran Doherty through a battery of memory tests to gauge the extent of the damage to his brain. He was able to answer most of the questions and the ones he couldn't he wouldn't have been able to even with his faculties fully intact. The doc shined his little light into Doherty's eyes and closely inspected his pupils. He moved his finger in several directions while he did this and asked Doherty to follow it with his eyes. Before he left he told Doherty they planned on keeping him at the hospital one more night for observation before releasing him. He showed Doherty his chart and explained how he'd come awfully close to having his skull fractured.

"If that had happened you probably would have suffered permanent brain damage," the doctor said in his most serious tone.

After he left Doherty ate some of the putrid hospital food and waited for the nurse to come by. This time it was a different nurse than the one from the day before. He asked if he could take a walk and she told him he could. She suggested that he watch his step closely because he could have a dizzy spell at any time.

When she left Doherty tossed off the hospital pajamas and put on his street clothes. Standing upright proved to be more difficult than he anticipated. He balanced himself against the wall while he slipped on his shoes. He didn't bother tying them because he was afraid to lean over too long for fear he wouldn't be able to get up once he did. He shuffled down the hall to a public phone and used it to dial the main number of the hospital. He told the answering receptionist that he was Rachel Katz's brother and wished to visit her. He needed to know her room number. After a brief search she gave him a number that put her two floors below his.

He moved slowly to the elevator bank and hit the down button. It took forever for the lift to arrive. He thought of taking the stairs but realized he was in no condition to do so. The elevator doors finally slid open and Doherty joined three other passengers. They each looked at his head wrap without saying anything about it. One was a nurse, another a doctor and a third, in civilian clothes, was either a visitor or a hospital worker of some sort. They were all headed to the lobby. He left them when he got off at the second floor. Once there he stopped at the nurses' station to ask for directions to Rachel's room. Two nurses were busy gabbing and could barely spare the time to look his way despite his turban bandage. They eventually pointed him in the right direction and went back to their gossip session.

Rachel's room was around the corner and halfway down the hallway. Most of the doors to the other rooms were partially opened. He could see women, mostly elderly ones, propped up in their beds. The sound of TVs rang through the corridor, all running the same daytime soap opera.

The door to Rachel's room was ajar and he could see two beds inside separated by a long curtain. Rachel's bed was the one closest to the door. Doherty stepped inside and was immediately confronted by a small man who put himself in his path. He was about four inches shorter than Doherty and a good twenty years older. He wore thick glasses and had a body shaped like a pear. Doherty tried to lean over the man to get a better look at Rachel.

"What are you doing here?" the man spit out of his tightened mouth. "It's your fault that my daughter was…" he didn't finish the statement.

"Please, daddy," Rachel said in a garbled voice. "Let him in."

Still the man stood his ground and refused to budge. Doherty was not about to push him aside. Finally Rachel's father said in an exasperated tone, "Okay, honey. I'm going down to the cafeteria to get some coffee." He wheeled on Doherty and said, "Don't you dare do anything to upset her."

Doherty pulled a chair up beside Rachel's bed and took one of her hands. The left side of her face was swollen and bore a darkish hue. The swelling caused her eye to be nearly shut. Her hair was disheveled and she appeared haggard.

"You look like an Arab with that thing of your head. That's probably what most upset my father."

"Sorry about that. I hear the Arabs and Jews don't get along too well."

Rachel tried to smile but she was only able to turn up one side of her mouth. He rubbed her hand softly. "You'll have to excuse my father. He's very upset. He thinks you should have protected me even though I told him you were almost killed."

"I really didn't think you'd get dragged into this," he said.

Rachel looked at him with about as much astonishment as she could muster under the circumstances. "Are you telling me you know who did this to us?"

Doherty nodded. "Please Rachel, hear me out. The only one I got a glimpse of was Stanislaw Krykowski, though I have a pretty good idea of who was with him." He didn't bother to tell her Krykowski was the one who muzzled her and probably raped her.

"Did you tell the police about him?"

"I can't do that, Rachel."

"For chrissake Doherty, why the hell not? You know who did this to me. They need to hear that."

Doherty tried to stroke her hand again but this time Rachel pulled it away from him.

"If I give Krykowski to the cops they'll lock him up for a few days and he'll be out on bail in no time. Then while you're going through all the legal rigmarole he could blow town, maybe even go back to Poland. Besides, even if they do charge him you know how these things can go. Before they're done they'll make you feel like it was your fault because of what you were wearing or for being drunk."

"So instead he and his friends just get to walk around like free men after what they did to us." Rachel turned her head to her pillow and a tear poured out of her good eye.

"Can you tell me about what happened after I was knocked out?"

"Why do you need to know?"

"Because something very bad is going to happen to Krykowski, something much worse than anything the police or the courts could do to him." Doherty leaned in closely and whispered, "He will be taken care of for good. I just need more assurance from you that it's the way things should go."

Rachel was clearly uncomfortable with Doherty's last comment. Nevertheless, she spun out her story. "He dragged me into someone's back-yard. He pulled up my dress, yanked down my panties and had his way with me from behind, on the ground like a dog. All the while his friends stood by laughing and rooting him on. They thought it was funny. I tried to scream but the bastard had his hands wrapped around my throat and across my mouth. After the smelly prick was done I turned over and spit in his face. That's when he punched me in the jaw for good measure." Rachel was gasping for breath as the words poured out of her. "I fell back on the ground and then he kicked me in the ribs while I was down."

"When I was finally able to get up I couldn't find my underpants. I crawled back to where I thought you were." Rachel's voice trembled as she rolled out her account. "I guess by then someone had called the police because I could hear sirens coming from every direction. By the time I got there a police car and an ambulance had already arrived. Jesus, Doherty, when I saw you lying on the ground I thought you were dead."

He was overwhelmed with disgust at Krykowski and at himself as well for bringing all of this down on Rachel. "Listen, you've got to let me handle this my way. We can't get the cops involved. Please trust me on this," he said finally.

Rachel turned her reddened face and looked at Doherty with nothing but anguish. "Just promise me you'll take care of that bastard. I want you to make him feel the pain and humiliation I felt. Will you do that for me?"

"Yes, I promise I will." Doherty took her hand, but could sense that Rachel was beginning to nod off. When her father returned he took the opportunity to leave. Mr. Katz gave him his meanest look. It didn't come close to measuring up to that of Stanislaw Krykowski.

On Monday morning the doctor came by with Doherty's discharge pa-pers. He wrote him a prescription for some painkillers that he could get filled at the hospital dispensary before he left. The doctor indicated that these par-ticular pills did not have a sedative added to them; they were merely intended to lessen the pain in Doherty's head. Once dressed Doherty hustled down to the second floor to check on Rachel. By the time he got to her room the bed she'd occupied the day before was empty and made up anew. He walked back to the nurses' station to inquire about her status. He was told that she was released to go home in the custody of her parents. The nurse in charge was indifferent to Doherty's concern.

He next stopped to have his prescription filled. When he finally descended to the lobby he was surprised to see Gus Timilty and another man waiting for him. They were both busy smoking cigarettes and checking out the nurses.

"It's about time, pally. I called upstairs twenty minutes ago and they said you'd already been released." Timilty's sidekick wasn't paying much attention to their conversation. He was too busy eyeballing the girls in uniform.

"I went downstairs to check on Rachel. Apparently her parents had already taken her home."

"C'mon let's get outta here. I parked your car in an emergency vehicle zone. Tony here'll drive me back to the office once I get you settled at your place in West Warwick."

"I can drive myself."

"I don't think so, pally. We can talk on the way. That way you can give me a bigger picture of what really happened up on the Hill. Besides driving down to West Warwick will give me a chance to check out my old stomping grounds." Timilty gave the guy named Tony directions to Doherty's apartment and they were soon on their way.

"How'd you get my car?"

"I called some people I know in the Providence PD and they told me where the incident occurred. Finding your car wasn't a problem. Nor was clipping the keys outta your pant's pocket while you were on your knock out drops."

On the drive to West Warwick Timilty probed Doherty as to what his plans were for getting revenge on Krykowski and his cohorts. Doherty didn't want to give Gus too much to chew on unless, or until, he needed his old buddy's help. Besides, Doherty hadn't formulated a solid plan of his own yet. He figured he'd need another day or two to let his head clear. Experience from the war told him that a good conk on the head can often cloud your thoughts for a few days.

Once at the apartment Gus got him settled in and then left without lingering. He told Doherty he was working a case, but that he should feel free to call him if something turned up where he needed help. Once Timilty left Doherty took two of the prescribed painkillers followed by a short nap. Afterwards he felt better and made himself a ham and cheese sandwich on some stale bread. It was still better than the hospital gruel he'd been eating. He then walked slowly into town.

Chapter Thirty-One

Agnes was pecking away on the old Remington when Doherty pushed the office door open. He was more winded by the climb up the staircase than he anticipated. Nevertheless, it was gratifying that his secretary was so glad to see him back in one piece.

"Hey, boss, you didn't have to come in today. I got everything under control here."

Doherty plopped down in the visitor's chair across from Agnes' desk. He was winded. "I know, but I didn't want to stay in the apartment any longer. I thought the walk would do me good. What're you working on?"

Agnes smiled, clearly pleased to be back at Doherty and Associates. "I'm just typin' up the notes you left on the Poznanski case. Should I assume this one is closed?"

Once he'd regained his normal breathing Doherty lit a cigarette. "It's as closed as it can be at this point. I tried to convince the man to go home even though it would be to a dead-end marriage. He didn't seem too anxious to do that," he said, not bothering to tell his secretary that Meir Poznanski was still in the hands of some Nazi hunters – or at least Doherty hoped he was.

"Listen Agnes, I got to talk to you about something serious."

The secretary immediately abandoned her typing and turned her attention his way. "I'm all ears, boss."

Doherty proceeded to tell Agnes about what had happened to Rachel, purposely leaving out the identity of Stanislaw Krykowski. He wanted to know if

Agnes thought the attack on Rachel would be a deal breaker in terms of their relationship.

"Jeez, I don't know how to answer that. Do you think she blames you for not protectin' her?"

"If she doesn't, her father certainly does. You know, when she and I first met and I told her what I did for a living I think she found it kind of exciting. She thought my being a private eye was the cat's pajamas; that my life was like what she'd seen in the movies. And, well, I guess I didn't say or do anything to make her think otherwise. Maybe I even used it as a way to get something going with her. Now that this other thing has happened, I'm wondering if she's having second thoughts about hanging out with a guy like me."

"Look, boss, you got to face some facts here. You're in a business where bad things can happen. Isn't that why that other girl, Millie, gave up on you? You know, most girls just want the quiet domestic life – a house, a bunch of kids, a hubby who comes home from work every night. You travel in a different world and it'll take a special kind of girl to wanna be part of that."

"No girl wants to get raped on account of what her guy does for a living," Doherty said, more emotionally than he intended. He hoped that Agnes didn't catch the real meaning of his remark.

Agnes shook her head. "No girl wants to get raped period. What happened to her stinks no matter how you slice it. But what about what happened to you? She got attacked and *you* almost got killed. I know it ain't pretty, but you read about random muggin's like this in the papers all the time. It could've been anybody. This didn't happen because of what you do for a livin'. It just happened. And if you're lucky, the cops'll catch the SOBs who did it and they'll get what's comin' to them."

Doherty felt bad about not clueing Agnes in on his previous encounters with Stanislaw Krykowski and for not telling her that the big Pole was the one that molested Rachel. But it was the way he had to play this out. He had to keep as many people out of the loop as possible. The game was now his and he'd finish it his way.

By Wednesday Doherty felt well enough to put his plan into action. His head wound had diminished to the point where he could cover it with a gauze patch rather than the turban he'd been wearing since leaving the hospital.

The new dressing could easily be hidden by his fedora and most of the discoloration below his eyes had pretty much disappeared. He spent the morning at Harry's barbershop getting a trim and spinning out the tale for his buddy, barber Bill. Before he got too far along Bill informed him that word of the attack had already spread throughout Arctic. Fortunately, nothing about the molesting of Rachel was being publicly circulated. Doherty didn't let on anything about that to his barber.

As usual Doherty took a quick lunch at the Arctic News and bantered there with the girls as if nothing had happened. Still he could tell by the way they were looking at him that they were disappointed not to see a more massive wound on his head.

Back at the office he'd forgotten that it was Agnes' day off, though that was probably for the better. He needed time to think and her presence would've been a distraction. Trying to contact Rachel since her release from Our Lady of Fatima was a problem. He didn't want to call her at home knowing how much anger her father bore toward him, and how much her mother bore toward just about everyone. He thought his best bet would be to leave her a message at the high school. He dialed the number for the school's main office and a pleasant woman answered the phone.

"Hi," he said in as inoffensive a voice as he could muster. "I would like to leave a message for Miss Katz. She teaches in the English department."

There was a short pause on the other end of the line. "I'm sorry but Miss Katz is no longer teaching at our school. She's taken a leave of absence for the remainder of the year," the woman added.

"Oh, I'm sorry to hear that." Doherty was at a loss as to what to say next.

"If you're the father of one of her students, Mr. Armstrong will be substituting for Miss Katz for the rest of the year. I can take a message for him if you'd like."

"No, that's okay. Thank you very much." He hung up.

Doherty could feel Rachel slipping away and he didn't know what to do about it. On the other hand, given what he was planning it was probably best to leave Rachel out of things for the time being. Yet he couldn't help but feel responsible for her leaving the job she loved so much. And he couldn't help how much he missed her.

Chapter Thirty-Two

It was nearly ten o'clock at night when Doherty pulled up in front of the Polish-American Citizens Club. This time he stayed in the car, knowing that he wouldn't be welcome there anyway after his previous performance. Besides, tonight he wasn't dressed for the occasion. He was wearing a pair of old black pants, a beat up gray sweatshirt, a dark blue windbreaker, athletic sneakers, and a black knit toque on his head. Almost forty minutes went by before Krykowksi and his pals exited the club in a noticeable state of inebriation. "Perfect," Doherty thought. He wanted his own sobriety to give him an edge.

As he'd done before, he followed their car at a discreet distance. Their driving was so erratic that he was afraid they would attract the attention of the Pawtucket police before they got to their house. In time they led him to the place he'd tracked them to before. On this occasion they didn't knock over any garbage cans once they got there, though not for lack of trying.

Krykowski staggered out of the back seat and stumbled into the house followed by his two cronies. Doherty parked caddy-corner to the house where he could see what was going on inside, but not be easily seen himself. He waited patiently. Lights came on and noise filtered out from the Polish bungalow. After a reasonable amount of time Doherty slid out of the Chevy and walked slowly toward the house, being careful to remain in the shadows of the neighboring homes and out from under the street lamps. He reached behind him and adjusted the .38 that was tucked into the small of his back under the windbreaker.

He slunk around the side of the house and peaked through a window that opened onto the kitchen. Krykowski was sitting at a small table with a pint of brown liquor in front of him. The place was a god-awful mess. Loud polka music was playing on a radio that sat atop the fridge. Krykowski's face was red and his chin drooped down onto his chest. The big Pole looked like he was pretty soused. It was a look Doherty'd seen many times on his own father's face.

He stealthily circled around the back of the house and peaked in a side window that opened up onto the living room. The other two men were sitting on a tired looking sofa watching TV. Doherty couldn't see the squawk box but he saw the white light from it reflected on their faces. One had his hand wrapped around a can of beer while the other guzzled some clear whiskey from a pint bottle. Everything was peaceful in the house. None of them suspected what was about to happen.

Doherty walked quietly back to his car and reached into the back and grabbed the brick that he'd left on the floor. He retraced his steps toward the house in a purposeful manner. He stood on the small front lawn and with all the force he could muster hurled the brick through the front window into the living room. The sound was louder than he expected. Within seconds there was a bustle of activity inside. When the front door swung open the two smaller men tumbled out ahead of Stanislaw Krykowski, but it was the big man that Doherty focused all his attention on. Krykowski pushed in front of the other two and came down the steps in Doherty's direction. It took a while for him to recognize the face under the knit toque. When he saw who'd thrown the brick through his window he laughed loudly.

"If it isn't the Jew lover," he said through his patented sneer. "You think you can take on all three of us you foolish bastard."

"It's you I want first," Doherty said firmly. "I'll deal with your two friends afterwards."

"It don't work that way, Irish. We are all for one, right boys," Stanislaw said as he looked at his two friends. He turned back to Doherty. "Not very good for you, huh. You know I should call the police and tell them you broke my window. Is good idea, no?" The big man laughed again, pleased by the irony of his comment.

"That might not work out so well if I give you up for raping my girlfriend."

"Ah the little Jewish girl. Such sweet meat. Just like the Jew girls back in Poland. In the war the Germans would let us do whatever we wanted to them. It was like taking candy from a baby as you say here in American."

Doherty took a step forward. "You rotten Nazi bastard," he said in a loud voice. Just then there was some movement in the bushes that surrounded the house. Three men appeared from one side and two more from the other. They all wore black from head to toe. Some light reflected off the pistols a few of them held in their hands.

A familiar voice rang out. "Antonin Bradz, I am here to arrest you in the name of the Jewish people for crimes against humanity. You will be taken to the state of Israel where you will stand trial for your actions." The voice was unmistakably that of Janisz the leader of the Nazi hunters.

Krykowski looked around obviously confused and frightened for the first time. He then turned his attention back to Doherty. "So you are with them. You are a Jew lover like I say, eh my friend?"

Doherty took another step closer and said, "I'm not with anyone. My business with you is entirely personal."

Janisz came up a few feet behind Doherty and said, "Please, Mr. Doherty, let us take care of this."

Without taking his eyes off Krykowski, Doherty said, "Not on your life. This pig is all mine."

In a split second Kryhowski drew a switchblade knife out of his pocket and made a lunge at Doherty. The knife pierced through Doherty's windbreaker and he could feel the blade cut into his forearm, but not deeply. When Kryhowski stepped back and readied himself for another parry Doherty slipped the .38 out from behind his back. Then without hesitating he shot the big man in the gut. Krykowski took a step forward before stopping cold. He looked down at his shirtfront, apparently surprised at the dark blotch that was beginning to appear there. He sat down in a lump on the grass. The dark stain spread wider across the light colored shirt that covered his large stomach.

Janisz stepped up next to Doherty and whispered, "Shoot him again or else he will live. Then the police will get involved. That will not be good for you. It will be his word against yours."

Doherty stood frozen with his gun at his side. He peered down at the despicable Nazi as the bloodstain continued to broaden across his shirtfront.

Krykowski looked up at both of them, the perpetual sneer still on his blubbery face. Janisz quickly wrested the .38 out of Doherty's hand. He then turned and shot Stanislaw Krykowski, or Antonin Bradz as he knew him, directly through the heart. The big man fell over backwards and uttered one last gurgle before he died.

Janisz then returned the gun to Doherty. "It will only have your prints on it as I am wearing gloves. You will tell the police that you shot this man in self-defense. As to why, that I will leave up to you. You must forget that we were ever here. Do you understand?" For the first time since the three men had stumbled out of the house Doherty took his eyes off the hateful Krykowski.

"What about the other two?" he asked blankly.

Janisz shook his head. "We will take care of them. Trust me, you will never see them again. We will drive a few blocks and then I will call the police from a pay phone. I will tell them there has been a shooting at this address. You will stay here to explain what has happened. As soon as it is safe we will release Meir Poznanski. Afterwards nothing more will be said about any of this, not by you or us or anyone. If Meir wishes to speak to the authorities, that is his affair. By then we will be long gone." Janisz took Doherty's hand and shook it. "I would have preferred for Bradz to stand trial and be hanged, but dead is dead. Justice has been done."

"Justice?"

"Good-bye, Mr. Doherty. We shall never meet again." With that the man named Janisz jogged across the street and jumped into a panel truck much like the one they had used to abduct Doherty. The other men had already hustled Krykowski's two friends inside it. Within seconds they were all gone and it was eerily quiet. No one had come out of the neighboring homes despite the two gunshots. Perhaps they were cowering inside. Doherty calmly removed his jacket and used it to stanch the blood leaking from his forearm. He could tell that the wound was merely superficial.

Fifteen minutes later two police cruisers and an ambulance arrived. The medics ran to the body of the big Pole who was laid out flat on his back. After a quick examination one of them looked at the uniform cops and shook his head. In the meantime Doherty was taken to the ambulance where he was made to sit on the tailgate while a medic bandaged up the cut Krykowski had administered to his forearm. As they were working on him one of the Pawtucket cops came over and took down his statement.

Doherty told them that once his head had cleared from his earlier injury he realized that it was Stanislaw Krykowski he'd gotten a glimpse of when he and Rachel were mugged up on Federal Hill. He explained that he'd had unpleasant dealings with the big Pole before and that he came to his house tonight to confront him about the attack. When the cops asked about the .38, which they'd immediately confiscated upon their arrival, he told them that he had a license to carry it and that he'd had no intention of using it until Krykowski came at him first with his knife. He said he'd only brought the gun along in case things got out of hand, which they obviously had.

While the questioning was going on another car pulled up to the scene and Jeru Squillante and his young partner emerged. Before approaching Doherty, Squillante exchanged some familiarities with the local cops. He then walked over to the ambulance.

"My, my, Doherty, you sure are having a busy week in the world of crime."

Doherty didn't say anything, knowing that the Providence detective was out of his jurisdiction.

"Now correct me if I'm wrong here, okay. Something tells me you knew all along that this guy lying here dead was the one of the men who molested your girlfriend last Friday night and cold cocked you. Am I right?"

Doherty remained silent.

"So, rather than letting the police do their job, you thought you'd take the law into your own hands. You came up here, provoked this big slob into attacking you and then put two slugs in him. One in the gut just to make him suffer a bit, then the coup d'grace in the heart. You coulda put one in his heart right away, but that would've been too kind. Or maybe you're a little outta practice so you shot him in the gut first by mistake. Then seeing that he was still alive you decided to take him out for good before the men in blue arrived."

Doherty didn't move or speak. He just stared off into space hoping news of the killing of Stanislaw Krykowski would somehow relieve Rachel's misery, all the while knowing that it never would be enough.

"Still not talking, eh Doherty. Well I'll tell you what I'm gonna do. I'm gonna suggest to my compadres here in Pawtucket that they take you down to the station and interrogate you for the next six hours. They might not get anything more outta you, but at least I'll know you had a miserable night." Squillante patted Doherty on the shoulder. "Be seeing you around, pal."

Chapter Thirty-Three

As Squillante recommended, the Pawtucket cops did take Doherty to their station house and put him in a small, sparsely furnished room where he was left alone for a good half-hour. Finally a thin, good-looking, plainclothes detective came in and sat on a chair across the functional wooden table from Doherty and smiled. He was in his forties, had closed cropped dark hair and a five o'clock shadow covering the lower half of his face. The cop introduced himself as Lt. Patton. Doherty just nodded in return. Patton began his questioning at the beginning of that night's events. He did not bring up Krykowski's and his pals' previous attack on Rachel and Doherty. Doherty was cooperative up to a point, but volunteered nothing about Meir Poznanski or the Nazi hunting party.

Patton's interrogation was low-key but persistent. It took until the second hour for him to finally turn his attention to the assault on Federal Hill. Doherty gave him the same story he'd given the uniformed cops: that it was later, only after he recovered from his head injury, that he realized the attack had not been random and Krykowski had probably been tailing him all along. Opening up this line of inquiry forced Doherty to explain why he was on Krykowski's shit list to begin with. Along the way he told the cop of his suspicion that the big Pole and his cronies were responsible for the killing of Billy James – a murder Patton was unfamiliar with nor seemed to have any interest in. When the detective asked about the man Doherty was initially searching for, he refused to give up Meir Poznanski.

At this point Patton showed some emotion, angrily telling Doherty that they had ways of finding out who this man was. Doherty knew Patton wasn't threatening to take him into the backroom and work him over with a rubber hose to get the information out of him. Rather he would only have to question a few key people in West Warwick before someone kicked Poznanski his way. For the time being, however, Doherty would do his best to keep Poznanski on ice until the Nazi hunters cut him loose.

After two hours of this go-round Patton excused himself and said he was going for coffee. He offered to bring Doherty one when he returned. While the cop was absent Doherty rested his head on the bare table. He must've fallen asleep because he hadn't heard Patton come back into the room. The cop shook Doherty awake and handed him a cardboard cup filled with tepid black coffee. Then they began the routine all over again. About twenty minutes into round two the inter-rogation room door opened and a uniformed officer stuck his head in.

"Hey, Lou, I think you better step outside for a minute." Patton seemed angry to be interrupted, yet acceded to the cop's request. A few minutes later Patton returned accompanied by two other men in suits. One took the chair Patton had occupied for the past two hours while Patton and the other guy stood against the far wall. The small room was now very crowded and began to smell of after shave and body odor. This new cop was about the same age as Patton but heavier and not as well dressed. He sported a military brush cut much like that of Squillante's junior partner only his was laced with gray stubble. He sat and stared at Doherty for an uncomfortable amount of time without saying anything.

Finally he began, "My name is Agent Montgomery. This other gentleman is Agent Delaney. We're from the FBI."

Doherty did not bother to introduce himself. Montgomery turned back to Delaney who handed him a manila folder. He slid a somewhat blurry 8 x 10 photo out of the envelope and placed it on the table in front of Doherty.

"Do you recognize this man?" he asked matter-of-factly pointing at a younger Stanislaw Krykowski wearing a uniform and standing with three other men in similar garb.

Doherty looked closely at the photo and then up at the FBI agent. "I think so. He looks like an earlier version of the man I shot a few hours ago." The agent was not amused by Doherty's levity.

"And his name is?"

"Stanislaw Krykowski."

Montgomery glanced over his shoulder at Delaney and then turned his attention back to Doherty. "Have you ever heard the name Antonin Bradz?"

Doherty shook his head. "Can't say that I have."

The FBI agent folded his hands and leaned across the table. "Stanislaw Krykowski was named Antonin Bradz when he was back in Poland. We've been looking into his file lately. It turns out this Bradz has been in the country illegally for some time now under the name of Krykowski. We believe he is, or rather was since he's now dead, the leader of a hate group here in Rhode Island among Eastern European immigrants. A group we have been tracking for some time now."

"I'm sorry, I don't know anything about any hate group. Not sure I can help you there."

Montgomery smiled, but not in a friendly fashion. "Oh, but I think you can, Mr. Doherty. You see we have witnesses that will attest to the fact that you called Krykowski out as an ex-Nazi at the Polish-American Club here in Pawtucket. I believe you even identified him as a member of the Granatowa Policja, translated as the Blue Police in English. You know what that tells us? That tells us you knew more about this dead man than you're letting on."

Doherty turned silent again.

Montgomery shook his head and then extracted two more photos. Both were recent snapshots of Krykowski's two cronies standing side by side on a street corner. Doherty made an act of looking closely at the pictures.

"I recognize those two. I saw them with Krykowski at the club the night I threw a beer in his face."

"Here's the deal in a nutshell. These two," Montgomery said pointing at Krykowski's cohorts, "live in the same house where you shot Bradz. And as of now they're nowhere to be found, though at least one neighbor swears she heard them come home in a car with Bradz shortly before all the commotion began. We figure they skipped out right after you shot their leader. That would make sense. But believe me when I tell you, we will find them and bring them to justice." There it was again, Doherty thought. That word. As if there could ever be any real *justice* in this world for those who had gone through what Meir Poznanski and Anna Koplowitz had.

Doherty thought if the FBI found them it probably would be with a bullet through each of their heads. His hunch, however, was that Janisz and his gang would dispose of Krykowski's two cohorts in such a way that they would never be seen again.

Delaney pulled another photo out of the envelope and placed it on the table next to the ones of Krykowski and his pals. It was a double police mug shot of Janisz, one front, one side view. He then placed a similar one of the man called Avraham next to it, and a third of a man from the safe house whose name Doherty never learned.

"Do you recognize any of these men?" Montgomery asked.

Doherty pretended to look carefully at those pictures as well. "No, I don't. Are they also part of Krykowski's hate group?"

Montgomery stared hard at Doherty. "We have reason to believe these men are in the country illegally as well, but with a different purpose. And unlike these others they have no intention of staying here. Our surveillance of them has led us to believe they are Israeli nationals in the U.S. tracking down ex-Nazis who live here. We know that they've already shanghaied some alleged Nazis out of this country as well as from countries in South America. Our information is that they somehow smuggle these men off to Israel to face their own form of justice. Let's just say the bureau has been tracking both of these groups, hoping they would intersect at some point so that we could round up all of them."

"And have they? Have they intersected?"

"That's where you come in, Mr. Doherty. We believe you may be the point of intersection."

Doherty shook his head, "Me! Sorry, Agent Montgomery, I think you've got the wrong man. I don't know anything about any Israeli guys. I've never seen these men before," he said, again tapping the three photos with his index finger. "My job was to find a missing man who set out to kill Stanislaw Krykowski because of some old grievance he had carried over here from Poland. I was just hoping to find my man before he did something reckless."

"You mean like kill Antonin Bradz? Well it looks like you saved him the trouble."

"I guess, but that wasn't exactly what I had in mind when I took on this case. You see, some of his friends hired me to find this missing guy. When I finally located him I tried to convince him to forget about Krykowski and go back home. Unfortunately, he refused. The truth is I was able to locate him by finding Krykowski first and then following my leads back from there. I tried to warn Krykowski that someone was out to kill him, but he wouldn't listen to me. He just laughed in my face. I believe he mistakenly thought I was the one who was after him. That was how the hostility between us began."

Agent Delaney stepped away from the wall and said harshly, "Do you really expect us to believe that load of bullcrap?"

"Believe what you want. I tried to warn Krykowski that somebody wanted to kill him and he returned the favor by threatening me and then attacking me and my girlfriend. If you want to know if I have any regrets about shooting the bastard, the answer is no. And from what you've just told me it looks like I might've done the world a favor."

"Why? You think you were justified because you believe he'd been a Nazi during the war?" Montgomery asked.

"And from what you just told me, the leader of a hate group operating here in Rhode Island that you guys were tracking. Look, I won't lie to you. I killed my share of Nazis in the war and Uncle Sam gave me medals for it. I don't expect a medal for what I did tonight, but don't expect me to feel bad about it either. Not after he and his pals cold cocked me and raped my girlfriend."

"And you don't know what happened to his two house mates?"

"I haven't seen either of them since the night I got into a beef with Krykowski at the Polish Club. As far as tonight is concerned I never saw them, nor do I give a damn about them. It was mainly Krykowski I was interested in."

"And this man you were hired to find? Where is he now?"

"Beats me. Last time I saw him he was living at the Y in Providence. I'm pretty sure he left there and that's why Billy James was killed – because he wouldn't or couldn't tell Krykowski where my guy had gone. My job was to find him and hopefully bring him to his senses. I found him, but he had no interest in going home. Maybe he will once he finds out Krykowski is dead. Otherwise I've got no idea where he is now."

Montgomery leaned across the table and said, "You know something, Doherty, right now you're like a carbuncle on my ass. I know you're not telling us all you know and I know that there's nothing I can do about it. I could try having your license pulled, but something tells me you'd hire some fancy pants lawyer and have it back in your wallet by next week. But trust me on one thing, we will find out who this man is you were looking for and we will get the straight story out of him. What I don't know is whether he'll implicate you anymore than we can." With that Montgomery stood with his hands leaning on the wooden table and said to Patton, "We're done here, lieutenant. He's all yours."

Chapter Thirty-Four

Doherty had a few loose ends to attend to before putting the Poznanski case to rest. The first required him to take the walk up Washington Street that he'd been dreading for months. The little bell rang as he entered Francine's women's clothing shop. Once inside he was immediately spotted by Millie St. Jean, the girl he'd briefly dated the previous fall. He hadn't seen her since they split up. His real mission was to speak with her boss, Morris Mendelson, though he knew a visit to the shop would inevitably lead to an encounter with Millie.

She was busy with a customer so Doherty just lingered by the door hoping to be scooped up by Mendelson before Millie was free. However, the little man was nowhere to be seen. Millie'd cut her blond hair back to neck length since the last time he'd seen her; otherwise she looked pretty much the same. The customer soon left the little shop and Doherty and Millie were alone. She gave him a sweet yet puzzled smile. It was the look that had hooked him the first time they met.

"Nice to see you again, Doherty," she said approaching him, though he couldn't tell if the words were sincere or not.

"Likewise, I'm sure. Is Mr. Mendelson around?"

"He's in the back. Would you like me to get him for you?"

"In a minute. How have you been, Millie?"

She hesitated, obviously made nervous by his presence. "I've been fine. You know, about the same."

"I hear you're getting married. When's the big day?" Doherty said trying as best he could to keep the sarcasm out of his voice.

"Next month, June 20th."

"What about Gerard?" he asked, though he knew the status of her husband who was in a vegetative state at the Howard Mental Institution was none of his business.

Millie looked away when she spoke next. "We've gotten the marriage annulled – on account of Gerard's condition." By *we* he assumed she meant her father-in-law, herself and some other interested party, like Judge Martin DeCenza.

"How did you pull that one off?"

Millie should have been offended by Doherty's tone. Instead she answered his question calmly. "My father-in-law arranged it, with the help of Judge DeCenza. I know what you think of the Judge, but he did help us with this so I owe him a debt of gratitude."

"Millie, knowing what I know about the Judge, you will owe him a lot more than your gratitude. He'll have you and your in-laws in his hip pocket now and forever."

"I read in the papers that you shot someone," Millie said, moving the subject of their conversation away from her annulment and Judge DeCenza's role in it.

"I did. Shot him dead, as I'm sure you already know." Millie didn't respond. Their interaction had now reached an awkward stage.

"They said it was in self-defense. Is that true?"

"More or less. The person I shot stabbed me in the arm with a switchblade knife. I think he would've done more damage if I hadn't shot him first."

"And are you all right? I mean are you okay in the head about all this?"

"If you're asking if I feel bad about shooting the guy I'd have to say no, I don't. He was a despicable human being whose absence from this world will not be missed. Maybe it could've ended differently, though I'm glad it didn't."

Sadness passed into Millie's eyes. "Oh, Doherty, you seem so angry. You didn't used to be like this. I hope I didn't have anything to do with…"

"Don't worry about me, I'll be fine. And no you didn't have anything to do with what happened. Let's just say my life has taken a different course since we last saw each other."

At that point Mendelson emerged from the back room and was startled to see Millie and Doherty engaged in conversation. For both their sakes his presence was a welcome relief. Doherty abruptly left Millie and walked over to the little man. Mendelson was wearing a clean white shirt, suspenders and a paisley necktie loosely wrapped around his collar. He appeared less than pleased to see Doherty in his shop. Doherty'd noticed of late that being known around town as a man who killed someone colored the way people looked at him.

"Can we talk in private?" Doherty asked, not wanting any of his business with Mendelson to be shared with Millie.

Mendelson stood aside and said, "Certainly. Let's go into my office."

The small cubicle in the back of Francine's contained a functional metal desk with a stack of papers on it and an adding machine. Otherwise the only other adornments in the room were a couple of pictures of Mendelson and his equally small wife and miniature daughter.

"What can I do for you?" Mendelson asked in a voice that lacked even a smidgen of warmth.

"I came to settle up on the Poznanski case." He then handed an itemized bill to Mendelson. "Here's a list of my expenses. As you can see it's mostly for small incidentals like parking, gas, bus fares, and a few meals. Nothing exorbitant." He'd included under *meal money* the cash he paid to grease Billy James for information.

Mendelson perused the list with the keen eye of a shopkeeper. "The hundred and thirty we already gave you doesn't cover these expenses?"

"It was my understanding that the money the minyan put up was for my services alone and did not include expenses. I found Poznanski like you wanted. It's not my fault he chose not to return to West Warwick. I guess that means you'll have to be the minyan breakfast's errand boy from now on."

Mendelson looked up from Doherty's itemized list and said, "Oh, but he did come home. Just yesterday in fact. Edith called me last night. She said he came home, packed his clothes and left about an hour later. He didn't even wait for his son and daughter to come home from school to say good-bye to them."

"Where did he go?"

Mendelson shook his nearly hairless head. "I don't know. You'll have to ask Edith. So I guess we can say that since he did come home, even if it was for just a short time, that you've completed your service." Doherty did not like the coldness in Mendelson's voice, as if it was his fault Poznanski chose not to stay in town or in his loveless marriage. He decided to let it slide if only to close out the case and be on his way.

Mendelson pulled a large ledger out of a desk drawer and carefully wrote a check to Doherty and Associates for the balance of what was owed.

"Are we jake now?" Doherty asked once the check was handed over.

"I believe we are, Mr. Doherty. This check should finalize all dealings we have with one another." And that was the end of it, or so Doherty thought.

He gave Millie a cursory wave as he exited Francine's. She returned it with an uncertain smile.

A half hour later Doherty found himself banging on the door at the Poznanski house. Edith Poznanski answered in an ill-fitting housedress that resembled a small tent. Her hair was once again an unruly bird's nest. She gave him a stern look when she opened the door and didn't toss him an invitation inside. They stood in the doorway for an unpleasant moment eyeing one another. He noticed that they were about the same height.

She sighed, "I suppose you might as well come in."

Doherty followed Edith Poznanski into the disorder that passed for a kitchen. Although the rummage sale boxes were gone, the room was still a mess. No coffee or rugelach were offered this time. Without being invited to Doherty took a seat at the breakfast nook.

"You'll be happy to know that my husband stopped by briefly yesterday to pick up some clothes and a few books. He left me an address where I should forward his mail. The only other thing he had to say was that he'd come by to get the rest of his stuff later. Twelve years of marriage and that's the kiss off I get."

"What forwarding address did he leave you?"

"Why do you want to know?"

"Because Meir and I have some unfinished business."

She gave him a disapproving look. It was a tough one. "You're not going to shoot him, are you?"

Doherty's first impulse was to answer this question in an angry fashion. He then thought better of it knowing that he'd probably hear similar comments in jest, and not in jest, over the next few months.

"No, I'm not going to shoot him. However, there are some last bits of information I need to get from him before I close his case file."

The big woman walked to the refrigerator and took down a piece of paper that was attached to it with a magnet. She handed it to Doherty. He took out his note pad and wrote down the information. It was what he expected. Saying a final good-bye to Edith Poznanski would be the most satisfying thing he'd do that day.

Chapter Thirty-Five

It was late May and temperatures were rising about as rapidly as the Red Sox were sinking in the standings. Williams was still laid up with a bum elbow and the rest of the team was having trouble getting a batted ball out of the infield. The Dodgers and Giants had moved to the West Coast where the former was tearing up the league while playing in a football stadium. Baseball in New York would never be the same again without the National Leaguers. Meanwhile the Sox were edging toward their first losing season in years.

Doherty parked the car in front of Anna Koplowitz's small house on Camp Street and walked slowly up the walk. He could hear the tinkling of piano keys as he stepped up onto the porch. It grew louder when Mrs. Koplowitz opened the front door. As usual she was nicely dressed as if she had just returned from a shopping trip or was about to go out on one. The Steinway piano that had been crowded with photographs the last time Doherty was there was now unadorned and had its top propped open. Meir Poznanski was sitting at the bench playing a classical piece that Doherty did not recognize. Anna Koplowitz took his arm and silently escorted him into the room. She pointed to the couch where Doherty should sit while Meir finished the composition.

Poznanski looked much better groomed than he had at the Y or the safe house. He gave Doherty a big smile beneath the blond pompadour that was now well oiled and set in place. Mrs. Koplowitz left the room and returned moments later with a tray of teacups and small pastries. She offered them to

Doherty while still maintaining a silence so as not to disturb Meir's piano recital. She leaned in his direction and whispered "Chopin." Doherty assumed she was identifying the composer of the piece Poznanski was playing.

When Meir finished she softly clapped her hands. Doherty did not join in the applause.

Poznanski stepped around the piano and gave Doherty his biggest smile and a firm handshake. He was wearing the same light gray suit with shiny black shoes. The white shirt under the suit was open at the collar and not adorned by a necktie. His smile was broad and he exuded self-satisfaction.

"Ah, Mr. Doherty, so very nice to see you again," he said still grasping his guest's hand. "I trust you have completed your business with the men in the minyan to their satisfaction."

"So it appears," Doherty said. "I did have to kill a man in the process. I hope it's not bothering you that I deprived you of doing the job."

Poznanski's smile grew even broader if that was possible. He slung a glance at Mrs. Koplowitz and said, "Why Mr. Doherty, I never had any intention of killing Antonin Bradz. You see I'm not that kind of man. I couldn't hurt a fly. Isn't that right Agniezska?" he added, without looking at the woman on the couch. She didn't respond to the question.

"Well you certainly had me fooled when we talked at the Y."

Poznanski let out a short guttural laugh. "Why of course I did. That was all part of the plan."

It took Doherty a minute to size things up. He looked at Anna Koplowitz who gave him a sincere smile and offered up another pastry. Poznanski remained standing in a position that indicated he was the king of this castle.

"So, am I to assume then that you were only acting as a decoy to flush out Stanislaw Krykowski, or Bradz, as you knew him?"

Poznanski smiled broadly again. "You might say that, Mr. Doherty. You see we wanted Bradz to think that I was planning to kill him so that he would reveal that he was who we suspected him to be. Then we hoped he'd do something rash. In that way the people tracking him would be convinced that he was the monster we thought he was. When I first saw him at the Shepard Company. I wasn't entirely sure he was Bradz. People can change in twenty years, and well, perhaps my own memory is not what it used to be either. But apparently he recognized me. Afterwards when Agnieszka contacted Janisz he convinced us that we had the right man. We just needed him to come forward and make a mistake."

"And that's where I came in, right? You made me think I was protecting you from committing murder when all along you were using me to wind up Krykowski. And that little charade where they whisked me off to the safe house to visit you confined in the locked attic?"

"Yes, as you say, a charade from start to finish. It was a means of keeping me safe from Bradz and to assure you that I was out of the game while you did what we thought you would do, confront Bradz on my behalf."

"How did Bradz and his pals find out you were staying at the YMCA?"

"Why, Mr. Doherty, they found out by following you. After you confronted Bradz in the shoe department he thought it was you who was the Nazi hunter. He never accepted the idea that you were trying to protect him from me. Instead he thought you were the one out to get him. When you called him a Nazi and threw beer in his face at the Polish club that only confirmed this to him. A small irony, wouldn't you say, because in the end you *were* the one who killed him?"

"And the family you lost in Poland? Was it true that Bradz was responsible for their and your deportation to the concentration camps?"

Meir Poznanski shrugged. "We knew he'd been part of the Granatowa Policja. I had seen the pictures that Janisz had of him in his uniform. Was he the one who sent my family away? This I do not know for certain. What matter does it make now that he is dead? He was one of them and now he and his friends have been disposed of."

"What about Billy James? Was he also part of your grand plan?"

"An unfortunate occurrence. However, from our point of view the old shvartze was expendable."

"Expendable!"

"Look, Mr. Doherty, it wasn't our fault that Billy was so nosy or that you got him involved in all this. If you hadn't preyed upon his predilection for informing on people in exchange for money and cigarettes he might be alive today. Besides it was my understanding that Billy suffered from emphysema so you could say his time was already limited. Bradz just hastened his death along."

"Goddamnit, Meir, a man was killed because of you!"

Poznanski's self-satisfied expression remained in place. "Yes, you've made that abundantly clear. Two men to be exact – and perhaps two others if Bradz's associates were disposed of as we suspect they were. But is it I who is responsible for their deaths, or is it you, my friend?"

"And how long has this been going on?" he asked waving his arm to take in Mrs. Koplowitz and her neat little house.

Poznanski looked at the woman and asked, "What has it been, Agnieszka, a year now?"

"Almost. It will be a year in July," the woman said without stirring from the couch.

"What about your wife and kids?"

Meir shrugged, "What about them? If it had not been for Edith I would not have been able to stay here in Rhode Island and be reunited with my dear Agnieszka. As for my spawn – they have no use for me, nor I for them. I gave Edith what she wanted. I gave children to a woman no other man would have ever procreated with. In return she gave me the opportunity to legally stay here in America. It was a fair deal. We have plenty of money from Herman's estate so we will provide for whatever my wife and children need. And, of course, I will work if a suitable job arises. But I will not return to the shmatte trade or to the business of a brother-in-law. That part of my life is over. Kaput."

Meir Poznanski seemed so pleased with himself that all Doherty wanted to do was smack the supercilious smile off his face. Instead he held his anger.

"There is one loose end you two are forgetting about. Rachel Katz and I were almost killed by your friend Bradz while all this was playing out. Who's going to pay for that? Were we expendable as well?"

Mrs. Koplowitz spoke for the first time. "We are very sorry for what happened to you and Rachel. If it is money that you want we would be happy to compensate each of you."

Poznanski interrupted. "What compensate? Bradz attacked you and the girl and you returned the favor by shooting him. Is that not compensation enough?"

Doherty stood and confronted Poznanski face to face. "That innocent girl could be scarred for life thanks to you and your *grand plan*."

"Please, Mr. Doherty," Mrs. Koplowitz interjected. "It was expected that Janisz and his people would capture Antonin Bradz before he could do any further harm. No one thought he would come after you and poor Rachel. I know how you feel, but you must remember the horrible things that were done in the camps to Meir and myself and many others because of men like Bradz. The world can be an evil place sometimes. It is regrettable that Rachel had to feel that. The Jews here in America, they have no idea what it was like. They have heard the stories, but the stories can't even begin to tell the truth of what happened over there. Now she and you are part of the knowing."

For once Doherty was at a loss for words. These Nazi-hunting Jews had snookered him. In the end he could not blame them entirely and knew that he was just as responsible as they were for the death of Billy James, the molesting of Rachel Katz and the bump on the back of his head that nearly smashed his skull. Indeed, the world could be an evil place and he could at least console himself with having taken one of those evil actors out of it. In the end, it was small compensation. He couldn't help but bear some measure of hatred toward Meir Poznanski and his European smugness. Yet he had to remind himself that it was Poznanski who had lost one family and forsaken another. Maybe war does make people callous to the suffering of others. As for himself, he would do his best to guard against such feelings.

Chapter Thirty-Six

I t was ten to six when Doherty pulled up across the street from Katz's Deli. Through the front window he could see Rachel and her mother cleaning the glass display cases in preparation for closing time. He wondered if Rachel was working regularly at the deli now that she'd taken a leave from her teaching job. He was reluctant to go inside though he knew it was something he was obliged to do. He wanted to see if Rachel was healing as best she could.

There were two large bodied female customers in the deli, each squeezing the loaves of bread to determine their freshness this late in the day. Mrs. Katz spotted Doherty before Rachel did. She was the kind of woman who had a permanent expression of dissatisfaction on her face. He wasn't sure if she remembered him from his visit when he first made Rachel's acquaintance. Rachel was bending over swabbing a wooden cutting board with her back to Doherty. He waited patiently.

"Can I help you," the mother said in a voice that sounded like she preferred to do just the opposite.

"I came to speak with Rachel," Doherty said softly. It was in that instant Mrs. Katz realized who he was.

"You've got your nerve coming in here," she all but shouted. This got the attention of the two women who'd been pinching the breads.

Rachel turned around slowly and looked up at Doherty. Her dark hair was tied up in a bandana and her white apron was smeared with mustard and other food stains. The swelling on her face had receded considerably, yet so had the gleam in her eyes. They looked at each other while Rachel's mother barked out some other insults. Finally the girl turned on her mother and shouted, "Will you please shut up. For once in your life will you please just shut your goddamn mouth!"

The two bread handlers were so startled by this exchange that they immediately bustled out of the deli. Mrs. Katz tried to make some comment about how Rachel had just cost them a sale until her daughter shut her up again. Rachel removed her apron, walked around the counter and took Doherty's arm. "Let's go outside and talk. I need some air."

Once out on the pavement Rachel asked him for a cigarette. Doherty slugged a couple of Camels out of his pack and lit them with his Zippo. Rachel drew in a lungful of smoke.

"I tried calling you at the school but they said you'd taken a leave."

Rachel inhaled deeply and blew smoke out of the corner of her mouth. "I wanted to go back. Once the principal and his assistant got a look at my face they suggested that I take some time off. It was close enough to the end of the year that we agreed it was best if I didn't come back at all."

"Will you go back to teach in the fall?"

"I don't know. For some reason just the way they looked at me gave me the impression they knew what had happened. I know that was probably just my imagination getting the better of me, but I couldn't help feeling that way."

"How are you doing?"

Rachel hesitated. "I'm not sure what you're asking nor am I sure how to answer you. Right now I'm just trying to put one foot in front of the other. I know one thing, if I was still working at the school I'd be out looking for a place of my own. I have to get out of my house. It used to be only my mother who bugged me, but now my father watches me like a hawk, always asking where I'm going whenever I go out and when I'll be back. I can't even go to the drugstore without getting the third degree." An awkward silence followed. She broke it by asking, "What about you? How are you doing now that you've killed somebody?"

"You know it was Krykowski I shot, the one who … who was part of the gang that attacked us that night."

"I figured as much from what I read in the papers. Did you shoot him dead right away or did you make him suffer?"

"I don't know. I only shot him in the stomach. That made him suffer, but it wouldn't've killed him. The Nazi hunters showed up and one of them shot Krykowski through the heart with my gun."

Rachel looked confused so Doherty spun out the details of the night he went to Krykowski's house where he was stabbed and the big Pole was killed.

"So the Nazi hunters, they were for real, huh? And they were onto this Krykowski all along?"

"Yes they were. They just didn't show up soon enough. Not soon enough to prevent Krykowski from killing the old Negro man from the Y or from attacking you and me. Yeah, he was killed in the end, but not before he could wreak more damage."

Rachel did not take this last remark well, knowing that she'd been the victim of Antonin Bradz's final act of anti-Semitism. "Whatever happened with Meir Poznanski? I haven't seen him or Anna Koplowitz in the deli lately."

"I have a feeling they'll be taking their business elsewhere from now on. You see Meir never had any intention of killing Krykowski. He and Mrs. Koplowitz were in cahoots with the Nazi hunters right from the beginning. They were hoping to flush out Krykowski, or Antonin Bradz, which was his real name. Their job was to insure that he revealed himself to be who the Nazi hunters suspected he was. When I came along they decided to use me instead to get at Krykowski. It worked perfectly as far as they were concerned. The only ones who got hurt were you, me and Billy James. But as Meir Poznanski so eloquently put it, we were *expendable*."

"Holy shit. So your whole case was a ruse from the beginning?"

"Not entirely. Meir had gone missing and I think the men in the minyan were sincere when they hired me to find him. He was lost, and they knew that finding lost people is what I do best. Though like a lot of missing persons I search for, Meir was missing on purpose. I guess you could say I walked right into it with my eyes wide open."

"But you were trying to prevent Meir from killing that man. You set out to do something good and..."

"And I ended doing the killing myself. And in the process I got another man killed - and you hurt."

Rachel was down to the butt end of her cigarette. She took one last deep drag and tossed it into the gutter. Doherty made a point of stepping on the fiery remnant.

"So what happens now, Rachel? I mean between us?"

"I don't know, Doherty. Right now I feel like damaged goods. Don't get me wrong, I'm not blaming you. I like you. I have since the first time I saw you standing in the deli looking out of place among all the Jewish women. I guess in some respects I'm as much to blame as anyone. You see, I thought it was going to be great fun playing your gal Friday. It didn't work out the way I thought it would, did it? I guess real life isn't like in the movies."

"No, I suppose it isn't."

"Let's just say I'll call you when I'm ready. And if I don't call you then that means I'm not going to be ready."

"I understand," Doherty said. He reached out and touched her arm; she flinched when he did and backed up. Then she came into his arms and hugged him in a way that said she really needed the hug. "I'll miss you," she whispered in his ear. She quickly let go and turned around and walked back into the deli. He could see her mother's steely gaze through the front window. Within minutes he was pulling away from the curb and putting the East Side of Providence in his rear view mirror.

THE END

GLOSSARY OF YIDDISH
AND HEBREW WORDS

Bar Mitzvah – A ceremony marking a Jewish boy's coming of age. Generally celebrated on a Sabbath day around his thirteenth birthday

B'nai B'rith – an international Jewish service organization committed to the preservation of the Jewish people and the state of Israel

Boychik – A term of endearment for a young boy

Bubbie – Usually refers to a grandmother; used in the book as a general term of affection more akin to the word bubele, a casual term of endearment

Czarmuch (Polish) – Polish equivalent of nigger

Goniff – a thief; often used to refer to a dishonest person, especially in business

Goy, goyim – Goy is singular for any non-Jew; goyim is plural. Synonymous with Gentile

Hadassah – a women's Zionist organization. Usually a charitable group made up of volunteers

Kike – an insult of a Jew. The term originated for Jewish immigrants coming to America through Ellis Island who were illiterate. They refused to sign with an X because an X was associated with Christianity. They made a circle instead. Kike is a shortening of the Yiddish word for circle.

Kosher – special Jewish dietary laws originally established in the Bible. Strictly followed by Orthodox Jews and other Jews by choice

Kvells – to be proud, usually of one's children. Bragging about them though not necessarily in an offensive manner

Meshug, Meshugana – Crazy, nuts. Can be used to describe a person or a behavior

Minyan – traditionally ten Jewish men over the age of 13 required to hold any kind of prayer service

Mitzvah – an act of kindness or a good deed; sometimes used to refer to something that is a blessing of good fortune

Oy Gevalt, Oy – A Yiddish expression loosely translated as "Oh, God" or "woe is me"; also an expression of surprise. Oy – a simple expression of exasperation

Putz – a penis. Used interchangeably with "schmuck"; Yiddish equivalent of calling someone a dick or an asshole nowadays

Rebbie – informal reference to a Rabbi

Rugelach – a small pastry consisting of dough rolled around jam, raisins or some similar type of sweet filling

Schmear – a spread of cream cheese; can also refer to a layout of food or a lavish meal

Schmuck – same as putz; most commonly used as an insult

Sephardim – Originally Jews who populated Iberia and North Africa during the Moorish period. Often characterized by dark hair and darker skin than Western and Eastern European Jews.

Sheeny – insult of a Jew; sometimes used interchangeably with shyster, an unscrupulous businessman, lawyer or politician

Shlemiel – a dorky person or someone who is physically inept or clumsy

Shlomo – a common Jewish name; used to refer to any Jew, often as an insult

Shmatte – literally a rag, but is often used to encompass the garment trade itself, or clothing that is sold in it. Can refer to anything that is shabby, usually clothes

Shvartze – a black person; the Yiddish word for black. Now considered too insulting for common usage

Shoah – the Hebrew word for the Holocaust

Shul – Yiddish word for synagogue; literally means "school"

Tallits – prayer shawls; always worn by orthodox and sometimes by conservative and reformed Jews at religious services

Tefillin – small black leather boxes containing verses from the Torah occasionally worn by observant Jews at morning worship services. One
box is worn on the forehead near to the brain, the other on the upper
left arm near to the heart.

Touchis (Tuches) – Yiddish word for the rear end, the buttocks, the ass

Trafe – any food that is non-kosher

Yamulkes – skullcaps worn at Jewish religious ceremonies

ACKNOWLEDGEMENTS

I would like to thank Anne Sherman, Office Manager of the Rhode Island Jewish Historical Association, for her help in providing me with information about the Ahavath Shalom Synagogue and its early founders in West Warwick. Along with written information she sent me several photographs of the interior and exterior of the synagogue when it was a fully operational house of worship. I would also like to thank West Warwick resident Denis Roch who provided me with information about the Jewish community of West Warwick in the decades after World War Two. Included in what he sent to me was a list of Jewish merchants who owned a large number of shops along Main and Washington Streets in Arctic in the 1950s and 1960s. Most of these merchants were good friends and acquaintances of my parents, Fred and Silvia Kafrissen. Several would remain friends with our family even after my father moved his business and family to Cranston, Rhode Island.

I would like to thank Midge Frazel, who I met online and is now a Facebook friend. Midge worked at the old Shepard Company in Providence and along with some of her friends provided me with a firsthand description of what that department store and its neighboring Tea Room looked like back at the time this book is set. I would like to acknowledge Israel "Izzy" Arbeiter, whose story of Holocaust survival was printed in the Boston Globe on June 3, 2012. I "borrowed" some of Izzy's tale to provide the framework for Meir Poznanski's and Agnieszka Koplowitz's stories of their own Holocaust experiences. Finally I would like to thank an old, long-lost friend, Paula Kessler, for giving me Rachel Katz.

In terms of researching Hebrew and Yiddish words, I found most of their definitions from online Hebrew and Yiddish to English dictionaries. Others I found in a book titled <u>Talk Dirty in Yiddish</u> (2008) by Ilene Schneider. I also consulted about all things Jewish with my good friend Bob Deutsch. Another friend, Julie Gordon, did yeoman service in helping me in the editing process as did my wife and best friend, Jeanne Berkman. In addition, I consulted regularly with my brother Don Kafrissen, who has penned two Holocaust based novels of his own, <u>Brothers Beyond Blood</u> and <u>Long Lost Brother</u>, both available on Amazon.

Made in the USA
Lexington, KY
10 November 2019

56728877R00136